SHIP OF PERILS

BOOK FOUR OF THE THREE HEIRS SERIES

JOHN W. FEIST

Inquiries should be addressed to:
John W. Feist, 2335 Dale Drive, Falls Church, VA 22043, USA, or jwfeist@aol.com

ISBN (print): 978-1-7357497-8-5
ISBN (ebook): 978-1-7357497-9-2

Book design and production: Domini Dragoone
Cover images: Bill Chizek/iStock, metamorworks/iStock, itakayuki/iStock,
    Andrew Beatson/Pexels, Nikolett Emmert/Pexels

PUBLISHED BY

Ocean! thou mighty monster!
That lies curled like a green serpent, round about the world!
To musing eye thou art an aweful sight,
When calmly sleeping in the morning light;
But when thou risest in thy wrath,
As now, and fling'st thy folds around some fated prow!
Crushing the strong ribbed bark as if it were a reed!
Then, Ocean, art thou terrible indeed.
—Oberon, Carl Maria von Weber

PART I

TEMPESTS

2005

The Swiss-flagged, dry-bulk cargo carrier MV *El Caballo* rode high on developing seas as it cleared the Santa Ana, Philippines, lighthouse. It was empty, returning on light ballast to Valparaiso, Chile, in a long voyage under charter to the Chilean maritime authority. After delivering Chilean-mined copper ore in Japan, she had sailed to Australia to lift the grain she then delivered at a remote Philippines terminal, using her shipboard unloading equipment. Aware of a fast-approaching August typhoon, the vessel's master, fifty-four-year-old Nils Dahl, had charted a course north of the weather system which would add five days to the journey. Dahl was slow-steaming her to conserve expensive bunker fuel he'd taken on at Mindanao, thus adding another week to the voyage.

Beside him on the bridge stood a thirty-two-year-old apprentice, American Thad Maxwell, nephew of Earl King. King was an influential consultant to the tiny Chilean maritime world.

Just before midnight, Nils felt himself coming down with a cold, probably the same one that had put the Chilean navigational officer down for the day. It would be open sea from here on. I'm going below, he said to himself.

"Thad, think you can relieve me for the next watch? I'm going to turn in."

"Sure, Nils, I'd like nothing better." Maxwell was tired of this whole damned trip and impatient with the skipper's cautious plan. He was keen to get back to the beaches and casinos on the sunny coast of Chile.

Nils should have seen something in the gleam of Maxwell's eyes, but did not, or chose not to.

Maxwell would really, really screw up on this voyage.

Maxwell's uncle, Earl King, had a unique job. When his company sold a fleet of military jets to a country, King's job was to help that country generate export dollars to pay for the jets. Called "offset and countertrade," it was a very gray shade of dark business the company kept under wraps.

He had learned that Chile's maritime industry was too small and local for the vanities of post-Pinochet bureaucrats. Globalization was passing Chile by in the shipping sector. So, he proposed that Chile charter a large vessel to deliver its biggest export, copper ore, to Far Eastern ports. He would hire instructional crew and officers to teach Chilean mariners how to operate the vessel and then expand the fleet. The first such vessel was the *El Caballo*. Nils Dahl was the first skipper/instructor, a highly regarded ship's master from Bergen, Norway.

This was the third such voyage of the *El Caballo*. Thad Maxwell was not part of the plan of the Chilean maritime authority, but was a singular part of Earl King's plan.

Maxwell had finally finished college and had taken a year longer than most to get through high school in his native Paris, Tennessee. He had his eyes on Stanford Law School. King firmly believed that his nephew first needed some grounding in the real world before starting law school anywhere. He put Maxwell's feet on the deck of this cargo ship because he damn well could. No one else liked the idea, but that only strengthened King's resolve.

An hour after Dahl went below, Thad Maxwell stepped to the side of the young Chilean helmsman. "Bring her twenty-five degrees starboard, and make your speed full."

The young Chilean gulped. "There's weather there, sir."

"I've been on the horn with the old man. It'll be fine."

He hadn't. It wouldn't.

After four hours of codeine-aided sleep, Nils rolled hard against his cabin's bulkhead as the ship yawed wildly in heavy seas and gale winds. His throat was on fire. He pulled on gear and fought his way to the bridge. His helmsman was panicked. Maxwell was nowhere to be seen. He had gone to his cabin an hour after the storm hit. Two apprentice Chilean officers gripped the rail with one hand and rosaries with the other.

"Where the hell are we?" Nils croaked breathlessly.

"We will die," answered the helmsman.

Aiko Watanabe was sixteen when she and her best friend and cousin, Mariko Isaemon, drew blood from their palms with a sharp edge, clasped their hands together to seal a forever bond, and decided to leave their homes in Kohoku, Japan, a small Saga Prefecture town between the coastal city of Fukuoka and Arita, the famed origin of Imari porcelain. Her father was the descendant of a proud merchant family who had made their fortunes exporting fine porcelains to Europe and America in the eighteenth and nineteenth centuries. The man yearned for their bygone glory—intractably, to the point of stupidity. He was incompetent. With flourish and flair, he would buy high and sell cheap just to foster friendliness, so lacking at home, with his opposite number in business transactions. He had drained the family's reserves. In his large, inherited estate, he insisted on wearing the robes and swords of the old aristocratic class. It further bolstered his esteem to abuse his wife and harass his children. His wife hid money from him to buy the Johnny Walker Red Label whisky that had braised her vital organs.

Aiko had had enough.

Her mother's brother, Fujio Isaemon, lived in Guam. Aiko believed him to be a happy person. She had secretly corresponded with him and confided her desire to flee the Watanabe compound. Fifty-seven-year-old

Isaemon, divorced, whose daughter, Mariko, lived in Kohoku with her mother, was a resourceful businessman operating in the penumbra of the US Naval base. He had encouraged Aiko to come to Guam, and even bring Mariko with her. He came to Japan to fetch them, posing as their guardians since they were underage, and paid for their trip to Guam, whereupon Mrs. Watanabe disowned brother and daughter as a final act of self-loathing.

Despite that daring dash to freedom, life in Guam came to disappoint Aiko. Isaemon's businesses were distinctly geared to lonely sailors and merchants who were transients in Guam's base and ports. He owned a jazz club, a massage parlor, and three detached houses containing only bedrooms. Aiko and her friend were apprenticed to each of these business units and forced into prostitution. He gave the girls Americanized names and made them dye their fine, long hair. Mariko became Bree, a blonde, and Aiko became Lydia; her hair turned out more henna than red. They wear it that way to this day. By 2005, they had been assigned to the house with the best view of the Pacific, and with the best guests who still behaved like swine.

Isaemon also owned a one-half interest in a cargo vessel, the other half-owned by Honshu Lines, a large shipping company in Japan. That ship had recently been put on bareboat charter to the maritime authority of Chile.

Imagine his surprise when the vessel limped into Guam in September 2005.

The typhoon had damaged the *El Caballo*'s hydraulics, electronics, and rudder so badly that she had to finish the last sixty-five hours of that voyage in tow of two blue-water tugboats. To help assuage bitter feelings, Earl King had arranged for all hands to get laid when they arrived in Guam.

It was thus that Thad Maxwell and seventeen-year-old Aiko met in a bedroom on the island of Guam. Maxwell was a stranger to any place not located in his native state of Tennessee. Maxwell carried a distinct distrust of foreign faces. But while he was in Guam in the last quarter of 2005, he shed those old biases. He fell in love with Aiko and with her stories from the folklore and poems of Japan. She made sure that Maxwell was a happy man in Guam, day and night.

Then, tragedy struck on Christmas Eve. Aiko was not with Isaemon-san, for she and Maxwell had decorated a potted palm for a private celebration in a hotel room, away from the house of beds. Presumably a brazier had tipped and started the fire that claimed Isaemon's life.

Fujio Isaemon had been fiercely proud of his role in removing Mariko and Aiko from their unhappy conditions. His superstitious and sentimental streaks had led him to think he had crafted with Shakespearean significance the circumstances allowing for Aiko's romance with the likable American sailor blown upon the shores of Guam by a storm at sea. He wasted no time altering his will to capture such significance for posterity. Under the new will, Mariko would inherit the local businesses but to Aiko would go the one-half interest in the *El Caballo*, which had brought her suitor into her life.

In a modest ceremony, Aiko became Mrs. Thad Maxwell, and had her name changed to Lydia. Aiko would leave Guam and her sordid memories behind and, as Thad's wife, gain US citizenship. She and Mariko wept when they touched their friendship scars together for the last time.

Those are epic episodes of ancient history—practically a quarter century ago—the people long since scattered and living in completely different worlds. But, what if …

CHAPTER 1

In the dinner hour on a Friday in late July 2027, Brad Oaks would like nothing better than to sit down to a salade Niçoise with his sparkling wife, Amaya, and provide their daughter, Kozue, with encouragement for her upcoming speech on gun control. He parked in the cramped old garage of his Russian Hill apartment building, just beneath where, on the rafters, rests the family's green aluminum canoe. He bonked the hull with his knuckle and smiled, knowing that in a few days, the three of them would be out in Marin County estuary marshland, their intimate sanctuary. There, the family can finally crouch together for bird-watching and deep conversation in the shallows. He trudged alongside the building's east wall up one of San Francisco's steepest sidewalks, mounted two flights of stairs as he fumbled his door keys in one hand, briefcase in the other, and pushed his way into his large apartment.

Brad, Amaya, and thirteen-year-old Kozue live in the same flat overlooking the Golden Gate Bridge where Brad's parents had lived. He finds the apartment empty, dark, and soundless.

Amaya and Kozue are in the Seattle hotel where the gun conference is underway, and where Brad should be, but is not. He couldn't get away from the steel plant in Stockton where he works—as the CEO, mind you, so you might think he could have kept to the plan to go to Seattle with his family. But, well, things came up.

At fifty-three, his hair now completely white, the former college pitcher cranes and bends to peer into the refrigerator for a familiar can featuring a pop-top and satisfying whoosh when pulled. His ankles crack and his bony wrists thrust out of his suit jacket as he reaches to the back behind bottles of green grass water ("it's not pond water, Dad") favored by his daughter, where he hopes to locate it by feel. He's wearing the wrong glasses for this search. Summer fog made the last half hour of his drive home a heart-pounder. Brad has about had it with the long commute between this apartment and Stockton, California, where he is chief executive officer of Elgar Steel, overseeing the operations of a fabricating plant specializing in long-distance, high-specification pipe for oil and gas, and a new venture, a coal mine in Western Canada.

His phone chimes. He'd dropped it with his briefcase on the table in the front hallway when he came in. *It's gotta be Amaya.* He can either sprint back to answer it or enjoy that opening whoosh and first cold swallow, but not both at the same time.

"Hey there, hon, how's your hotel? Yeah? How's Kozue holding up?" Brad grins from wall to wall. The happy sound of Amaya's voice pleases him far more than the whoosh of a pop-top can.

"We are fine, Brad, and settled. Kozue has reconnected with the kids she sees at these events. How are you, and those *things* that keep you from us?"

"I'm a lot better now that you called," says Brad as he makes his way back to the fridge for his secondary objective. "You know I'd rather be there with you."

"I do know that, my Man of Steel, and I also know that the steel will not melt nor the pipe mills crunch without your command and presence in person." Brad waits for it … ah, there's that giggle.

"Amaya, it is you who melts my steel-cold heart and Kozue who makes me smile just saying her name."

In Japanese, "Amaya" means "night rain," and "Kozue" means "treetop."

"Good. She is here and smiling back. So, will we be seeing you this month sometime?"

"Tomorrow, Amaya. Yay! I have my tickets and should be there by lunchtime."

"We will have a surprise lunch on the patio of this tall hotel. We have to go now to meet Aunt June for dinner. Love, love."

Brad Oaks feels happier now than at any time in his life since the day before he graduated from law school. He had finished in the high end of his class and had won the heart of the woman he expected to spend the rest of his life with. His parents and fiancée were to join him at the graduation ceremonies at UC Davis School of Law. But then, they didn't.

All three died in a foggy pileup on the freeway en route to Brad's ceremony.

That was twenty-two years ago. It sucked away Brad's life purpose and almost took his soul. Ernie Elgar, the owner of Elgar Steel, snagged and hauled him back from the edge of the pit. Ernie and Diedre Elgar had raised twins, Sarah Jane and June, on their vineyard and winery estate in Napa Valley. He took on the devastated Brad Oaks as the son he never had. The twins, ten years older than Brad, helped with the clucking, although June tired of it after a few months. He made Brad the steel company's first general counsel and coaxed his spirit back to life with hard work. Otherwise, Brad remained a loner, whether in his canoe watching shorebirds or on Lone Mountain with his telescope watching the ancient light of stars finally reach the retinas of backyard astronomers.

Brad could do his job and considerably more. He could see bright solutions to intractable problems at Elgar Steel. Take the Wishbone Pipeline project, which he landed fourteen years after his tragedy. Elgar would need that job to fix a world of hurt from declining projects for the pipe mill. The pipeline would carry Canadian oil from Alberta tar sands across the breadth of America for export from Galveston Bay. But the pipeline didn't do anything good for America and, hence, was stuck in bureaucratic mud. Brad and Ernie decided that if one Wishbone Pipeline was bad, two of them would be great. The second one would carry

Canadian water to Great Plains drylands east of the Rockies, on range land and wheat fields overlying the heavily depleted Ogallala Aquifer.

Just as Brad starts to pop the top of his can of lager, he flinches at the sound of an insistent car horn outside. It's unusual in this quiet neighborhood. Brad puts the can down again, strides to the front of the apartment, and peers out the rounded front bay windows to find the commotion. A Tesla sits double-parked on Larkin Street, a familiar figure leaning against it. Brad raises the sash window.

Over a foghorn's deep keening from San Francisco Bay, he hears, "Brad Oaks, just the man I'm looking for."

"Alden Knight, I've heard that line before," says Brad. "Park that electricity-guzzler and come upstairs. Can you stay for supper? It's just warmed-ups, and it's just me. My wife and daughter have left me."

"Park it where? I've circled this corner for twenty minutes, and there's nowhere to put it. Except for that, I'd love warmed-ups. Or you could hop in, and we'll go somewhere."

"Mr. Ambassador, see that white-painted curb? I won't see you park there, and neither will anyone else. I know it'll offend your law-and-order sensibilities, but everyone around here does it."

Ten years older than Brad, Alden Knight was United States trade representative when Brad sought him out to steer the new Wishbone idea through bureaucratic bramble bushes in the US and Canada. Today, Knight lives in Napa, married for five years now to Sarah Jane Elgar. He is five eleven, still sturdy and fit from a lifetime of playing squash. He combs his silver-and-black hair straight back from a tanned forehead. In his dark blue trousers and burgundy work shirt, he looks for all the world like a French vintner. He likes that because he and Sarah Jane run the prestigious winery that the Elgar family has operated since the Great Depression.

No sooner had Brad and Alden met at a State Department reception in Washington than Ernie Elgar died at his Napa Valley home. His will revealed yet a third daughter fathered by Ernie, one known in his Napa family only to him. Ernie's will divided the common stock of Elgar Steel into three equal shares: one-third to Sarah Jane, one-third to June, and one-third to Amaya Mori, ten years younger than the twins and raised in Japan. The twins sent Brad off to Tokyo to buy back Amaya's inheritance.

Brad had just dodged an assassin's bullet, but he did go to Japan. He found Amaya and, in her, found a love that he never thought he could experience again. He met Amaya, gained her trust, then her love, then lost all the Elgar stock, then lost Amaya to Iranian kidnappers, and then regained her and the stock through wile and wit. He returned from Japan leaving behind a marriage proposal for Amaya to chew on.

Sarah Jane Elgar, successor to running the steel company, knew Brad was ready for a bigger job. She made him chief operating officer to produce the pipeline he had so deftly brought back to life. The daily nitty-gritty of his new job ended all those trips to Japan he had been counting on to be with his beloved Amaya. In the end, it was Amaya who uprooted and came to San Francisco to marry Brad. Three years later, they adopted a Canadian-Japanese girl named Kozue.

Kozue Tory was eight years old when a troubled man sprayed AR-15 bullets into a small church in the Toronto, Ontario, suburb where she lived with her parents. Both her parents died in that incident while Kozue was home with a cold. Her dad had been a counterintelligence officer with the Royal Canadian Mounted Police. June Elgar had known Tory because he helped her into a protection program when Iranian terrorists were targeting Elgar executives to gain a competitive edge in the Wishbone Pipeline project. June's connection with Tory led her to inform Brad and Amaya that Kozue would be a candidate for adoption.

As Kozue grew, she acquired her nickname, Tree.

Before starting this family, Brad relied on his work to save his sanity. With the arrivals of Amaya and Kozue, Brad became central to three points of view, not just his own. Every day is a balancing act. More and more, it seems Brad has to shift his center of gravity away from the business to maintain the balance.

Brad hands Knight a glass of Elgar winery's "Ambassador" label. Knight accepts it with a warm smile. Sarah had named this merlot blend for this very Knight. He was then a special envoy to Japan. She had created the new label as a marriage bribe.

Brad goes to the refrigerator. From the plastic containers with colored-marker labels and emojis, he picks Kozue's Awesome Curry, passing up the delicately ink-brushed Amazing Amaya's Aji Niçoise. Soon, awesome fragrances of spice and lamb broth fill the apartment.

Alden wags his finger in a mock scold. "Why aren't you in Seattle?"

"I wanted to go more than anything, Alden, believe me." Brad waves off the scold with one hand in annoyance with himself and karma in general. "Then one of those 'anythings' came up at the plant that needed me more. I couldn't go and I couldn't stay all at the same time. So, I sent the girls on without me. It's been the same old story for me, Alden. I almost didn't get Amaya because I was spending all my life with my job. I navigate between those sirens every day, tied in knots, just like Odysseus. There is a purpose at home and a purpose at Elgar Steel. I know both, and I need both.

"Anyway, that's more answer than you were looking for. I'll fly out tomorrow and bring 'em home Sunday, right after Tree's speech. What brings you to me tonight?"

Knight loses his jovial smile and stiffens. He frowns and clenches one fist.

"Brad, I'm here to curry an unusual favor."

CHAPTER 2

Surprised, Brad lifts his eyebrows and says, "I owe you more than one, my friend. What's on your mind?" He has always felt indebted to Alden for helping push the Wishbone project through red tape. And he has always admired Knight as an international lawyer and a man of honor.

Alden is on his feet now, pleading as if to a jury to emphasize a point. "You need a boat bigger than that canoe of yours. You need it to haul the coal Elgar Steel is mining from Canada to Japan. You need it because that way you can make regular coal deliveries rather than wait for the Japanese to send a ship whenever they're good and ready to collect it. It's a great investment."

Elgar Steel expanded its operations a year ago to include a coal mine near the Alberta-British Columbia boundary. It hadn't been a planned acquisition. Instead, Brad had pulled this rabbit from a hat by turning a June Elgar bad debt into a promising mining venture. It turned out to be a good deal. The coal is such a superior grade that it is used in steelmaking—called metallurgical coal—and commands three times the price of coal used by power companies. Carbon from the coal chemically bonds with molten iron ore to make steel. Brad Oaks sells the coal to Japanese steel mills.

Brad looks into his wineglass. "Does it come with an extended service warranty, or do I buy that from you separately?"

Silence.

Brad looks up now. Alden is frowning. "Hey, man, forgive me. It was a lame joke."

Alden sighs, then chuckles. He settles into the couch again. "No, Brad, it was a good one, and I deserved it. I'm real uncomfortable doing this."

Brad nods. "I can tell."

Alden sits forward now and spreads his arms from his elbows, palms upward. "Let me start at the beginning."

"Please do. And you're right about the shipping situation. It's been on our minds as well. Take your time, we've got all evening—and there's an empty bedroom if you need more time."

"So, a former law school student of mine is in a delicate situation. I knew him and his wife pretty well when I taught at Stanford, but I had lost track of them until I went to Washington as USTR. By that time, he was a rising star in Congress. We used to get together now and again. We both were in turmoil over how the party was being hijacked. A lot of us felt that way. As you know, I decided to get out of town. But he decided he'd give in to the new tide. I'm afraid the undertow of that tide is very dangerous."

Brad cocks his head quizzically. "Who're we talking about here?"

Alden stands and refills his glass. "Thad Maxwell, Speaker of the House."

Brad exhales. "In all the time I've known you, you've never said you were close to that guy."

Alden shrugs defensively. "Well, there was no need, and I never felt inclined. Now there's a need—his need. I'm still not inclined, but here I am. This is not easy."

Brad reaches to touch Alden's arm. "I get that, Alden. Let it out. Don't struggle so. Maybe now's a good time for me to plate Kozue's curry. Bring your glass to the table. If this is going to be a long night, should you call Sarah Jane? I'll be a couple of minutes in the kitchen."

"Sarah knows I'm here, and why."

Brad brings generous portions of aromatic curry and rice to the table. The men smile, remembering. It was Alden who had taken Brad, Amaya, and Kozue to Tokyo's India House, which Kozue then declared to be her favorite restaurant in the world. Kozue was eleven at the time, and it was her first trip to Japan. This is her remarkably accurate reproduction of the "rather more important" curry from its menu.

"OK, Brad, so here's where I have to tell you about Thad Maxwell and his wife."

Alden picks up a glass of water after reaching the part in the story where Tennessee boy meets Japanese girl on a tropical island beneath the stars. He finishes by telling Brad that the charter-hire payments to Lydia from the ship have continued right up to the present day. The steady income to the Maxwells financed three years of Stanford Law School for Thad and eight campaigns for election to Congress. Thad rose like a rocket through the ranks of his party's caucus in the House of Representatives as a confident and affable man and a vote-whipping genius.

"And here's where the history lesson ends and the one on current events begins," Alden says. "I'm now going to tell you why I camped out on your doorstep tonight. A week ago, when I was in New York, Thad phoned me. He had just left a meeting with a couple of his staffers. Because of what he'd heard at that meeting, he pressed me to come to Washington. I went as soon as I could, and I listened. Afterward, I decided I needed to bring you into it because of your background in Japan. You think Washington was nuts when you had your office on K Street there? Here's what he told me."

CHAPTER 3

On the morning of that staff meeting in Alden's story, Thad Maxwell had quickened his pace walking from the Capitol Building's garage to his office next to the House chamber. That was his token, daily aerobic duty. Hurry lived inside him, born of perpetual impatience. He rarely squandered impatience on himself, but was generous with it with others. In his eighth term in Congress, and at age fifty-four, Maxwell's girth and cynicism had enlarged his persona considerably from the days of romance and discovery way the hell off in Guam. He had moderated his Tennessee whisky intake and frequently quit smoking, so he was content with his lifestyle. Thad lost his merchant marine tan a long time ago. His face does redden and glisten after a long golf game in the sun. He had adopted the gait and visage of a wise, gray elder, despite the fact that he was one of the youngest House Speakers ever. Always conscious of being third in succession to the presidency, he had much to smile about. Today, though, he did not smile. It was with a fixed frown that he clumped into his office's conference room for a meeting with his ethics lawyer and his campaign finance staffer.

"Drew Wallace," the Speaker said, elongating the name in his Tennessee accent, "I hired you to handle this ethics inquiry because you look like a choirboy. However, I don't want you to think like a choirboy. Have you read Machiavelli?"

"Yes, I have," Drew responded brightly. Twenty-seven-year-old Drew is fair skinned and avoids long exposure to the sun to prevent the burning that red-haired people are subject to. Lanky, five eleven in height, Drew has the frame of a tennis player, but he has never played any sport. He walks three or four miles a day, always alone. He is a quick study of hard-case legal problems. What he knows of the world, business or otherwise, he gains from books. Romance has played no part in his real life, so far.

"I know you have, Evelyn." Thad didn't so much look at Evelyn Hutton as leer.

"Yes." Evelyn looked like an ad for a high-priced shampoo. She was Drew's age, self-assured, blonde, tanned, and smart—make that very smart. Evelyn started working for the Speaker five years ago after graduating with honors from the Total Carbon Institute for Advanced Studies. Her thin cotton dress was the color of lilacs, appropriately paired with the scent she had chosen for the day.

"So, Drew," Thad said, again with that drawl, "what's your game plan for this inquiry?"

Wallace developed his skill for seeming confident even when unprepared or out of his element during his Provo, Utah, high school debate team days. "Mr. Speaker, since I just onboarded two weeks ago, I'm still going through documents. The ethics panel staff is doing the same thing. Before I can answer your question, I need to know what's not in the documents."

"I figured you'd say that, and I don't hold it against you, Drew." This time the drawl accompanied a wide smile. "So, that's why I set aside some time today and brought Evelyn into the meeting. We are both up to our eyeballs in more important stuff, so please don't tax our time. A little later, I'm going to call in Nancy Booth, my chief of staff, whose time is more valuable than the three of ours put together. She'll give you a rundown on the legislative thicket we're in. Drew, you are going to need to know as much about that as anything else you learn here today. That's going to give you important perspective when you struggle with all this dry ethics stuff."

Drew stood. "Well, sir, then I'll get right to it." Summoning his debate-team-captain stance, with hands thrust into his side pockets, Drew enunciated in a low tone, "I cannot find the source of some of your annual income. If I can't, then the committee staff can't either, and that will gnaw at them."

"Keen eye for detail, Drew." Maxwell's smile disappeared as he assessed the cut of this new kid on his staff. "You have a need to know, so, Evelyn," he said, turning to her. "I want you to be completely cooperative and open with Drew."

"All right, Mr. Speaker," she replied with a practiced smile.

"Either of y'all using a recording device?"

"Of course not," said Evelyn, quietly shaking her head.

"No, sir."

"Splendid. Now, both of you hand me your smartphones."

Reluctantly, Drew handed him his. Evelyn quickly reached into her purse, her smile unchanging, and gave him hers. Maxwell looked at the phones, then scraped his chair back and left the room to secure them in his desk drawer. When he returned, he carried a steaming mug of coffee—for himself.

"Now you can begin the cooperative openness, Evelyn," Maxwell grunted. "Let's start with *El Caballo*. From there, we'll bring in Nancy to open the rare earth elements can of worms."

Evelyn moved to the seat next to Drew Wallace on his right. She glanced at Maxwell, who nodded quickly. She turned the chair slightly and leaned forward. Drew inhaled the scent of lilacs.

"Few people know that the Speaker has a merchant marine background," she began.

"I was unaware of that," murmured Drew.

Evelyn nodded brightly. "He was an apprentice master on the *El Caballo* when she made port in Guam for repairs in 2005. Mrs. Maxwell was employed there. They met, and it was love at first sight. Thereafter, Mrs. Maxwell inherited a one-half interest in the ship he was working on. After a whirlwind wedding in Guam, they came to America to begin life's adventures together."

Drew arched his eyebrows in surprise. "Doesn't his biography say that they met at a Stanford football game?"

"Yes, it does." Evelyn's voice and smile were unchanging, "So, you see, this particular vessel has great sentimental value to them. It is a nostalgic piece of their life."

Drew tilted his head to one side. "They've done a good job of keeping it a secret."

Evelyn frowned. "Not so much a secret, Drew, more like a treasured keepsake."

"A cargo vessel?"

"The vessel and its *business*," Evelyn said earnestly. "Nancy and I have been doing some research of our own. If someone else were to do the same research, someone less charitable than Nancy and me, they would find that the cargo revenues don't quite add up. It would appear at first glance that the *El Caballo* transports half again as much tonnage as she was built for."

Now Drew frowned. He made an entry in his notebook, "phantom cargo." He looked up at Thad. "Mr. Speaker, I would like to ask you how that comes about and where the, um, phantom freight is recorded, accounting-wise?"

Thad fidgeted and looked away. Before he could reply, Evelyn said, "Drew, this is a very thorny issue. A great deal of the money earned by the vessel is paid by Total Carbon Corporation for cargoes of various ores carried all over the world. TCC is an extremely enthusiastic supporter of the Speaker's political agenda. The surplus, or phantom, freight revenue doesn't actually show up on the accounts of either TCC's political action committee or the Speaker's campaign finance reports. It simply arrives as deposits to Mrs. Maxwell's bank account as earnings of the ship. What Nancy and I saw at first blush is that the total freight money paid far exceeds the capacity of the vessel to earn by way of actual cargoes. So, if you'll recall the words, 'warts and all,' this phantom freight, as you put it, constitutes our warts."

"I can see the warts more clearly now, Evelyn," said Drew, his head tilted slightly. "The concern, of course, is to find a cure as well as cosmetics because the ethics panel will argue ..."

Speaker Maxwell thundered, "I know damn well what those pirates are going to say about it. That's why I brought you here to our team. I need you to do whatever is necessary about this troubling condition."

Unfazed by the Speaker's outburst, Drew leaned back in his chair, his eyes half-closed. "Mr. Speaker, my strong instinct would be to consider selling your wife's interest in this vessel. Once the committee hearings start, it will be increasingly difficult to keep this under wraps. I'm thinking with the proceeds of that sale, you and your wife could own several romantic yachts, along with a nest egg that would make your pension benefits pale in comparison."

Evelyn placed her hand on Drew's wrist and said, "You see, the Maxwells have only a one-half interest in this ship. The other half is owned by a giant Japanese shipping company. They probably do not want any change in current ownership."

"Why not? Business is business." Drew shrugged. "Ships are floating real estate. If the other owner is so large, what could possibly be the attachment to this particular one? It's hardly new."

With a meaningful squeeze of Drew's wrist, Evelyn said: "Cargos. As long as Mr. Maxwell is who he is in Congress, and Mrs. Maxwell maintains ownership of her half, Honshu Lines never has to concern itself about the vagaries of the charter and cargo markets for this ship. I daresay this venerable cargo vessel earns consistently higher revenues than any other vessel her size in their entire fleet." Evelyn winked. Drew was thinking of lilacs.

Drew looked at Speaker Maxwell and said levelly, "You are handcuffed."

"Keen eye again, Drew." This time the name came out clipped.

Drew continued, "Mr. Speaker, this ship could sink you."

Maxwell stated flatly, "No, Drew, your specific assignment is to avoid that outcome."

Drew dismissed a sudden thought about running away to a carefree life at sea and said, "You mentioned something about rare earth elements? They've been in the news this year."

Maxwell considered an impromptu lecture over who sets the agendas in his meetings. Instead, he stepped to the door and motioned for Nancy Booth to come in. Thad Maxwell took his seat and smiled at his chief of staff. "Nancy, Mr. Wallace has requested a briefing on the scarcity of rare earth elements, and our legislative position on that issue."

Nancy Booth had lived in the same Capitol Hill apartment from the day she started as a staffer for Maxwell, handling his Tennessee constituency correspondence. She remained infected with Potomac fever throughout her fifteen years on his staff. Forty-year-old Nancy Booth's hair had grayed and frizzed, but she still made it into a French roll. She wrapped her neck with a silk scarf from her collection of Hermes, a mad-money indulgence. Otherwise, her suits and ecru blouses all looked alike, and her gum-soled shoes hopelessly scuffed. Unlike Evelyn, Nancy did not fuss with makeup and scents. But behind her simple visage was an organizing and meticulous mind. Her stiffly erect gait emphasized her station as the "head Fred" of the office, in her words.

"Nancy, before we get into briefing Drew," said Thad, "what's the pending business on the floor?"

She turned and smiled. She made a dismissive circling motion in the air above her shoulder. "They are debating the assault weapon resolution. Our friends are vehemently opposed." Thad grimaced with a nod.

"How's your cubicle, Drew?" asked Nancy with a warm smile. Before he could answer, she continued, with a wink, "I've got my eye on an office in the Cannon building that will give you more breathing room. I'd be happy to walk you over there to take a look whenever you're ready."

"I think I'd like that," said Drew quietly.

Beaming, Nancy sat in the open seat on Drew's left. "Drew, are you familiar with rare earth elements? Most people aren't, so you needn't hesitate to say." Evelyn had not withdrawn her hand from his wrist.

"I'm a quick study, Ms. Booth."

"It's Nancy. Here's what I know. Rare earth elements are ubiquitous but only in deep, thin scatterings around the world. They are recovered as a byproduct of mining basic ores like bauxite, iron, coal, and even salt. They're used in computer chips and electric cars. Demand for them is growing exponentially."

Drew finished making an entry in his notebook. "So, how is that the business of Congress?"

Nancy nodded. "Right, ordinarily it wouldn't be. But there is a proposed bill making the rounds to assure America's supply of these vital resources. Mr. Maxwell is the lead sponsor of the bill. There have been articles and books lately putting forth the idea that greening and transforming the energy infrastructure, together with the voracious demand for computer chips, make these commodities the weak link in the chain of commerce. And nearly half the world's supply of key rare earth elements is under Chinese soil or under control of Chinese-owned mining companies elsewhere in the world. In a nutshell, the Speaker's bill would: subsidize American processing plant investment; place restrictive export controls on any computer chips and batteries made from un-American, imported rare earth elements; and place tariffs on foreign chips and batteries coming into our republic."

"So, it becomes a supply chain issue," Drew said.

"Exactly," said Nancy. "But the environmental community is pushing a different position. Mining and processing that stuff are ecological and carbon-emitting nightmares. They want to stop or regulate the business. But, if rare earth elements are as scarce and essential as our industry claims, that argument would help defeat environmental legislation. The environmentalists insist we should 'conserve' these elements in place. When there's a conflict on scientific views like this, we turn to the Congressional Research Service to give an unbiased report. Then, the name of the lobbying game is to influence the contents of that report."

Thad Maxwell stood. "Drew, let me cut to the chase. Total Carbon Corporation is the most modern and largest American conglomerate operating in the field of mining basic ores, the ones that also contain rare earth elements. They have started investing in huge processing facilities in the United States. They have committed millions' worth of research time at their university to prove the case for moving ahead with US dominance over these vital elements. I personally know the folks at Total Carbon, and they are the right kind of people. Evelyn and Nancy both went to school at their university. This office is one hundred percent committed to defeating the environmental lobby on this issue."

Drew put down his ballpoint. "OK, so this sounds like a separate issue from the one we were just talking about. How does this bear on the ethics committee inquiry?"

Evelyn leaned in. "The warts, Drew; the phantom freight. Total Carbon keeps the *El Caballo* steaming full speed with full cargos and more, month in and month out, with no end in sight. And, from what we hear, the Congressional Research people aren't too concerned about the danger of shortages or China-dictated prices in the open market."

Drew asked, "What are these cargos, please? In cooperative and open language."

Nancy answered, "Nothing fancy, nothing illegal, and mostly dirt mixed with copper or coal."

Drew exhaled. "No wonder Honshu Lines is a happy partner, Mr. Speaker."

"Lydia and I value our friends and colleagues in Tokyo," said Maxwell. "Have you ever been?"

"No, sir," said Drew. "But someone has to go there now. Actually, yesterday would have been better. We absolutely need to know whether Honshu will agree to either buy Lydia's interest or let her sell it to someone else. We cannot remain in the dark. This is imperative. Your political future depends on it."

———

"So," says Brad. "Is this where you come in, Alden? Or, I guess more appropriately, is this where I come in?"

"You'd think so," says Alden with a shrug. "This would be the logical place for me to ask you the favor I came here to ask you; but not just yet. The picture gets murkier, and darker. You need to hear about your old friend Earl King and what he's up to here."

CHAPTER 4

The evening of the day of Maxwell's ethics meeting, he and Lydia have dinner with Earl King at their country club in the rolling, fox-and-hounds countryside not far from Dulles airport. Earl King comes to Washington every two or three weeks. That is way too often for Lydia's taste.

King is a short, squat lecher. Habitually, he honks his nose into his soggy handkerchief, something profoundly impolite in Japan and to Lydia. His small condominium near the torpedo factory in Tullahoma, Tennessee, is a comedown from homes in the tony Bel Air section of Los Angeles, where he had a spectacular rise in fortune working for that aircraft manufacturer, and a more spectacular fall from its grace after being caught red-handed bribing South Korean air force officials. He comes to Washington to promote the killing power of the torpedoes he earns commissions from. But those commissions are not enough to sustain King's lifestyle. That's where his decades-long relationship with Lydia and Thad comes in.

The little that Lydia Maxwell knows about golf disgusts her. She remembers her father's infatuation with the game. He owned an abundance of clubs, bags, horrible spiked shoes, and loud clothes for his bad habit. When he went to a nearby practice range, he would change into this gear, straight from the brown-and-black kimono with the bespoke family crest he had commissioned to replace the two-hundred-year-old one that symbolized bygone decades of success in the Watanabe export business. He would frequently leave home for the golf courses outside

Tokyo, or the precious valley of courses in Karuizawa. It was after returning from three days of golfing there that her father was especially vile. He would drink throughout the bullet train ride into the Hakata station in Fukuoka, where he would buy vending-machine sake before boarding the local express that jerked him back to his Kohoku home life. He then usually put on his spiked shoes when he entered the house and punctured the tatami mats. Her mother soon gave up protesting such boorish conduct; the spikes left bluish scars on her smooth, desirable legs.

So, it is not with a gracious, open mind that Lydia sits in the Nineteenth Hole bar at a country club course that weaves through Virginia vineyards planted a mere sixteen years ago. Lydia has retained the youthful frame of her days as Aiko Watanabe. Her face is long and narrow, with a small nose and sunken cheeks. She has also retained the henna dye of her hair, which she wears to her shoulders. Tonight, she wears the jodhpurs and lily-white silk blouse of the hunt; the jodhpurs show off her legs and meet with Thad's special fancy.

She sips Pepsi Zero as Maxwell and King bray over conquering such things as sand traps and the rough between gulps of cheeseburgers. To Lydia, there is nothing rough about this landscape. It is a mowed, rolled, and sprinkler-nourished flatland. It is nothing like the wetland rice fields where she and Mariko would romp among muddy egret feeding grounds.

King managed to keep his fingers in the *El Caballo* pie after the end of her charter to the Chilean maritime authority. He convinced Lydia that she should insist on getting him the management operations contract for the vessel. When Thad was a law student, she had no leverage with Honshu Lines for such a sinecure. However, as Thad became more and more successful in the House, and rose higher in the leadership of his caucus, Lydia became more persuasive with Honshu, at King's coaching.

A ship management agreement between joint owners is not at all unusual. What is unusual about this one is that Lydia doesn't know one end of a boat from another, whereas Honshu Lines employs thousands of experts in ship management. What Lydia has, of course, is Thad. Thad has eager cargo shippers lobbying him. Thad also has Uncle Earl King, who is an expert at messy stuff. The operating contract between Honshu and Lydia is private, and her subcontract to Earl King is very private.

Following the cheeseburgers, the chat between Maxwell and King turns down in volume and becomes more slurred by young wine. Earl King does not like this chat.

Thad explains to King that he needs to divest Lydia's half of the *El Caballo*. This comes as a surprise to Lydia and as a dark storm-cloud's thunderclap to King. King tells them that the ship is temporarily out of his hands. For some reason, Honshu intervened directly with the ship's master and countermanded King's instructions. King demanded an explanation but was told nothing. They still don't return his phone calls.

Sullen, dehydrated, and frightened, Thad digs in. He says he will damn well see to it that either the vessel gets sold off or it never sails again. He says that he will start by calling his friend Alden Knight to get over to Japan and shake things loose in order for Lydia to sell her interest to a private buyer.

The sun, the losing at golf, and the alcohol has also darkened Earl King's brain. He calls up the adrenaline on tap whenever survival money is at stake. He forms the seed of an idea.

"I have a good notion to go to Tokyo and find out for myself what's going on with Honshu. I know Japan. I can get things done there. I can shake things up."

Lydia looks away wistfully, thinking, *I don't want this man meeting with Honshu! He is offensive and would ruin everything.*

<hr>

Thad Maxwell's face is blistered and haggard when he reconvenes his staff huddle with his ethics lawyer the next day. He has not slept well. It is a miserably hot day. His rare earth elements bill is still stuck in committee. Total Carbon is rattling his cage. He knows he needs them badly and their money even more badly, but he also knows the days of that easy monthly fill-up into Lydia's bank account are about to come to an end, and that he is going to have to end them himself, if he can. It is a rare predicament to have to work so hard to turn off a firehose of dark money.

With Drew Wallace, Evelyn Hutton, and Nancy Booth smiling at him at the conference table, Maxwell begins his grumble with a dry and tense voice.

"There's a new development. There is no joy in divesting Lydia's interest in the ship. Normally she is in charge of the movements of the ship and her business. She has an operating agreement with Honshu giving her that job. She hired Earl King to actually carry out that job since he has had a long career with the kind of business that benefits me. But last night, Earl told me that Honshu has stepped in and taken over the ship. He doesn't believe Honshu would be in the mood to sell, but he can't even talk to them. I'd sure like to know why. I'm going to work on that through an old friend from my law school days."

Drew looks at Maxwell with frightened eyes. "You've lost effective control of the ship, and Honshu's not talking to you?"

Thad nods. "That pretty well sums it up."

Maxwell watches Drew stand and pace. At the far end of the conference table, he stops in the corner of the room to look at the scale model of an oceangoing cargo vessel on a tall pedestal. The model is about thirty inches long and ten inches wide amidships, with a large superstructure rising over its stern. It is painted deep orange to its waterline maroon band, and black below that. Drew steps closer to the prow to squint at the small lettering: *El Caballo*. Maxwell sees him shake his head slowly.

When Drew returns, Maxwell is sitting with his arms folded and a deep frown on his face.

"Mr. Speaker, there is only one ethical game plan."

The room is quiet. "Well?" booms Maxwell.

"I need you to listen to me in private, Mr. Speaker."

Nancy scowls. Evelyn clenches her fingers.

"Could you girls give us a minute, please? I'll catch you up later. I'd like to hear Mr. Wallace's ethical thinking."

Thad does not watch Nancy Booth and Evelyn Hutton leave the room. He is watching Drew. He resumes drumming the mahogany tabletop.

"Well, choirboy, what's on your ethical mind?"

"So, Honshu refuses to permit the private sale?"

"I have to assume that, Drew. Honshu has gone dark. I'll try to reestablish communications with them using Alden Knight as a go-between, but there is no assurance that's going to work or on what timeline. What are our options now?"

Drew shakes his head with a scowl. "For the last twenty-four hours, I have thought about little else than options to salvage your political future from this meddlesome ship and to rid you of this affliction of warts. There are no good options, Mr. Speaker."

Maxwell grows annoyed. "Well, give me the less-than-good options. Don't just go limp on me!"

"As I said yesterday, ships are like floating real estate. If this were some warehouse or barn we needed to get rid of, we'd light a match."

Maxwell's eyes widen, and he sits back in his chair. "You do think outside of the box, don't you? OK, that's fine as an analogy, but I need something in the real world."

"Mr. Speaker, consider the analogy of a barn. What is the analogy for burning down a ship?"

Maxwell shrugs. "It sinks."

Drew nods gravely.

"Wait a damn minute …"

Drew paces in a broad circle in the manner of one of his most feared law professors in pitched Socratic battle. "What causes a ship to sink? You were the merchant marine apprentice."

"A bad storm, but you can't make one of those just happen. They could scuttle her, I suppose, but why would they?"

Drew stops dramatically and leans toward the Speaker of the House. "Anything else?" he asks, drawing out each syllable.

Maxwell is not only annoyed but also uncomfortable and impatient all at the same time. "Dammit, get to your point, and don't be so coy. This isn't some game." He starts drumming his fingertips again.

"No games, I agree. So, what is Earl King's day job when he's not booking more freight than your wife's ship can carry?"

Maxwell turns his head and scoffs, "You know the answer to that, Drew. He's always up here lobbying for that … oh."

"That torpedo factory in Tennessee? Is that what you were about to say?" Drew's eyebrows are in high, melodramatic arches now.

Maxwell's heart beats faster. His thinking slows. He looks again at Drew and meets his beady-eyed stare. "Torpedoes, Drew?"

"Sink her, Mr. Speaker."

Maxwell's fingers freeze; their drumming stops. He hears Drew speak in a husky, rustling whisper resembling a snake's rattle.

"Insurance proceeds are not reportable as income. They can be put in a blind trust. Yes, your future earnings would drop off, but your political future would not. Ethics committee proceedings proceed slowly. By the time they get to this issue, there's no bone for staff to gnaw on. No odor. The air would be fresh and clear. The past would be past. The future would be unblemished."

Maxwell exhales as though released from a choke hold. "Honshu Line's consent would not be required," he rasps.

"Exactly."

"How, Drew?"

"Once again, I defer to your superior knowledge in the merchant marine service. I suppose there would have to be a submarine." Drew crouches, looking over first one shoulder, then the other, and snakes his hand in front of him. "Bubble-lubble-lubble-lubble."

Maxwell cannot remain seated. He stands jerkily and grips the edge of the table to steady himself. Then he marches to the other end of the room, where he stares at the ship model. He turns, animated now. His words come in a rush. "Not a submarine. Two of them; need to confuse the issue of blame. A joint submarine exercise. A misfire. A misfortune, but one that involves shared embarrassment by two countries. Maybe Japan. The naval authorities play up the rescue, not the loss."

Out of earshot, Drew moans as if in admiration of a slow student's insight. "Yes! Maybe Japan, indeed; that is genius, Mr. Speaker."

Maxwell returns to shake Drew's hand warmly. "I'd like you to meet my old mentor from my law school days, Alden Knight. And to meet Lydia, of course. Would tomorrow night work for you? Evelyn can drive you out."

Clouds in the late afternoon and evening sky catch and hold the colors of molten iron as the sun dips below the horizon in the woodlands of northern Virginia. Drew and Evelyn bring uproarious laughter to the table with inside jibes and gentle pokes at the "boss." Thad is an accomplished giver of toasts, most often as a means of heaping surplus praise on his guests. It is his remarks about Drew that catch Lydia's attention especially. Thad drawls an unctuous, rambling account of how Drew is working on the single most important matter of the Speaker's long career. Drew and Evelyn are rapt as the compliments flow like tidewater. Lydia is so struck by Thad's intensity that later, she moves to Drew's side and takes his hand.

"May I please know the nature of your exciting and important work for my husband, if you think I could understand its complexities?" Drew has never before held hands with a beautiful, graceful woman of Lydia's age and remarkable exotic charm.

"It has to do with an upcoming ethics investigation. It also relates to the business of the *El Caballo*." He does not need to explain further.

Lydia grasps the point and its significance immediately. Instinctively her interior gears slip into survival torque. She understands immediately why Thad brought this choirboy to her on a warm summer night.

"Have you been to Japan, Drew-san?"

"No, ma'am, although I am enchanted by the way you have applied its craft and art to your own look."

"You are so observant, Drew-san. I am impressed. Please, let me bring us another glass of the champagne. You will wait here for me, won't you? Thad rarely brings guests to me with such cultivated taste."

"Oh, yes."

CHAPTER 5

"That's quite a story, Alden," says Brad. "So you were with all of them? They weren't serious about torpedoes, were they? What happened then?"

"I flew from New York to Dulles. We had dinner out at his country club. We spoke very little about the issue during dinner. Afterward, Thad excused the three of us men to the ladies, and we went to the cigar bar. It was weird. I've been in English homes where they still do that, but not here. Anyway, it was in the cigar smoke that he and Drew went through their whole nutty plan. I told Thad he was as crazy as a loon. He told me that if I didn't unlock Honshu's silence and get their consent, he would get the Pentagon up and running on this."

Brad is incredulous. "But torpedoes? How could he even do that?"

Alden raises both arms. "I know, you're thinking it is too ridiculous to take seriously. But Maxwell is serious. Torpedoes tie into defense spending, and Maxwell is a master at that. For eight terms in Congress, Maxwell has raised astonishing campaign funding from mining interests, fossil fuel and petroleum associations, and finally from an unexpected sector. That sector is one of the most successful and feared influencers upon the United States Congress: the gun lobby. Every manufacturer of munitions from handguns to torpedoes supports Thad Maxwell. And Thad Maxwell supports every one of them. Do I think he could actually pull such a stunt off? Not in a million years. Still, he's a loose cannon now, and I can't ignore it."

For a long moment, Brad's apartment is silent except for the ticking of an antique Seth Thomas clock atop an oak bookcase.

"Well, this was a terrific dinner, Brad. I'm going to write Kozue a note."

Brad starts clearing dishes. "She'll like that, Alden."

"I knew you were all going to Seattle. I'm not sure what for."

"It's another convention on gun violence. Kozue's giving a presentation on Sunday morning. That's her new passion, gun legislation; well, the close second to law enforcement. I'm not your guy if you're serious about torpedoes. You know her story."

"Oh. Yeah, of course I do. Hmm."

"What's wrong?"

"Nothing is wrong with Kozue or her passion. Every thirteen-year-old should have a passion for important issues. It's just …"

"Just what?"

"Well, it's just something I failed to factor into the favor I was about to ask."

Brad says nothing as he finishes loading the dishwasher. Alden steps through the small dining room and takes a seat on the sofa facing the parlor grand piano that fills the semicircular southeast corner of the living room. The floor-to-ceiling windows surrounding the piano are dark except for a streetlight, its fog-blurred glow falling on his Tesla in a no-parking zone.

Brad joins him. "Don't tell me you want Elgar Steel to buy that same vessel, the *Caballo* one. Are you thinking if we do that, Thad Maxwell won't have to launch torpedoes to finance his opposition to gun reform?"

Alden shifts his gaze to the oil painting over the fireplace—a weathered Kansas barn and wheat stubble. He stands to inspect the signature in the bottom left corner. He stares at the painting but thinks about what else is on his mind. He turns to face Brad.

"Thad Maxwell has sold his soul, Brad. He panders to the dark money that now fuels craziness in what used to be my political party. Just like the party, Maxwell doesn't have an agenda. He is weak on principle but addicted to power. He is not some lone, corrupt outlier. He is one in a herd of others just as weak. In that context, perhaps torpedoes do not sound so outlandish to him. But dark money comes from the likes of the Total Carbon Corporation you became so acquainted with a couple of years ago. Dark money has agendas."

"I think I have a pretty good idea where Total Carbon's coming from. That's part of the business jungle. But guns? That's a different kind of evil, Alden."

"Yup. Well, I'm not going to ask the favor I came here to ask. Yes, it was to buy that ship. Technically, it'd be Lydia's deal, not Thad's, but that won't make a difference to you."

"Alden, why are you involved? There are shipbrokers everywhere. If the ship has a value, it will have a market. I don't follow that market, but I know that whenever we decide to charter, or even buy, a ship like that, we'd go through a broker."

Alden stretches his legs forward. "Remember, he's locked into Honshu Lines. It's those cargoes, Brad. That vessel is never unemployed, no matter what the market's doing. If he cashed out of that ship, he and Honshu would never get near the same amount of income. The *El Caballo* gets top dollar and more, even when newer ships in her class are laid up without any business. That's not all. When it comes time for maintenance and repairs, she puts into US Navy facilities. No one knows what he's charged if anything. There's never a broker involved in her cargo and charter contracts. Well, there's a manager on retainer, so it's a fixed cost. No other cash cow that I know of is as fat as this plain-looking cargo vessel."

"Alden, listening to this makes me want to take a shower."

"Oh, it does me too."

"Why does the Speaker of the House of Representatives spill all this to you, Alden? You should back away from this. You have a great retirement and a great life at a prestigious Napa Valley winery. You earned your position through integrity and professionalism. You're too much a square shooter to step in this dog shit."

Alden stands and walks to the circular windows. He speaks to the streetlight. "Brad, my party—my former party—is at a tipping point. Some think it's tipped too far to be set straight again. But I—and people like me—think otherwise. A group of us desperately wants to salvage the party and make it viable in the public square again. That party has lost its purpose. Some of us are trying to restore purpose to the party. The country absolutely needs two political parties. Right now, it has one party and one animal house. It's now or never, Brad."

"Nobly said, Alden. But you'll never convince me that Maxwell is going to go along with that."

"You're right, of course. He's too far gone. But the thing is he's not *actually* gone. We need to make him fade away, but not in a financial scandal that will stink up the whole party even more than it is now. I'd rather he lose power and influence quietly, not in a ruin. Rebuilding the party with vision will be hard enough as it is."

Brad throws a dish towel across the room. "Spare me the talk about leaders with vision, Alden. We've had competing, soaring visions way too long, and in the meantime, the government is falling apart, just like America's infrastructure. Give me a president who can follow his oath and simply uphold and execute the laws already on the books. Give me a president who can manage the system professionally and honestly. After that, maybe there's room for vision. The 'vision thing' these days means taking the eye off the ball. Sorry, but I've seen too many good—and too many bad—chief executives in business; to me, 'vision' is a secondary attribute. You can't reinvent a vision every four years."

Alden stoops to pick up the dish towel and tosses it back to Brad. Then he claps his hands slowly. "That's the best campaign speech I've heard in years, Brad. Why don't you run for office?"

"Ha! Why don't you?"

Alden falls silent, lips pursed. He rocks twice on the balls of his feet.

"Wait a minute! Are you even thinking of that, Alden? Really? I'm in for a contribution if you are."

"I've been approached, Brad."

"Wow. I see we've moved off of boats."

"Sit down, Brad. Yeah, that's enough talk about something neither one of us knows anything about. It's been on my mind to talk to you about something more in your wheelhouse."

Brad looks at him with a smile at that reference. But he does sit and gives Alden his full attention.

"I've admired you ever since you came to my reception when I was USTR. You took on a new kind of job, and you went after it very well, with no experience in the Washington scene. You have the right bones. You have a synthesizing mind, and I said so to Sarah Jane."

Brad is quiet now. "I know, she told me later."

Alden takes a step toward him. "Now, let me tell you what she said to me. She said you also have a directing mind. She meant you can bring others into the fold and point them in the right direction. You can give directions that are apt and don't sound like you're giving orders. You make people feel they can contribute if they do something you've suggested. British law uses the term 'directing mind' as a negative, more like what we would call a ringleader, or the brains behind a criminal plan. She meant it in a positive way, and as a compliment.

"I'm dead serious about remaking a dignified political party," Alden continues. "I don't accept that it is too late to fix it. The repairs will take many people with the kind of qualities you have, Brad. For too long, the party has been caught up in the false charisma of a few. The people I am talking to about this welcome other smart people who have synthesizing, directing minds. I'd like you to think about playing a principal role in the change we're working on."

Brad bows his head quickly. He walks to the bay windows. "I don't know what to say, Alden. Thank you, of course. That is high praise." He turns to look back at Alden. "I have a capacity problem with what you're suggesting. I was a hundred percent busy with the steel plant, and then the coal mine came along. All that came on top of putting together my own family. There aren't enough hours in a day as it is. I have to say, I like the direction you're going in, Alden. Not long ago, I would have gotten excited about being a part of it. Now, it strikes me as a disruption. I'm trying to avoid any more disruptions. I couldn't do that to Amaya and Kozue."

Alden holds his arms out from his sides, palms up. "Brad, I just want to show you where there could be a new opportunity and a way to help your country. For example, my old job. Brad, assuming we pull this off and I have something to say about it, would you like to be the US trade representative?"

"Oh, man, you found my sweet spot. Don't tempt me. Can't we just go back to talking about sinking freighters?"

CHAPTER 6

"Are you nervous?" June asks Kozue at dinner. Her presentation is the next morning.

"No, Aunt June. There was a time I was, but not anymore. Look around the restaurant. Over there are college kids from Florida. When they give their speeches, they talk about their friends at Parkland who died when they were my age. When I think about that, I have no fear of giving a speech."

"You are growing up too fast," says June, softly.

"Will you go shopping tomorrow, Aunt June?" Kozue is wide-eyed. June is the most awesome shopper Kozue has ever encountered.

"No, Kozue. I plan to return to Toronto right after your presentation. Besides, this conference sort of blunts my shopping appetite."

June Elgar's long auburn hair falls to the shoulders of her serious-business khaki skirt-and-jacket suit. Pinned to her lavender cotton blouse is the insignia of her environmental organization, the American Canadian Environmental Alliance (ACEA). Her interests lie in that direction as well as the direction of men who fascinate her—any younger man, and a man of any age who is attracted to her.

June lives in Canada, fundraising for do-good environmental projects. Her personal exposure to environmental activism ends there. She does not venture into forests or wetlands. Since their father died, the twins see less and less of each other. Sarah Jane is well grounded; June a gadfly, shamefully flirtatious, spiced with mendacity. Workers at the steel plant and the winery hardly know June because she's never around them. Sarah Jane's caller ID for June reads, "Evil Twin." It's a love-exasperation relationship between the two. In 2019, after their father died, June had fouled her nest, trying to trick Amaya out of her inheritance. Brad managed to fix that one, but June was harsh in her dealings with Amaya until Kozue came into the family, when she warmed considerably.

June Elgar has always felt a unique bond with Kozue. That closeness has led to spoiling her with attention and confidences for the five years Kozue has been in the family. Thus, it was June who organized the excursion to Seattle, knowing of Kozue's fervor to quell gun violence. Most of the featured speakers at such events make heartbreaking outpourings about young lives lost in schools. Kozue brings her own point of view.

———

Brad's phone buzzes. He holds up one finger and quickly says, "Amaya?"

"No, Sarah Jane. Where the hell do I park around here? I brought you guys some fresh fruit and encouragement. Both will spoil before I find parking. I haven't heard those foghorns in years. Beautiful."

Brad rolls his eyes and grins. "See where the Tesla is? Well, go up the hill one block. There's another no-parking curb near the cable car tracks."

"Good thing I made you COO and got us another general counsel. I like you a little bent. Be there in a minute."

Sarah Jane Elgar, June's fraternal twin, is the steadier hand and the one who became more firmly attached to Brad, but in a platonic, sisterly way. Sarah Jane retired as CEO of Elgar Steel some three years ago. She still keeps herself up to date on the business but spends most of her time running the family's winery in Napa. A metallurgical engineer, she creates massive architectural sculptures for new buildings around the world. Amaya knew of her artwork before actually meeting Sarah Jane. Recently, Tokyo commissioned her for a three-dimensional cherry blossom in front of a new skyscraper in its sister city, Berlin. During the early days of Wishbone, she and Alden Knight took a liking to each other, and five years ago they married. Brad still consults with Sarah Jane, occasionally, when it comes to very personal questions, arm in arm in a stroll around the exercise area of Sarah Jane's horse barn.

"This curry is heavenly! Where did you order it from?" Sarah Jane is shamelessly spooning the last of it straight from the saucepan. The fruit she brought rests in an Imari bowl on the dining room table where Brad and Alden sit, waiting for her to join them. Sarah Jane's white hair clings stylishly to shape her narrow face. She is five feet four inches tall and has been trim and fit her entire life. She still uses one of the fabricating bays at the plant to weld steel sculptures, some as tall as fifteen feet, commissioned for the facades of skyscrapers and performing arts centers in major cities throughout the world. That plant space might just as well be called her private gymnasium for molding her taut physique.

"Kozue made it for Brad before they left," says Alden. "We agree with you."

Brad is subdued. He looks at a bowl of ice cream topped with huckleberries picked from ancient scrub at Point Reyes, a national seashore north of San Francisco. His hand doesn't move to lift the spoon filled with his favorite dessert. His mind swirls with: corruption at the top of government; an impending disaster at sea; a sales pitch from a former ambassador for a vessel employed in shady freight; and the intriguing suggestion that the same former ambassador is considering a comeback of some sort. Somehow, berries and ice cream don't fit in.

Saucepan still in hand, curry stain on her upper lip, Sarah Jane joins her favorite men at the table. "Did Alden fill you in on his trip to Washington?"

Brad adjusts a chair for her and kisses her cheek. "Oh, yes."

"So, what do you think?"

"I guess 'damn the torpedoes' would be in poor taste." Brad's hands gesture an explosion.

Alden and Sarah Jane sputter. Alden says, "OK, but really, Brad, I'd like to hear what you think about all this."

"Let's go back to this cargo vessel since that seems to be the most explosive issue." Now, they just groan. "Elgar Steel would never buy half a boat."

Alden tilts his head. "Well, you told me earlier you have thought about the coal delivery point. Putting a ship like that under your control means you could start selling the coal on a delivered basis, not come-by-and-pick-it-up-when-you're-running-low as things stand now. If Japan's coal demand slows down, the pick-it-up slows down, and you don't have a sale. If you sell it delivered to Japan, they stockpile the coal, and you stockpile the sales dollars. The other thing is that the Maxwells could sell their half on a more private basis than if a shipbroker is involved and it goes on the open market."

Brad taps Alden's arm. "Alden, you never did say, but I need to know how you left it in Washington. Who did you meet with, and what are their expectations?"

"Yeah, well, I saw Lydia at the dinner at Maxwell's country club. I was glad to see her again. She wants it both ways. She wants Thad's troubles to go away without giving up her half of the *El Caballo*. Lydia got more adamant as the discussion went on. She definitely got along well with Drew Wallace. I think Thad likes Wallace's crackpot plan, but some part of him tells him, 'No way.' That's why he called me back there, to find another way."

Sarah Jane stands and puts her hands on Alden's shoulders. She gives him a little shake. "Come on, you don't really think he could pull this sub attack off, do you?" Sarah Jane asks.

Alden cranes his neck to look at her. "Definitely, Sarah. He has the connections at the Pentagon and in the industry. He can pull the right chains in the Defense Department. He's lived in that patch his whole career."

"It's as loony as it is wrong," she declares.

"That's what I said to them. So, as for you, Brad, I told them you and Sarah run Elgar Steel and the Canadian coal mine. Maxwell knew about the Wishbone Pipeline, of course. He admires your ingenuity. All I did was to ask them if I could consult with you and see if you had a better idea than a hunter-killer sub."

Brad paces, worried that Alden may have started a commitment Brad can't finish. "I have to ask you again, what are Thad Maxwell's expectations that I take his ship off his hands?"

"Zero, Brad. Maxwell is open to anything that keeps him out of the soup with the ethics panel. My idea, which I haven't mentioned to him, is for you to contact Honshu Lines, find out what's going on with the vessel, and nail down their position on Maxwell getting out of it."

Brad stops pacing and stands in front of Alden. "Well, what's your opinion about Honshu Lines? Why have they suddenly taken drastic action with the ship, and why aren't they telling King or Lydia about it?"

"I sure don't know, but that's the heart of the problem, Brad. The only reason Wallace and Maxwell are thinking about sinking her is that they can't even talk to Honshu, and they don't have a better plan." Alden's on his feet now, a note of desperation in his voice.

"Brad, I'm out of other good ideas. I'm begging you to go to Tokyo and work your magic with your Japanese friends. As things stand now, King has said he'd go to Tokyo himself. You know that could be a real disaster. More than anyone else I know, you stand the best chance of getting the true story. Maybe there is some sort of scratch-your-back possibility involving your cronies in the steel industry over there."

Brad sees it—which is not to say he likes it much. But he does see it. Brad has been traveling to Tokyo on steel business ever since Ernie brought him in as the company lawyer. Ernie was a good mentor, but Brad had even better help from his counterpart at Shin Steel, Jiru (Jerry) Hiwasaki. Jerry and Brad hit it off right away. Both enjoyed contemporary literature, and both had a gift for probing moral issues in business settings.

Brad's openness and genuine respect for his Japanese counterparts earned him the most valuable quality in Japanese business: trust. It turned out that his wife, Amaya, had gone to college in Kyoto with a woman from a prestigious steel family, Yuko Kanawa, who later became Yuko Kagono. After her husband died, Yuko turned her full attention to politics and advocacy. Their paths had parted briefly when Amaya went to London for graduate studies, but later came together after Yuko had become Japan's first female prime minister. Japan had been suddenly thrust in an energy crisis when half its liquefied natural gas (LNG) storage reserves blew to smithereens. Yuko arranged for Brad and Amaya to come to Tokyo in a hurry to help sort out the aftermath of that mess. During the course of that mission, Brad also became a trusted source of good advice to the prime minister. His already highly valued stock in Japan as a person soared after that.

"Well, there's going to be no mad dash to Tokyo for me," says Brad. "Those days are in my past. But the idea of selling coal on a delivered basis is appealing. So, buying this ship from Honshu and Lydia could be interesting. Since a couple of the coal customers are also part owners in the coal mine, it might be appealing to them too."

Alden relaxes into a smile. "No mad dash to Tokyo, but maybe a thoughtfully planned one? Soon?"

"We'll see." Brad stops and turns to face his friend. He is worried. "In the meantime, you should be thinking about what's in the deal for Total Carbon. It seems to me the invisible heavy hand in all this is TCC and their leverage with the Speaker. Just from what you've said so far, you've got the TCC powerhouse channeling flood levels of dark money into the household account of the Speaker of the House. Since they call it freight, they can try to deduct it from their income taxes. You and I call it political contributions which Maxwell hasn't reported. You think about that, Alden, before you get too caught up in trying to rescue Thad Maxwell. He is swimming way too far away from the shore. He's thrashing and scared. He's likely to pull down anyone who tries to pull him back. This isn't some political shenanigan—it's tax fraud and illegal campaign funding." Alden is silent as the two men lock eyes.

Brad breaks the tension. "But, while you're taking a hard look at that, I'll think about the Japanese angle. You guys can hang out in Kozue's room tonight. There's no better place to hear the foghorns."

As Brad starts to walk away, Sarah Jane puts her hand on his wrist. "Brad, I know you and your thinking. But I also know something about the Japanese mills. When I went there with Daddy, I wasn't just the 'touristy daughter.' I had ears and a brain. Don't assume too much about the steel mills agreeing to the delivery terms you guys are talking about. Daddy went there as a seller of steel scrap before he went there as a buyer of steel plate. He always said it was a hundred times harder to be a seller than a buyer in that country. You've been a buyer there all your career up to now. Now, as of last year, you're trying to sell them coal. You absolutely have to find out if they will accept your delivery terms before you start thinking about buying or even renting a ship."

Alden says, "Sarah, I think the next best step would be for Brad to go to Japan and see Honshu. Then he can talk to his coal partners about a direct purchase of the vessel before Maxwell blows it up."

In a stronger voice, Sarah Jane says, "Alden, don't get too far ahead of yourself. After all, Brad's running my businesses, and that's a handful."

She turns to Brad. "You, too, Brad, don't get ahead of yourself. You get grand ideas in your head and on paper. Maybe you're even thinking about backhaul cargo. But the Japanese steel industry has imported its raw materials its entire history. They would probably be unwilling to change a damn thing. I implore you to first consult with them before you run off to buy a boat."

Alden puts a calming hand on her shoulder. "Fair enough, Sarah. But in any case, Brad has to take a trip to Tokyo."

Brad stands and says, "Alden, if I'm going to take that trip, don't you need to tell Maxwell about it?"

CHAPTER 7

Three people sit in Thad Maxwell's office Saturday morning. None of them wants to be there. Maxwell clenches his teeth and then his fist. In tight-jawed, measured low tones, he says, "In thirty years, Lydia and I have never heard a peep from anyone about this ship. Now, I get a phone call from the West Coast saying that someone we don't know will be going to talk to Honshu about the *El Caballo*."

Drew asks, "You mean Ambassador Knight?"

Maxwell slams the clenched fist on the table. "Alden Knight is going to outsource that to someone else!"

"Want me to go and talk to him?" Drew asks with a warm smile.

"No, Mr. Wallace." Maxwell stabs a forefinger toward Drew's face. "You are to stay here and focus on the ethics committee. I need someone I can trust absolutely. Alden's on his way to Seattle and I've told Nancy Booth to get on a jet to Seattle this afternoon to find out what she can. She's no happier about it than I am."

Evelyn sputters, "But she keeps this office afloat."

"Exactly right," booms Maxwell, "that's how serious this thing is with me. So, instead of wrangling the unruly herd of my caucus, the job I'm good at, I now have to try to run my own office staff. What a damned nightmare."

"What would you like us to do, then?" asks Evelyn.

Maxwell takes a deep breath. At times like this, his first instinct is for money. Calmer now, he looks at Evelyn. "You need to step up fundraising, big time. Things are moving fast. I need you to replace those ship revenues from our usual sources, not spend time finding new ones."

Evelyn relaxes a bit. This is a task she's good at. "This wouldn't be a good time to hit up Total Carbon. We'll have to see how the ship issue plays out because that's their favorite channel. If we need to find it somewhere else, that leaves gun makers. But they're going to want something."

"Something more? After what I've done for them, what more is there?"

"Mr. Speaker, that's what I'll have to find out. But that's the best sector for a quick fix."

"Then get on it, Evelyn," barks Maxwell, pounding the table again. Evelyn flinches from the sound as if he had struck her.

"And me?" asks Drew, hoping there is at least something.

"Drew, you have to get nimble with the numbers on the *El Caballo*'s cargoes. Find flexibility. Make assumptions. I also want you to get up to speed on what we've done for defense appropriations over the last ten years. I have a feeling you're going to need familiarity with that history. You're going to spearhead the push for joint submarine exercises in the Pacific. It's your idea; now you're gonna make it happen." Maxwell knows he has other people more experienced for this, but he needs to put Drew Wallace in a box he can throw overboard if need be.

Wallace exhales and smiles in satisfaction. He's more an idea guy than a go-to-war guy. "I'm glad you are taking my suggestion seriously, Mr. Speaker."

"I don't play games with stuff like this."

<hr>

That same morning, the Tesla and Sara Jane's pickup pull away from their respective curbs and head south down Hyde Street to the freeway that will take them to San Francisco International Airport. Both had parking tickets under their windshield wipers. Alden needs to jawbone

Brad in the Tesla. Sarah Jane needs to pick up some things at the airport shops for her overnight in Seattle.

"I talked to Maxwell again before breakfast," Alden begins, his voice light and brisk. "He's on the warpath, and I mean that literally. He's sending his campaign funding staffer out into the gun world to pick up new campaign donations. His new ethics guru has started with the Pentagon to organize the submarines. And today, his chief of staff flies to Seattle to intercept me and try to figure out more about you and what role you're going to play."

"Things are moving fast, Alden." Brad scrunches lower in the passenger seat, frowning.

"Yes, they are. And of course, I thought about this thing off and on all night."

"Me too, Alden. You first."

Alden glances over and says, warily, "I've asked you to go to Japan. What do you think?"

Brad looks straight ahead, not saying a word.

"At least talk to me," Alden snaps.

Brad looks out the car's window to where the old Forty-Niners football and Giants baseball games were played, often in gale-force winds, at Candlestick Park, back in the days when he went there with his dad.

Brad sighs. This is it. "I reached the same conclusion, Alden. I'll get a flight out of Seattle tomorrow afternoon after Kozue's speech."

Now it's Alden who is silent.

"Well?" Brad sits up straighter.

Alden shifts his shoulders a bit. He gingerly gets to the point he realized in the middle of the night. "See, the thing is, that would put you in Tokyo at close of business Monday. It'll take you at least two days to organize your meetings, best case. In the meantime, Drew Wallace is getting the Navy locked and loaded. Because Maxwell is who he is, Wallace has a better chance of getting to the right people in the Pentagon sooner than you can organize Honshu Lines and the steel companies who buy your coal."

Brad is increasingly uncomfortable. He, too, can figure all that out. "Yeah. So?"

Alden dips his head. "So, if today you go to Tokyo instead of Seattle, you cut some of that time disadvantage."

"Alden, Kozue's speech is Sunday morning," Brad says flatly.

"I understand ..."

With considerably more energy, Brad says, "Good. What you also have to understand is that I promised Kozue."

Eyes straight ahead, Alden says, trying to maintain calm, "I am not saying what you should or should not do. I am not asking you to do one thing or another. I am simply saying what I think is the best way to do something about this mess, based on the facts and a timetable not of our choosing. There's a potential international incident brewing. There's the possibility of loss of life at sea. You happen to have a unique affinity with influential people in Japan. I don't know any others."

Brad shakes his head slowly. "Here we go again, Alden. Do I break my word to Kozue? I know she'd be forgiving, but is that any reason to hurt her? Does that make it fair somehow?"

"I wish I didn't have to say all this. I'm certainly not going to apply pressure—just giving you my analysis. I'll shut up and drive now so you can think."

Sarah Jane stands to greet Alden at their departure lounge. "You're wearing that? Well, you can pick up a blazer and decent slacks at SeaTac when we get in. Where's Brad?"

"I dropped him off at the international terminal. He's getting a walk-up ticket to Tokyo."

CHAPTER 8

In Japan, mid-morning on Sunday, Yuko Kagono is panting but smiling. Eight months into the year, she has never missed her daily bicycle climb across the Kanmangafuchi Abyss and up the winding, steep, narrow road of Mount Nantai to reach this spot. It overlooks the vast Senjogahara marshlands spread across a valley of overgrown volcanic debris near the town of Nikko, Japan. The breezy mountain air is exhilarating for those who pause at this lookout before continuing their trek to the summit.

The air in the prime minister's private gym is somewhat less so. Her workouts are on a stationary, recumbent bicycle, the wilderness experience provided by a high-definition video and recorded birdsong. The climbing angles result from resistance controls on the equipment, automatically coordinated with the video. The bicycle is recumbent because her orthopedic surgeon doesn't allow actual bicycling or even stationary bikes after her hip surgery a year ago.

Kagono is fifty-seven years old, shedding weight gradually, and toning her legs back in the direction of their fitness when she danced ballet in Kyoto. Yes, she should have been doing this exercise routine regularly ever since her college days, but, well, she was too busy breaking gender barriers in Japanese politics. She is five feet, three inches tall and still moves quickly. Her deep actor's voice was developed through years of chanting performances in Bunraku, Japanese puppetry.

Ordinarily, she chooses solitude on her Sundays as often as possible.

She is a widow. Her brother, Iseo, lives about an hour away in Kamakura. When they see each other, it is usually on a Sunday, but Yuko is content to keep those occasions infrequent. Today, however, she will have another visitor.

She dresses today in a linen lemon-colored skirt to the knees and a silk blouse the color of new grass with covered buttons. *I am slimmer,* she thinks as she smiles approval to her image in the tall mirror. She gathers her hair in the same tight bun she wore in her ballet dancing days, and her soft, dark eyes have a sparkle of anticipation. Satisfied with her look for today, she turns to the task of wrapping the *ochugen* (summer gratitude gift) she intends to present to her caller.

Marcel Bourquin, ambassador to Japan from Switzerland, clears the security desk at the residence and office of the prime minister, and follows the uniformed Japan Self-Defense Force marine to her residence. Although the meeting will not be attended by her usual entourage, protocol does require a uniformed guard to blend into the wallpaper, on alert. This duty is assigned as a special honor in the Self-Defense Force. Today, the honor falls to Chief Petty Officer Kimoto, one of ninety marines of the navy's elite Special Boarding Unit, for a special reason. Kimoto keeps a passive, stern face as he escorts the ambassador to the small parlor adjacent to Kagono's bedroom. Once inside, Kimoto takes up a position against the far wall, feigning invisibility.

On a small, raised platform at one end of the room rest instruments of Japanese stage music: a small, square banjo-like shamisen with its long neck holding three strings and strummed with a large plectrum; a wooden flute; and a koto, a horizontal thirteen-stringed harp with rounded wooden top, resting low to the floor, and played by a kneeling musician. The two long walls of the room are a solid mustard color, and the end walls are checkerboards of fifteen-inch-deep blue squares alternating with white ones of the same size. The corners of the room hold tall vases of ferns and deep purple irises. The furniture is distinctly comfortable: Western, leather-seated wooden armchairs. A polished, black-lacquered Chinese chest with large pewter pulls decorating the drawers serves as a sideboard for a bowl of fruit and tea service.

Bourquin is six feet tall, fifty-five, with brown, gray-streaked hair and tan eyes. He is a former equestrian and has the nicks and scars on his face to show for it. He keeps fit with frequent squash games. He is in tan slacks, a steel-gray polo shirt open at the neck, and a sports coat the color of pine bark. He carries a courtesy gift he hopes will delight the prime minister. Bourquin, a bachelor, has been at the Swiss embassy long enough to know that she has a fondness for Gruyere cheese and Bavarian *weisswurst*.

After courteous greetings, exchange of the gifts, and Yuko's service of tea, the two open the business of the day, which is distinctly confidential statecraft.

Yuko settles into her armchair. Her face glows with a combination of happiness and admiration for her guest. She sits tall with shoulders squared. Her voice is low and warm and displays a trace of affection. "Mr. Ambassador, this humanitarian mission is a matter that I deeply appreciate. It sets a high-water mark in my agenda as prime minister. It is ironic that modern geopolitics dictate that we keep it out of the public eye."

Bourquin smiles broadly. "Madam Prime Minister, I am delighted that my government may be of some small service in the matter. We have a long, rich history of carrying out humanitarian services, whether popular or not. In fact, the less popular and more humanitarian, the better, in our perverse thinking."

"*Independent* thinking, surely, Marcel. I can't imagine a perverse thought crossing your mind," says Yuko with a twinkle.

Bourquin resists an impulse to squirm. He chooses to dodge the temptation for repartee and get right to diplomacy. "I have in this portfolio the documents necessary to transfer from my government to yours official control over the particular assets involved in the mission. We shall defer to you any public release of information, or, if you prefer, we will assist in your complete secrecy."

Yuko sighs. Oh, how she would like to shout and dance and broadcast the whole thing, but she knows it would cause such uproar as to badly damage her nation and his. "First things first, Marcel. Let's accomplish the mission without incident. Then, we'll see about what we say publicly or whether we'll just bury it in obscurity. So far, only you and I know what's going on."

Marcel frowns. He has seen efforts to keep government actions private fail before. "But, at some point, Yuko, you must involve others. The sheer logistics and the many lives affected will dictate that. What are you going to do about that?"

Yuko nods in recognition of the stark truth. "You are right, of course. I am gathering trustworthy friends who are passionate about what we are doing but are not connected with the government at all. They should be able to meet the initial civilian needs. Moreover, Chief Petty Officer Kimoto you see behind me will be on the front line of the non-civilian effort. I have every confidence in its success."

Twenty-eight-year-old muscular Kimoto blushes invisibly.

Bourquin stands and gathers the wooden box holding the gift from Yuko. "You have humbled me with this exquisite Kakiemon bowl. Your spies are very effective to have learned I do have a modest collection. This one is truly exceptional."

He is right, of course. Yuko has presented him with an eleven-inch-diameter white porcelain bowl, which was thinly potted two hundred sixty years ago in Arita at the legendary Kakiemon pottery compound. One side of the bowl holds the image of a branch with persimmon-red berries. The color is the signature feature of the Kakiemon kiln, "kaki" being the persimmon shade of the enamel created there.

Yuko says quietly, "Five years ago, this bowl was nearly destroyed by a North Korean thug who broke into the art gallery where it was displayed. The manager of the shop was very badly injured in her struggle to save the bowl. As you can see, she succeeded, but not before suffering a frightful injury to her neck. The shop owner, Amaya, is a dear friend. She was visiting from America, where she lives, when this harrowing incident occurred. Some months after, I went to the shop on a Sunday afternoon, like this one. I purchased it. Marcel, the mother of the injured clerk may be one of the individuals our humanitarian mission might save. I hope so. This bowl is therefore very significant. I am not a collector like you are, Marcel. You should have it both for that reason and for the very significant role you play in our mission."

Bourquin bows. "Again, you humble me with both the object and its attachments. Let us speak of this again when we have succeeded."

Yuko places her hand on Marcel's wrist. "Yes, that's the right way. I hope to introduce you to my friend Amaya, if only I can entice her to leave San Francisco to join me here and become a part of what we're doing. Now, let's get down to granular details of the project. Chief Petty Officer Kimoto, please become visible to tell us the tactics."

CHAPTER 9

In Seattle on Sunday, Kozue has been awake since six. June has booked a two-bedroom suite on the ocean side of the hotel. Amaya, Sarah Jane, June, and Kozue sit in its living room, the walls adorned with photos of orca whales breaching, and watch the clock advance to the time of Kozue's presentation. She is already in San Francisco's private Quadrangle School's upper division uniform, a French blue pleated skirt well below her knees with ivory windowpane plaid, and a white long-sleeved shirt with a rounded collar, into which she has tied the school tie. Amaya and Sarah Jane are combing her hair, again, and brushing unseen lint from the hunter-green blazer. Kozue's succession of hair lengths and styles has gone from ponytail when she was adopted at age eight, to two braids, to short bob in the same style as her policewoman friend in Tokyo, Inspector Hiradi, to today's cut, which is to the nape of her neck in the back with two prominent, half-moon chin-length strands down her rounded cheeks, similar to but not exactly like Amaya's style. In five years, Kozue has grown strong and solid in San Francisco's invigorating air which invites long walks, boosted by her enthusiasm for Quadrangle baseball as a utility infielder, with unrealized aspirations to pitch. In this environment, her self-confidence has also grown like a tree, not a weed.

Hers will be a five-minute speech. She has rehearsed it at home and at the hotel. If she's said it ten times a day since she finished writing it a week ago—just counting the out-loud times—that comes to seventy.

Then, of course, the unspoken run-throughs might bring the aggregate well over twice that. She practiced in front of Daddy-Brad in the apartment, and in front of Mom in the apartment and at the hotel. Last night, she said it in front of Mom, Aunt Sarah Jane, and Uncle Alden.

But not in front of Daddy-Brad last night.

Sure, she gets it. Uncle Alden went over it softly and carefully, always the same way. He must have rehearsed it on the plane Saturday morning. She gets it. Getting it doesn't replace what's missing. Tokyo? He couldn't even wait a day? She gets it. Sometimes it had been like that with her birth daddy, too.

Amaya holds the blazer over one elbow. Kozue sits across the bed. Her voice and spirit are strong for her age. "I get it, Mom. He heard it last week. It's no biggie."

But it is.

Amaya puts the blazer down and moves to Kozue's side. She absently draws her fingernails over Kozue's arm, an endearment she started five years ago when Kozue became her daughter. Amaya is slender and graceful, slightly taller than Sarah Jane, and her long black hair falls below her shoulders, a few wisps against her high cheekbones, past full lips and sculpted chin. Amaya's thoughts always develop into solid ideas before she utters them, softly. Her ready smile is often accompanied by a turn of her head downward and away. Today, she wears a summer skirt suit of pearl-gray lightweight wool with faint chalk pinstripes, black pumps, a celadon-colored silk top with a jade brooch, and matching tiny ear pins.

"Mom, I always get scared when Daddy-Brad's away on business."

"I do, too, Kozue. Well, not scared as much as melancholy. The English word is 'glum.' The American slang is 'bummed.' It's as if colors have faded and empty rooms have gotten larger. Everything seems emptier when he's gone."

"Emptier, yes, that's it. With me, there's also this feeling it might be the last time I see him."

Amaya leans away, an alarmed look on her face. She shakes off her own glumness to focus on her daughter. "Do you still think that way? Do you think we should go back to the counselor?"

Kozue shrugs. "Well, the last counselor explained it, but that's different from really helping. She explained there are triggers. I'm sure you feel that way at times about your mother you lost, and then your foster mother. When he's on a trip, and everything here is the same except he's gone away, the absence is a trigger. I am incredibly sad."

"I had my art, my ceramics. I had museums and concerts and violin. Even all that didn't stop the double emptiness that I felt: first, when my mother died, and again when my foster mother died. It never goes away. It is a condition of life—like having black instead of red hair."

"Mom, people would give anything for your hair. It is beautiful, just like everything else about you. But red? Not blonde?"

"There was a time I wanted blonde, Kozue. But later it was red."

"You mean red because of Cindy Atherton?" Kozue pokes Amaya. "You think that because of Daddy-Brad?"

Cindy Atherton showed up in Japan when Brad and Amaya were there, and Brad needed an engineer. There is no doubt about Cindy's stunning good looks and imposing figure at nearly six feet, her hair indeed the color of sunlight on maple leaves.

Kozue pushes against Amaya's arm. "Mom, he says Cindy Atherton is like molten steel. He keeps a safe distance. Besides, she's totally married now."

"And living in Japan. Where he's just gone. I'm sorry, but I can't ignore it." Amaya laughs.

Kozue giggles and digs an elbow against Amaya's arm. "You. You're as bad as I am."

Sarah Jane has been listening. She replaces her coffee cup on the room service tray and lets out an exuberant "Hah! Kozue's right. He doesn't go looking for redheads when he's alone. He goes in his canoe looking for ducks. June has red in her hair, and they can't stand to be together in the same room alone." She takes a chair on the other side of the table. "I used to envy June's hair. All it ever got her was into trouble. Do you ever worry about Brad when he's away for so long in Japan?"

"Absolutely not, Sarah Jane," Amaya says with energy. She shrugs. "Oh, I know the stories. I come from such a story. But I never give it a second thought about Brad."

Sarah Jane, in mock astonishment, "Not even Cindy Atherton, before she married Iseo?"

"No, never. I used to tease Brad about her every chance I got. He always ignored it and said nothing. That was perfect. I would have worried only if he had protested or denied or something like that."

"Aha. You do have an intricate mind, Amaya." Sarah Jane settles into an armchair and smiles her approval.

Amaya turns. "What about your mother, Sarah Jane? When Ernie-san went to Japan so much, did she ever say anything like that? Did they discuss it ever?"

Sarah Jane looks out the window. "She hated him being away. That's all I remember. I honestly don't know. I never heard a thing. Frankly, that's one of the reasons you were such a surprise to June and me, sister. Forget about red hair," Sarah Jane scoffs. "Brad has his triggers, but it's not red hair or engineers."

"Oh?" Kozue looks up expectantly. Amaya knows what's coming.

"Yeah, it's driving cars. You'd never know it from all the effort he put into fixing up that old Caprice he drives."

"Brad's an awesome driver," says Kozue, remembering a two-week-long road trip three years ago and a hectic chase in its last half hour.

"That's Brad, conquering his fears, his demons, his triggers. When he first lost his parents and fiancée, he never went near a car. We had to drive him everywhere. Then he fought back into it when Daddy gave him a company car. He took his driving to a new level. He moved to San Francisco, into his parents' empty apartment, and commuted an hour each way to Stockton, just like now."

Amaya gathers her gleaming dark hair and rolls it carefully into a bun a little off-center at the back of her head, leaving a few wisps to fall against the sides of her face. Sarah Jane watches, admiringly.

"There, Amaya, just like that. You need never worry about blonde or red hair, sister. Brad told me exactly how you looked in that hotel restaurant where you first met. It was just that way then. He will never stray. That's the look that has him locked into you forever."

Amaya turns her face downward and away. "You should have some breakfast, my love-Tree."

Kozue selects three red grapes from the room-service trolley and an orange segment. She picks up a short bottle of water. "We need to go down now, Mom."

Amaya started attending such events as this one in Seattle when Kozue was in her clingy stage of grief. Before she uprooted from Japan to marry Brad, Amaya had no comprehension of the gun madness that gripped America. She soon learned not only about that contagion, but also about the ugly harassment attendees at these events invariably suffer.

Alden scans the small ballroom and figures there are about forty people—he's good at counting the house. A woman in a blue suit, an ecru blouse, and scuffed shoes slips into the room after Alden looks away. She sits in the rear. She seems to know no one.

The dais holds: the chairwoman of the conference, a college-aged survivor of the Parkland shooting, and an adult who survived the Stockton, California, shooting in 1989. It was she who knew of Kozue because the Elgar Steel plant is in Stockton, and it was she who got Kozue to join the panel for today's session of the conference. She has just given her remarks, reminding the audience that the Cleveland Elementary schoolyard shooting in Stockton preceded the Columbine one that many refer to when describing the history of these incidents. When Kozue steps to the podium, and to the small footstool she has brought for the occasion, she will speak about adults, such as her mother and father, a decorated Mountie, killed in an AR-15 massacre.

These conferences always feature speakers who promote sensible new gun laws, including universal background checks and safety buffers that could be incorporated in the manufacture of new guns. Always, the most compelling presentations have to do with the easy availability of military assault weapons, as though they are BB rifles.

She then introduces Kozue before returning from the podium. Kozue waits for her to sit and for the applause to die down, then stands, walks to the podium, and places her footstool behind it.

"Thank you for your introduction. You are a survivor of a school shooting. I'm about the same age now as you were then in Stockton. I'm a survivor of a church shooting in Canada. No, I wasn't in the church at the time, but I'm a survivor nevertheless because both my mother and my father were killed by AR-15 bullets.

"You and others at this conference speak about kids being victims of so many mass killings in this country. I can't imagine the lifetime terrors of parents and teachers and schoolmates who lose their children or ones they knew and were close to. I won't try to add to what they've said at this conference. But I can tell you what it's like to lose adults—in my case, both my parents. In other cases, it would be one parent. Perhaps it would be a single mother, like a woman who stopped by a supermarket for some groceries in Boulder, Colorado, on her way home one spring day in 2021, or the ones at the store in Buffalo, New York, in 2022. When you shoot mothers and fathers, you leave kids who constantly ask themselves, 'What am I supposed to do now?'

"I got lucky. Two Americans adopted me, so I live in San Francisco and go to a great school there. One of them, my now-mom, was born in Japan just like my own birth mother was. I was pretty messed up. Not only didn't I know what I was supposed to do, I had no confidence that I could do anything at all. To call me shy would be a compliment. I wouldn't even change out of my old school uniform from Ontario, Canada. I didn't have low self-esteem, I had none whatsoever. Part of that is because I don't look like most everyone else in my schools, whether in Canada or San Francisco. My now-mom understands that and is always there to help. But that's the point: kids need adults. Adults who lose kids in shootings have lifelong pain. Kids who lose adults have that, plus they become adrift with no solid mooring in sight—ever for some of them.

"Yes, I got lucky because my adoptive mom looks like me and had lost her mother when she was young. Her mom was a victim of the war. She eventually died from a disease caused by the atom bomb that was dropped on Hiroshima.

"But the shooting victims we talk about in this conference were all killed in peacetime by guns of war. How can that be? When there's a war, and it ends, how can it be that the guns made for war can kill kids, teachers, moms, and dads? Not why, but how can the government allow it? Over and over again?

"I also got lucky because of my adoptive father, Daddy-Brad. All kids should be so lucky as to have a dad like him. A year ago, he did something for me that really helped with my shyness I told you about. He took me to see a play, just him and me. It was *The Glass Menagerie* by Tennessee Williams. He knew the play, and that's why he wanted me to see it. You probably know it as well. So, in it is a twenty-four-year-old girl, Laura, who has a bad limp and is afraid of any part of the world outside her apartment where she keeps her glass animals. Her mom, who's a mess herself, dumps it on Laura. She calls her a cripple. She says, 'What are you going to do with the rest of your life?'

"The mother wants to fix Laura's life by getting her a 'gentleman caller.' Her brother and her mom contrive a dinner party with someone from his work. It goes badly. The gentleman caller is already engaged. But he tells Laura what she needs to hear and that no other adult in her life has told her.

"When they are alone together, the gentleman caller talks about people who are 'different,' the way Laura is with her limp. He says: 'The different people are not like the other people because other people are not such wonderful people. They're a hundred times a thousand. You're one times one.'

"That's what Daddy-Brad wanted me to hear and understand, one times one. Hearing it in a play like that was powerful for me. Kids need to hear that, and they only hear it from adults.

"By the way, it takes a powerful actor to play a leading role on stage in front of an audience, someone full of confidence and life. Imagine how good you have to be to play the part of a shy girl with a limp and an inferiority complex. That woman who died in the Boulder shooting was an actress who trained in New York and wound up living in Colorado. One of her best roles was Laura in *The Glass Menagerie*. I'm sure that her son, who was grown and out on his own by then, had to wonder the same way I did, 'What am I supposed to do now?'

"Thank you."

Afterward, during the break, Kozue joins the family. "Yeah, thanks, it went pretty well. I'd practiced enough. I'm glad you came, Aunt Sarah, Uncle Alden."

June holds her close and rocks her gently. "You were magnificent, dear Tree. So grown up. So poised and in control. I am glad we could all be here to see you, well, all except Brad. I don't know what there is about Tokyo, but that's another topic altogether. I'm booked to return to Toronto at two fifteen, so I really have to scoot. You're in good hands now, and there's no more excitement on the horizon. I'm off, everyone."

As June nears the door to leave the ballroom, the gray-haired woman in the blue suit scurries to catch up with her.

"Excuse me," says Nancy, "I noticed that you are part of the family of the girl who just spoke. Do you have a minute to talk?"

June stops and faces her. "I'm June Elgar. She is my niece. Actually, I'm on my way to the airport."

Nancy motions for June to continue walking. "I thought you might be. You're with ACEA, aren't you? I have followed your work. I'm Nancy Booth. I'm Thad Maxwell's chief of staff. Didn't I see you at a presser for the Wishbone project years ago?"

June remembers that clearly. It was her preemptive announcement of the agreement reached between Canada and the US to add the water pipeline to the one for oil. The family was not happy about the way she jumped the gun on a public announcement, but it gave June a bit of undeserved glory, just the kind she loves.

"Well, Nancy, nice to meet you. I'm amazed something like that sticks in your memory. I know that Congressman Maxwell did support the project. I hate to hurry this conversation, but ..."

Nancy says, "No, not at all. I'm leaving for Washington right away. Would it make sense if we share a cab to SeaTac? It'll give us at least forty minutes to talk."

June smiles. "Sure, why not. I have to get things from the room. Shall we meet at the front desk in fifteen minutes?"

"That would be great. See you then."

<hr>

"Tree, do you want some breakfast now?" asks Amaya as the family gathers at the rear of the conference room.

"I sure do. When do we go back?"

Alden looks at his watch. "You three should leave the hotel at three; your flight's at six. I'm not going with you, though. I've decided to join Brad in Tokyo."

Kozue thinks, *It's just coming on three a.m. tomorrow in Tokyo; I'm gonna do it anyway.*

"Would you please excuse me? I need to make a call." Kozue pushes open the heavy door into the hall. She walks to an empty corner.

Wakened from a deep sleep, Brad mumbles, "Hi, Tree. Look, I am so sorry ..."

"Daddy-Brad, I know you had to go because it's the right thing I know and you need to do the right thing without worrying about me and Mom and you are the best there is and I know you love me and Mom but you do the best you can and you shouldn't worry about when you can't be at my speech and stuff and anyway you've heard that speech a zillion times at home helping me like you always do and I'd rather have you doing the right thing somewhere like Japan instead of mooning around after my speech like I'm just a kid ..."

Her knees give way. She is sobbing. She hears Brad's alarmed voice on her phone, "Kozue? Are you all right?" She nods but blubbers stifled words. She looks around and sees Amaya emerging from the conference room. "Mom's coming," she manages to say.

Brad controls his voice, "You go to her, Tree, then call me back. I know you are strong like the tree you're named for. Call me back after."

Kozue watches Amaya come into the hallway from the conference room and look around. She sees her start to rush toward her. Amaya's phone rings. She doesn't look at the screen. She gathers Kozue in her arms. Her phone rings again. They say nothing, but simply hold each other. Kozue's tears flow. Amaya is stricken less with worry than with utter love for her brave daughter who has just relived the trauma of losing both parents to another person's sick mind. Again, the phone rings. Kozue reaches for it to take a look at the screen.

"Who's Orchid Petal?" gurgles Kozue as the phone slips from her tear-wetted hand to the carpet, where it continues to ring persistently.

"I'll call her back."

"Wait, you know an Orchid Petal? What's that about, Mom?"

"Another time, I will talk to her. Tell me how you are, Tree?"

"Yeah, I'm getting a grip. I talked to Daddy-Brad like a blithering idiot. I was on the phone with him. I knew I was gonna lose it, then I did lose it. Then I went into a heap on this hotel carpet." Kozue sits up straight now. "Who is Orchid Petal?"

Amaya reaches for her phone. "It's a long story. Don't worry about it."

Kozue holds the phone behind her back. "Don't worry about my mom's Orchid Petal? That takes my mind off all my other worries and into a new direction. So, who is she?"

"It's just a silly name," says Amaya, flustered.

"It sure is, but whose silly name, Mom? Don't think I'm gonna give up." Kozue is halfway in tears and halfway toward howling in laughter.

"I'd rather not say." Amaya is trying to be defiant, but it's gotten too funny for that.

"I've picked up on that, Mom, but you're either gonna say or I'm gonna trash your phone in a toilet bowl."

"Tree!"

"Mom! Orchid Petal: Who? Right now, WHO?"

CHAPTER 10

Tokyo swelters in late summer. Its air hangs heavy and sodden. Relief will come in September, but not before the typhoons. Brad arrived late Sunday afternoon, Tokyo time, with a carry-on packed for Seattle. He had spent an hour in the Mitsukoshi department store picking up summer attire for business meetings he had not yet organized. He checked into the Hotel Grand Palace, older than other high-end hotels, but comfortable and familiar. Located near the north wall of the Imperial Palace compound, it is not far from the Marunouchi district of Tokyo, the business center where Honshu Lines makes its headquarters. Within the Imperial compound resides the Imperial family in the palace of Emperor Meiji, who ended the dark, feudal isolation of Japan and ushered in the beginning of industrialization, Western style. Brad, Amaya, and Kozue have spent many happy days and nights at this hotel.

Two years ago, they were here to try to sort out a terrible mess that June Elgar had put the entire family in. She thought she had found the last, great love of her life in a guy who was out to fleece her. A mining engineer, he manipulated her to cosign the debt to finance a new mine in Canada, and also to pledge as collateral for that loan her one-third of Elgar Steel's common stock. There was no way the mine or June or the engineer could service that loan. To avoid the disaster that would have resulted if the lender took over the Elgar stock, Brad arranged to pay it off early using Elgar Steel money. He then set out to sell most of the rescued stock to two Japanese companies. The move also rescued June but at the cost of thirty percent of her stock in the company, leaving her three-and-a-third percent. Its income keeps most wolves from her door, unless she invites them in.

After checking into the hotel Sunday afternoon, and as the prime minister is admiring her gift of *weisswurst*, Brad heads out in a taxi to meet the CEO of one of those companies. They have decided to meet at the Tokyo American Club's casual burger and bar service on the third floor. Jerry Hiwasaki is also his best friend and was best man at his wedding. They got to know each other when Brad was traipsing around after Ernie Elgar on frequent trips to Tokyo to meet with Shin Steel. Ernie was a great friend of Shin's chairman, Saito. Brad hit it off right away with Hiwasaki, who was head of Shin's sales for North America. They were the same age, and both had interests outside the steel business. Hiwasaki had studied comparative literature at UCLA, and both were avid readers. Today, Hiwasaki holds the job Saito once held, and Brad holds Ernie's old job. They have become even closer over the years through tough business negotiations. Shin Steel supplied the flat steel plates which Elgar Steel formed into pipes for the Wishbone project. At Brad's suggestion, both companies shared in the sales profits on that project through a joint venture. Two years ago, Shin Steel bought fifteen percent of Elgar's common stock and thus acquired a stake in that Canadian mine. Another fifteen percent of the stock was bought by KNN Steel of Japan. Brad knows the head of the pipe-making unit of KNN, Iseo Kanawa, and, significantly, Amaya knows Kanawa's sister, Japan's prime minister.

Hiwasaki is five feet ten, his black, thick hair now showing strands of gray. His shoulders and neck are wide and strong. He was a competitive swimmer in college. He wears a maroon short-sleeved polo shirt and khakis.

"Jerry, I really hate to break into your weekend, but something's come up. I appreciate you coming into town to meet."

"It is Yoko you must make your speech to, and a generous *ochugen*. She sends her best to you and to Amaya and Kozue. Are they here?"

Brad scratches his head and makes a wry smile. "Well, that's a bit of a sore point. No, I had to jump on a plane without them. That caused me to miss an important event Kozue's involved in, and her speech on gun control."

Jerry has had to do the same thing during his years in sales. "Oh, I can relate to that. In Japan, long separations can be hard on family life. But those separations are also hard in other ways. To the Japanese, a long separation to, say, America or Canada or Australia can have a subtle effect on the perception of others. Such separations can be regarded as diluting one's Japanese character traits. It's as though 'foreignness' has rubbed off on the one returning. Quite ridiculous, I know. Still, it's there."

Both men are silent as they look out the windows of the club. In the distance sits the redbrick nineteenth-century façade of Tokyo Station. The men watch sleek, aerodynamic trains enter and leave on tracks elevated above the Ginza District's streets and rooftops of neon-clad buildings.

Jerry continues, "So, Brad, is there a problem at the mine? Is that why you had to come here so suddenly?"

Brad settles back and smiles. "No, not the mine. It's a new subject altogether. It's not even steel or pipes. I'm here on a mission involving Alden Knight and a high-ranking member of Congress. It stinks. I just want to ask you to help me figure out who I should see."

Jerry holds his arms out at his sides, his face filled with astonishment and humor. "You come on another man's business, leaving your family's big event, not knowing who to meet, and it involves American politics. Ordinarily, I would be surprised. You always bring surprises to Japan. Is this going to be a long story?"

"Yes to all of your questions, including the long story. Another drink?"

His arms withdrawn, Jerry nods enthusiastically. "That would be essential."

"Do you know anyone at Honshu Lines?"

Jerry tilts his chin. "Yes, I do. That is certainly a different subject. Tell me your long story."

—

"Kozue, get hold of yourself. I cannot make a spectacle of saying her name out loud in a hotel hallway. Come back in my arms; I'll whisper it."

By now, Kozue is limp again, but with giggles. She returns to Amaya's lap, face upturned. Amaya gradually draws her fingernails along the girl's arm.

"Mommm … enough. Out with it."

Amaya gives the girl a tiny shake and whispers, "You know Orchid Petal, my Tree. But you know her as the prime minister of Japan, Yuko Kagono."

Kozue's eyes widen as she shrieks with laughter. She pushes the phone back into Amaya's hands and says, "Well, call her back, Mom. That place could have burned down before you get around to returning her call."

Amaya looks around. The hallway is empty. She speed-dials.

The prime minister of Japan mumbles sleepily, "Aya-chan, it's the middle of the night. I'd about given up. But I'm glad you called."

Amaya instinctively bows her head slightly and lowers her voice. "Forgive me, but my daughter was going through a meltdown in a public place."

Awake now, Yuko's actor's voice kicks in with energy. "And now? Can you talk now? Or at least listen?"

Her face animated by the excitement of speaking again with her friend, Amaya hurries her words. "Yes, of course. It is so good to hear your voice. Are you all right?" Amaya pushes Kozue's arm away from her ribs.

"Amaya, I am calling because I need you. Here. Right away. It's about Emiko Sugawara." Emiko managed Amaya's gallery shop in the arcade of the Palace Hotel. It was she who was injured by the North Korean and who prevented the Kakiemon bowl from smashing on the floor.

Amaya draws away from Kozue and gasps. "Is she …?"

Yuko hurries to say, "No, she is fine, this is not a bad-news call. Quite the opposite. However, I cannot disclose over the phone why I need you and why she will need you. Do you understand me? It is imperative, and that's all I can say."

Amaya's mind races. She says, "Brad is there now on business. Would he …?"

Yuko stifles a laugh at the irony. "No, Aya-chan, this is for you alone to do. But since he will be here, how can you refuse me?"

Amaya knows Kozue is scheduled to meet her school-little-sister. "I must put out a certain fire of my own here, Yuko. I shall do my best. But I need some time before I can make it happen."

There is silence on the other end of the line. "By 'some time,' do you mean days from now? Weeks? Minutes? I need you in the here and now."

Amaya says, "My dear friend, of course not longer than a few hours. Expect my email when you waken, and please have an untroubled sleep. I will do my utmost."

"Then, Aya-chan, I shall sleep peacefully knowing you will somehow find a way."

CHAPTER 11

After ending the call, Amaya pulls Kozue to her and explains in verbatim detail the message from Orchid Petal. Then they join Sarah Jane and Alden in their hotel room for a family conference. June is already on her way to catch her flight to Toronto.

A room-service trolley of sandwiches sits under the window that overlooks the Seattle cityscape and beyond to tree-covered islands dotting the Strait of Juan de Fuca. Amaya has gone over the problem for Sarah Jane and Alden.

At times, pretty much everyone has glanced over at Kozue to assess her reaction to the new demands on her parents. Before Kozue's adoption, Amaya used to travel to Tokyo at least three times a year. She still maintained not only her art galleries but also a position on the board of directors of a sizable trading company, Sunrise, in which she had inherited a significant investment from her foster parents. But five years ago, Amaya severed ties with both businesses to concentrate on starting a family. Yuko Kagono herself had advised her to do so. So, everyone recognizes the unusual nature of the call. But everyone is thinking foremost of the impact the request will have on Kozue.

Amaya turns to her and says, "Kozue, I don't want you to be separated from us, so would you like to go to Tokyo with me? You'll be with us and can see your friend Hiradi-san and your friends on staff at the hotel."

Kozue looks straight into Amaya's eyes. "Mom, I'm supposed to be a big sister to a new girl at orientation next week. I know you haven't forgotten that. How am I going to do that from Tokyo?"

Amaya smiles. "No, I certainly haven't forgotten, and I explained that to Yuko. So, if that's where you want to be, then that settles it. We go back home tonight as planned."

Kozue mimics Amaya's smile. "Well, Mom, how are you supposed to help Yuko and this Emiko from San Francisco?"

"Yuko has lots of help, believe me."

Kozue leans closer. "But, Mom, she told you this was a secret operation. You don't just put tons of 'other people' on a job like that. She wants you for a reason."

She stands and walks to the trolley to put together a chicken sandwich. "Look, I'm not really a basket case. I'm a lot different from the way I was when I first came to live with you. Yuko needs you in Tokyo, and some kid who's scared about a new school needs me. Both next week. It seems pretty simple to me. We do what we have to do."

Sarah Jane beams. She likes the attitude. "I don't mean to butt in, but I could stay at the apartment until you guys get back. I'd be delighted to have some quality time with my niece."

Amaya looks carefully to catch any sign of hesitation, but Kozue just slathers mayo on rye bread. She then reaches to clutch her half-sister's hand and give it a grateful squeeze.

"Yeah, Mom, that's a perfect solution. I'd like that a lot. Aunt Sarah, I have dibs on the top bunk. When's your flight, Mom?"

"Oh, Tree, I haven't even looked. You really are growing up."

"Mom, lots of kids I know stay at home all alone when they have to. I'm not a fragile flower. Look how lucky we are as it is. That's the main thing I take away from these conferences. Maybe some of that luck can rub off on the new kid in school and your Emiko friend."

At six o'clock that evening, Alden sits in the lounge near the bell captain's station, having just checked out at the front desk. He is on the phone with Maxwell.

"Thad, just cool it while I get things sorted at this end. I don't know exactly what I'm going to do next," (actually, he does) "but when I figure out a plan, I'll get back to you."

Alden hangs up. He walks to the elevator and punches the button for parking level 2, where a black town car is idling near the elevators. He opens the door and slides in next to Amaya.

"Where to, Mr. Knight?"

"SeaTac International, please."

"You got it. What time's your flight? Where're you two off to?"

"Eleven fifty, to Tokyo."

"Wow. So, when is it that you arrive?"

"About four in the morning on Tuesday, Tokyo time." *I'm getting too old for this.*

CHAPTER 12

Brad is in his hotel room on Monday, bewildered. He's just been wakened again by a phone call, this time from his wife. He has just learned she's leaving in a few hours for Tokyo, but will probably not have much time to be with him.

Amaya tries to be soothing. "Brad, my love, I have no idea how long I'll be there because I have no idea what I'll be doing. All I know is that I'm needed, and that it is 'hush-up-hurry-up.' I will find out as soon as I have met with Yuko after I arrive."

Brad is standing now. "What about Kozue? Are you sure …?"

Amaya breaks into a smile; Brad can hear it in her voice. "You know I would not leave her unless I was sure! She surprised us all. She has an *on*, Brad. You know, an obligation she acquired at school. She will be meeting with a new student before the school opens. She does not want to cancel that. She is taking responsibility, showing independence. It is no different from your feeling about Alden's request. It is the same thing for me. I'm coming because of Emiko, even though I don't know what it will involve. She took risks for you and me and received a dreadful injury as a result. I must come."

After a pause, Amaya quiets her voice. "We should be grateful that Kozue feels such things and is safe doing so without having to cling to me. Besides, Sarah Jane won't let her out of her sight. Now, what are your plans for Tuesday when I arrive? I would be very grateful for a quiet bedroom for my sleeping—you know, after. We are about to board. She'll be fine."

Brad had been waiting for a call from Jerry when this news arrived. They left it last night that Jerry would call his contacts at Honshu Lines and try to get a short-notice meeting. Jerry might be able to do this because of all the freight his company passes on to Honshu year in and year out. Ordinarily, the Japanese prefer *nemawashi*, or prior consultation in great detail for any meeting. It means literally "prepare the root," and rarely anything comes of a meeting without proper *nemawashi*. This may be extraordinary business for Brad, but it's not for Honshu; just a difficult case. Jerry's the customer, so the difficult case becomes a meeting scheduled for four that afternoon—in the chairman's suite.

Brad answers his phone again. Jerry explains the plan for the day. He and Brad will meet at Honshu at one o'clock with Jerry's principal contact there, along with department managers from vessel operations. Brad must tell his whole damn story to them before three o'clock, when the Honshu people will write up a document called *ringisho* to give to the chairman. That document will brief the chairman on the facts, the issue for Honshu to decide, and staff recommendations. It will be a skeleton *ringisho* because of the time crunch, and no one expects a decision from the chairman until the document is fully formed and carries the approvals of, perhaps, two dozen Honshu executives, a process of indeterminate length.

"Jerry, I'm amazed you could do all this on a Monday morning. I owe you, big time."

With a wide grin, Jerry says, "Yet another *ochugen*, Brad. Think big."

Brad dresses in his new lightweight dark gray slacks, a striped dress shirt just unpinned from the Mitsukoshi package, a pale yellow linen tie, and an off-the-rack light blue summer blazer. On his flight, he had looked up Honshu Lines. Their logo and vessel stack colors are light blue and pale yellow. Armed with ample *meishi* (business cards), his spiral-bound notebook, and trepidation over his own uncertainties about this mission, he steps out of the hotel's air-conditioned lobby into Tokyo's summer atmosphere, nearly a hundred degrees, with stale air laced with exhaust fumes. The taxi is fastidiously clean and air-conditioned.

Jerry greets Brad at the front security desk of the Honshu Lines fifteen-story gleaming headquarters in the center of the Marunouchi.

Jerry says, "This is where you lay the foundation for your case. The people at the next meeting are crucial to your mission. Tell them everything."

"Including the torpedoes?"

"Especially the torpedoes."

In a few minutes, they are in a conference room on the ninth floor, the center of fleet operations. Outside the conference room, cubicles and work spaces are placed in a pattern which would exactly reflect an organizational chart of the departments, with each department head positioned at the end of rows of workers and desktop computers. The conference room is closed off from the busy "bullpen" floor, and holds a metal table in its center with scores of armless chairs lining the walls. The long side walls hold framed photos of vessels of all classes, ranging from harbor tugs to coastal trading break-bulk freighters, to oceangoing vessels that move grain, coal, ores, oil, chemicals, and liquefied natural gas around the globe. On a screen filling the far wall of the room glows the projected image of the *El Caballo* at sea on a sunny day, low in the water, with a pristine wake. Her colors are black below the waterline and dull orange above. Below the image, in Japanese and English, are her specifications: built in Kobe, Japan 1999; length overall, 273 meters; beam, 44 meters; 120,000 deadweight tons; speed 16 knots; manned by four officers and nine crew. With such dimensions, she cannot transit the Panama Canal but must sail around the Cape of Good Hope—hence her description as "cape size."

Around the conference table sit six men and two women. *Meishi* are exchanged all around in slow, courteous introductions. Tea is brought in. Brad feels itchy at the slow pace, but knows it is necessary and cannot be altered. Jerry Hiwasaki is introduced as a valued customer of Honshu Lines. Jerry speaks in Japanese, and his remarks are translated into English for Brad's benefit. Jerry compliments the spirit and quality of Honshu Lines and thanks all attending the meeting for interrupting their hectic schedules to accommodate a special guest. Then he introduces Brad.

Brad is no stranger to meetings of this sort. He presents the facts as he knows them in short, declarative sentences. He waits for translation into Japanese. He scans the table for signs of confusion. The faces are impassive. He pauses for water. *All right,* he thinks, *here come the torpedoes.* When he has finished this segment, the faces are no longer impassive.

Heads turn in disbelief. Ballpoint pens clatter to the floor. Questions come at Brad from every direction. Brad spends the next half hour explaining to everyone that he believes the torpedo plan to be a serious threat and would best be averted if Honshu Lines were to assist Lydia Maxwell in making a quick, private sale of the vessel. Amid mutterings about needing the *bengoshi* (lawyers), one of the managers fairly sprints out of the room to fetch some from the legal department.

The two *bengoshi* he returns with avert their eyes when introduced to Brad. They sit, arms crossed, glaring downward at the table. Brad and Jerry wait as several in the meeting speak their minds to their lawyers. Finally, the hubbub settles. A young man in rolled-up shirtsleeves stands and addresses Brad.

"Our lawyers mostly work with charter and cargo contracts. The ones you have just met cannot advise us. Please wait until next week so we may consult with outside law firm."

Brad has also experienced the "long deliberation" barrier. The Japanese way of doing business does not easily accommodate the pace most Western business executives are accustomed to. But it can be done.

"I have one question for your *bengoshi*."

Brad's statement is translated and discussed at length. One of the lawyers glares briefly at Brad, in disbelief that she is going to be asked a question in this meeting.

Brad stands and walks to the image projected on the wall. He points to the vessel. "Before I get to my question, please understand that I am here out of a sense of affinity with the business principles followed by Honshu Lines and other Japanese companies I know. Your company's principles are well summarized in your mission statement, which I have studied before this meeting. As Hiwasaki-san mentioned in his generous introduction, I have been coming to Japan as a buyer for over fifteen years. Most recently, I have come here for Elgar Steel as a seller of metallurgical coal to Shin Steel and KNN Steel. Again, the more I engage in business with Japanese companies, the more I appreciate what Ambassador Edwin Reischauer wrote in his book fifty years ago, that the key Japanese value is harmony.

"I seek to foster the same that you do, namely, harmony in relationships as well as in life. I believe there may be a path for mutual and harmonious success for all parties at this meeting, despite the shocking and alarming suggestion being considered in some quarters about destroying this vessel. The question I am about to ask is in that spirit, and not in any antagonistic spirit. You need to know the answer as much as I do."

Brad stops for the translator. During the translation, Brad looks directly at the Japanese lawyer who has been glaring at him. Only after she looks back and bows her head does he ask his question.

"What's going on with the *El Caballo*?"

CHAPTER 13

Sarah Jane rattles Elgar Vineyard's legacy pickup back from San Francisco airport to the apartment on Sunday afternoon, with Kozue beside her. Kozue tugs her down the long hallway to her bedroom overlooking the Marina district, San Francisco Bay, and the Golden Gate Bridge.

They make up the bunk beds with fresh sheets. Kozue hands Sarah Jane one end of a handmade quilt to place over the top sheet of the upper bunk. It has the look of a nineteenth-century American quilt but with distinctly Japanese symbols: a pine bough, a bamboo stalk and leaf, and a plum blossom. It is unfinished and thready at the bottom edge. Sarah Jane holds it carefully and looks over to Kozue. "This is beautiful. What …?"

Kozue quietly says, "Thanks, Aunt Sarah. Yeah, it means a lot to me. Mom's making it out of my birth mother's clothes. It is still rough, but I use it anyway. She has more time to work on it when Daddy-Brad's away on his long trips. We can put it on your bed tonight if you want."

Sarah Jane looks out Kozue's window at the orange-lit outline of the Golden Gate Bridge. The foghorns swell. "No, hon, let's keep it on your bed where it belongs."

Kozue puts her girl-band tunes through the speakers, and the two of them switch into Kozue's game-green Quadrangle shorts (they fit S.J. just fine) and team-logo polo shirts for their meal of Amazing Amaya's Ahi Tuna Salad Niçoise. Sarah Jane figures she's in for a late night of chitchat. She is not wrong.

"Aunt Sarah, do you like Japan?"

"I do. I get there maybe every two or three years. I've just seen the tourist spots, in and out again after a few days. I don't know it the way Daddy did, or the way Brad does. They formed friendships; I just saw the surface."

"Why do you think they do that? Friendships like that?"

"My father always told me that relationships are at the heart of doing business there. Our company depends on long-term business in Japan. That is impossible without personal relationships."

"Daddy-Brad is addicted to it. Now Mom's there. Why don't we just move there?"

"I need him here, Tree!"

"I do too."

Sarah Jane breaks a long silence. "You are very good at public speaking. Today you were really good. I've heard a lot of speeches, Tree. I've given them, too. That is a gift and a skill. If you keep up the skill, it will serve you well through life. Just like writing does."

Kozue turns to lean over the edge of her bunk. "Thank you, that means a lot to me. Yeah, Daddy-Brad says most of what he did as a lawyer was to write stuff. I think most of what he did was to go to Japan."

"Well, he found Amaya there."

"That's a blessing. Do you have guns in your house, Aunt Sarah?"

"Nope. My dad never did either."

"An assault rifle can shoot four hundred bullets a minute. How can people defend themselves against that? My birth daddy was a Mountie, and he couldn't. Aunt Sarah, what you said about public speaking is great. I feel good when I do it, but it's not enough."

Sarah Jane props herself up on one elbow and pushes the upper bunk where it sags the most. "Oh yeah, so what are you going to do about that, Tree? What's more?"

Kozue gives her mattress additional shakes. "Who do you know in Congress, Aunt Sarah?"

"I know Joyce Gregor, who represents the Napa area, and Phil Perry from the Stockton district. That's about all. Alden is buddy-buddy with the Speaker of the House. He was back there to see him last week."

"The Speaker? *THE* Speaker? I wish you hadn't told me that. He's holding up a big thing in Congress."

"What big thing?"

"It's a resolution opposing assault rifles."

Sarah Jane is quiet again. "Do you have a copy of that resolution?"

"I can go print it out right now. Want me to?"

"It'll keep till the morning. I'd like to look it over then. I'll kick it around with Alden. My brain is paralyzed, Tree. Let the foghorns put me to sleep, OK?"

PART II

PERILS

As his daughter and her aunt drift off to sleep to the oddly timed sequence of foghorns, Brad and Jerry sit in the Honshu Lines food court, killing a few minutes before their meeting with its chairman. The court's open floor plan of stalls and vending machines surrounding small tables and chairs is filled with a blend of aromas, from barbequed chicken yakitori, bubbling pots of soups with vegetables and fish in simmering dashi fish stock, and the priciest of lunch offerings, hamburgers of Kobe beef.

Brad studies Jerry's laptop screen, which shows a short company bio of Masako Daigo, the scowling lawyer who came in late at his last meeting. The profile is in Japanese hiragana, and Jerry translates. She is thirty-eight years old and went through the Doshisha school complex in Kyoto, which includes a four-year university.

Jerry looks up and points to the screen. "Oh my, look at this. She's admitted to the California Bar. Wow. She also worked for three years in London with a maritime law firm. That's pretty strong. Her surname is the same as the chairman's. Could be a coincidence, but I wonder. You definitely want her on your side."

"I've heard of that school in Kyoto. Amaya told me about it. Her friend Yuko Kagono went there and married one of her teachers."

"Maybe you can chat about that with Masako over cocktails as you try to break the ice."

"You're nuts, Jerry." Brad scrapes his chair back and stands. "Let's head up now to get there a few minutes early."

The *El Caballo* is one of ninety cape-size dry-bulk vessels among the total of 220 vessels in Honshu Lines' fleet. Thus, in perspective, one would not think that Honshu's half-ownership interest in *El Caballo* would be at the top of the pile in urgency for a global transportation company. It has always been a privately held company, but if it ever went public, it would have a market capitalization of $56 billion. One would expect its chairman, Kenji Daigo, to have more pressing business this Monday afternoon than to meet with an American CEO of a steel fabrication plant, no matter how connected he might be with Shin Steel. Yet Brad has been moved to the top of the schedule. He and Jerry now are being ushered into Daigo's corner suite on the top floor of the Honshu headquarters.

The suite has commanding views sweeping from Tokyo harbor, over the downtown sparkle of Tokyo's Ginza and central financial district, and into the moated, walled Imperial Palace grounds. The special glass walls of the office automatically adjust to filter direct sunlight. A handwoven carpet from eighteenth-century Persia, in muted indigo with songbird designs of pearl gray and moss greens, covers the floor of creamy bamboo laminate. A *tokonomo* (display alcove), made from Japanese cryptomeria cedar in the sixteen hundreds, stands in one corner. Ordinarily, the center space of a *tokonomo* holds a simple basket with flower stems, or a scroll of calligraphy. This one holds a black-and-white, once-glossy photograph of a uniformed officer in the Imperial Navy, taken in 1943. Beneath it, a twisted-trunk pine bonsai sits on a black iron tray, its roots entangled in damp moss dotted with minute white blossoms.

Daigo sits at his desk adjacent to the *tokonomo*. Actually, the desk is a long, time-darkened communal dining table made by inspired woodworkers in a Massachusetts Shaker village. The desk holds only an orchid the color of burnished pewter and Daigo's folded hands.

He rises to greet Brad. The chairman is a commanding presence by girth, not height. He was adept at sumo wrestling in school and then briefly in amateur bouts. He is bald except for a ring of black, crew-cut hair resting like a fallen halo atop his ears. Most striking, though, is that his spectacles hold one smoke-gray lens over the eye blinded in his final sumo bout. He wears a bespoke summer-weight suit of lightweight tweed the color of bracken. His tie holds Honshu blue and yellow regimental stripes. His handshake is firm and long. Each man extends his *meishi* in both hands with a short bow. The same respectful introduction follows for Jerry Hiwasaki.

"I believe you have already met my daughter," says Daigo, nodding toward Masako, who sits to Daigo's right. She wears her shoulder-length raven hair in a braided bun pinned with an ornate tortoise comb made in Kyoto a hundred years ago, but with soft, loose tendrils over her ears. She has high cheekbones and bright dark eyes. She wears an oyster-colored two-piece linen suit and a seafoam silk blouse on her slender frame. Her jade brooch was made in China before the American Revolution. She stands five feet two inches tall in gray-green heels.

Brad grins. "Yes."

Daigo continues, "It is the shank of the afternoon, Mr. Oaks. Please, what may I offer you as a cocktail?"

"Oh, no thanks ..." Brad begins until he feels Jerry's shoe press urgently on the top of his. "But that is so kind of you. Um, a whisky on the rocks, please."

"Mmmm?" asks Daigo. "More specifically, please, Mr. Oaks?"

"A Rittenhouse rye would be very welcome."

"Hiwasaki-san?"

"The same for me, sir, and thank you."

A tuxedoed waiter disappears behind a standing, six-paneled screen of gold leaf medallions, decorated with white cranes standing in clusters of purple iris. Ice cubes clink into crystal tumblers. The waiter returns with a tray holding a yellow rose stem, three rye-on-the-rocks for the men, and a flute of champagne for Masako. They all lift their glasses. Brad might easily get used to this.

"My daughter is usually quick with answers to any question. It seems that this afternoon, you stumped her."

Brad hates it when he starts to redden and can't, by force of will, prevent it. He does the next best thing.

"That question has stumped my associates and me so thoroughly that I had to make this rush trip to Tokyo to ask her."

Daigo's face grows into a wide smile, which becomes a laugh. Masako blushes.

"In that case, let us enjoy our cocktails. Masako, did you understand the question, and can you answer it?"

Masako calmly rises. "I do understand the question. I can only answer it partially, for reasons you know very well, Father. As Mr. Oaks and his associates have surely discovered by searching the official records, the vessel's owner is Honshu Hull 33, Limited, incorporated in Switzerland in 1999. The issued and outstanding stock of that entity is held, as to one-half, by Honshu Lines, and as to the other half, by Mrs. Thad Maxwell, nee Aiko Watanabe, by a 2006 transfer from the estate of Fujio Isaemon pursuant to the probate of his will in Guam. This vessel's peaceful and tranquil status has been unquestioned for over twenty years, until today, when Mr. Oaks brings us the suspenseful tale of foul play being plotted by the United States government. His tale is worthy of the Kabuki stage." Her dismissive flick of one hand is accompanied by a smile, not a smirk.

Daigo clears his throat and says patiently, "Mr. Oaks, I canceled my afternoon plans in order to study the *ringisho* prepared by Masako-san. I need to hear about your torpedo scheme and the involvement of the Speaker of the House of the United States. Please be concise, Mr. Oaks. I am expected soon in a meeting at the Japan Self-Defense Force headquarters. We are assisting JSDF in a delicate government mission."

Brad carefully sets down his glass on a coaster. He takes a step closer to the chairman. "Thank you, Daigo-san. First of all, it's not my scheme. It was cooked up by Speaker Maxwell's staff. I'm a nobody in that saga, and my information comes to me as oral history. I have it from the very reliable Ambassador Alden Knight, who helped your government conclude the World War II peace treaty between Russia and Japan just five years ago. He is in the air, on his way to join me tomorrow with more secondhand hearsay from Washington. Anyway, here is what I know at the moment."

When Brad finishes his abbreviated report on the torpedo threat, the room is still. Daigo's face suggests disbelief. He turns to Masako. "What's her present position?"

"She's six days out of Australia, half-laden with grain and bound for a port north of the East China Sea. She is light in the water and making twelve knots with thirteen souls aboard. Weather will keep her course west of the Philippines," Masako states flatly.

Daigo looks up to Brad. The volume of his voice is stronger as he intones, "We live in the era of conspiracy thinking and folk wisdom at the forefront of political discourse in your country, Mr. Oaks. Such a remarkable country it is. The American military defeated our military and demilitarized our citizens. Then, your government swore to protect our disarmed people, but its own people went on to arm and militarize themselves. I'm not sure I can bear to listen to Ambassador Knight's additional report, yet I cannot ignore the need to do so. Have naval orders been cut for this folly?" Daigo's eyes bore steadily into Brad's.

Brad stands tall, still, and unfazed by the chairman's slightly condescending tone. "So far as I know, they have not. I came to Tokyo on an hour's notice, without luggage, as soon as I spoke with Alden, in order to help avert disaster."

Daigo blinks. He gestures to the *tokonomo*. "I am not a complete stranger to submarine service. That photograph is of my grandfather. He was a cabin boy on the flagship *Mikasa* in the Japanese blockade of Port Arthur in 1904. Forty years later, he trained teenaged submariners to pilot *kaitens*, two-man suicide subs—essentially steered torpedoes. When his last cadet class sailed to their missions, he sailed with them to his last."

Brad walks to the windows facing Tokyo Bay. Without turning around, he says, "Who controls the vessel's movements?"

Brad turns to look at Masako.

She says, "There is a vessel manager for charter and cargo fixtures who works on full-time retainer, not commission. The skipper takes his orders from him."

"Who is that?"

"A Mr. Earl King."

Brad lets out a pained groan.

Daigo says, "Do you know of this person?"

"Oh yes, Daigo-san, indeed I do," Brad states. "He is very, very bad news." Brad turns slowly to fix his eyes on the chairman's. "But I've heard that the vessel management situation changed recently. Isn't it true that Honshu Lines has assumed control? Isn't it also true that Honshu is not fully reporting the vessel's business to Mrs. Maxwell?"

Daigo frowns and rises suddenly. "As I said, Mr. Oaks, I am running late for another meeting. Please have a pleasant stay in Tokyo. I'm afraid I am unable to continue this conversation at this time. Perhaps the time may come when you will learn why I cannot respond to your question. I regret that I must leave you with doubt and uncertainty about it now. I beg your forgiveness." With a short, polite nod, Daigo extends his arm to the door. Brad and Jerry nod in return and leave the room as directed.

Masako walks beside Brad after the meeting. "Your associates are truly colorful, Mr. Oaks, from an American ambassador to the likes of Earl King, and seasoned with our prime minister and your Speaker Maxwell. Quite impressive, if I may say as one California lawyer to another. You must feel we are your second home. But, even so, there may be a quiet restaurant you have not yet visited. Perhaps you would join me tonight?"

Brad tenses. "I assume you will abide by Daigo-san's confidential approach to further information about the vessel. So, if I may have a rain check, I think not tonight, although you are kind to invite me."

"This is the time for relaxation, Mr. Oaks, before the torpedoes are launched."

"I know very well the customs of relaxation following a business day in Japan. I hope you do not think me impolite in declining for tonight."

"Not at all … for tonight."

CHAPTER 15

Kozue is up and at 'em, multitasking on Monday morning in the apartment. The incessant grinding of the rollers of Kozue's printer awakens Sarah Jane.

"Here it is, Aunt Sarah, the resolution."

Sarah Jane blinks, then squints from the daylight filling Kozue's bedroom. "Good. Wonderful. I shall be able to read it after I've dressed, and to understand it after I've had the coffee I smell brewing. Thanks for printing it, and especially for starting the coffee."

Kozue is overjoyed that she and Sarah Jane will have the day to talk about the House resolution. Sarah Jane calls the plant to check on what's ahead this week on the pipe mills since she is CEO pro tempore.

Steaming coffee in one hand, and with Kozue pressed against her and reading over her shoulder, Sarah Jane says, "OK, let's take a look at this thing, Tree. It's very unambitious. It's a long litany of what's wrong about the availability of assault weapons and says Congress should do something about it. I don't see anything in here I'd call actually doing anything though. It's all grand sentiments; all sizzle, no steak."

"That's what I think, too, Aunt Sarah." Kozue's energy seeps into Sarah Jane, or possibly it's the caffeine. "So, why is it such a problem for the Speaker?"

With a quick cheek-kiss, Sarah Jane searches for a good answer. "I haven't had a minute to talk to Alden about it, hon. You know, the gun lobby exerts tremendous pressure on the Hill. It would be even stronger pressure on the leadership. They won't like words against these guns even if the words don't actually prohibit them."

"But those guns are made for only one purpose: war."

"I get it, Tree. I'm with you on this."

"Aunt Sarah, how do you explain Speaker Maxwell holding up the simple assault weapon resolution?"

Sarah Jane sighs. "For that, you have to look to the man's deep-seated first principles."

"The Second Amendment, Aunt Sarah?"

"No, Tree, it's more basic. Greed. As long as I've got time to kill in your lovely home, let me make some calls to some people I know in Washington."

⸻

Amaya arrives at the room at five in the morning on Tuesday, bushed. Brad is eager to welcome her in the night stillness. She is not too jet-lagged for love.

At eleven, as he quietly goes about dressing for the day, he marvels at the weird movements of his family the last few days. Assured that Amaya is deeply asleep, he's on his way to meet with Alden.

In the cozy Wadakura Japanese restaurant in the lower lobby of the hotel, Alden waves chopsticks in a sort-of greeting. The walls of the restaurant are plain, the color of rice stalks before harvest. The booths are of pristine bare pine. The kimonoed waitstaff are as gracious as family.

"You like this hotel, don't you, Brad? It's the first time I've stayed here." Alden looks around, impressed.

"It's great for a lot of reasons, mostly because of its centrality. I couldn't get us into the Okura, your favorite." Brad tears the paper folder holding his chopsticks and rubs the edges together.

"I'm glad you booked my room here for the day before I arrived," Alden continues. "Otherwise, I'd still be camped out in the lobby waiting for checkout time. So, catch me up on Honshu Lines. I'm surprised you got in there on such short notice."

Brad gives Alden the details of both his meetings with Honshu, and hands him a printout of his notes.

Alden studies, then puts down the report. He frowns and shakes his head slowly. "I came to Tokyo because I want to be able to give Thad a solid alternative. I still think the best one is a private sale of the ship. You are the best prospect." He looks up hopefully. "You've had time to think about that; what are your next steps, Brad?"

Brad pours himself another cup of green tea. He can't really concentrate much on ship ownership at the moment. "You heard Sarah Jane; I'm going to have to get some buy-in from Shin Steel and KNN Steel. They may be partners in the coal mine, but they are primarily customers of it. She was spot on. There's no way we can talk about buying this ship until we sort out whether the coal buyers will agree to new transportation terms. I saw Jerry Sunday evening. He assured me Shin Steel would study the matter, but I'm not encouraged. The next meeting is KNN. Are you up for a meeting this afternoon? I've got Iseo Kanawa staked out for four o'clock. You don't have to, but you're welcome."

Alden finishes the last of his tempura. He smiles. It's kind of good to be back in an international business setting, no matter how much he's adapted to earthy vineyards. "Sure, Brad. I'm going up to the room for a quick nap, and I'll meet you in the lobby at three twenty."

Brad says, "By the way, I've been thinking about Kozue's project. I've got an idea I want to kick around with you later."

CHAPTER 16

Vice Admiral, Retired, Howard Copeland has been secretary of defense for two years, seven months. He had been a cautious climber of the ladder of naval command, and in retirement became a steady hand at the helm of the Patroclus Torpedo Works in Tennessee. His wife, Carolyn, has been of enormous help and support. Yes, as a wife, but significantly as trustee of her father's family trust, from which she draws generously to make campaign contributions beneficial to Howard's career. It is thus that Thad and Lydia Maxwell became so well acquainted with Howard and Carolyn during the run-up to the 2024 elections. A barber calls at Howard's home every Friday evening to ensure an unwavering steadiness in his straight, sculpted white hair. His face shows the effect of sun at sea, and of the careful ministrations of a dermatologist to erase the most troubling results. Nevertheless, he has a genuine smile and captivating light blue eyes which focus exclusively on the person speaking with him, no matter who or in what capacity. He likes his Defense Department rank and the deference of his retired Navy buddies. On Saturdays, he plays golf at the Army-Navy club. He would not normally choose to spend a lot of time with Thad Maxwell, but, well, he is Speaker of the House. He used to play customer golf, but these days, it's he who wins most rounds. His wrists of raw power keep his drives straight and long. On Sundays, he and Carolyn can always be found in their own polished oak pew in a glass-and-stainless-steel megachurch in Virginia's horse country near Middleburg.

Monday morning, he has to rise early to be driven to Capitol Hill to meet with Thad Maxwell, Evelyn Hutton, and Drew Wallace. Howard has discovered that Drew never served in the military, and so he keeps a wary eye on this staffer who looks like a high school choirboy. It is not from a hymnal that Drew has chosen the text for this morning's meeting.

Copeland is on his feet now, pretty steamed. "You've got to be kidding, Thad. There is no way in hell we can do that."

Thad Maxwell sips coffee and says nothing. His worries are divided. The assault weapon resolution is on the floor again. It's picking up steam in his caucus because it is so popular in the polls. *How do they persist?* he is thinking.

Evelyn says softly, "The DOD's five-year procurement of armaments cycles around again on October first. We are being pressed to open up to more bidders for torpedoes, Mr. Secretary." Howard does not need, and does not appreciate, the reminder.

Thad clears his throat. "Howard, just what is our readiness level should things heat up between Taiwan and the mainland? I mean, we have this kinda-sorta understanding about the independence of that island, and also have this kinda-sorta one-China policy."

Copeland leans his knuckles on the tabletop and thunders, "We are in high readiness in every theater, Mr. Speaker."

Maxwell grows calmer as Copeland reddens. "Right. But I'm talking about readiness in the sense of possible joint engagement in which we and the Japan Self-Defense Force are working together. Would we work as a well-oiled machine?"

"Joint exercises do not trouble me." Copeland slams his hand palm down on the table, which resonates like a drum. "Dammit, live warheads, unarmed merchant vessels in international waters, and coordinated misfires absolutely concern me."

"Continuity in House leadership should absolutely, absolutely concern you, Admiral," purrs Evelyn.

Copeland feels his emotions escalate. He sits and thinks a moment. "Carolyn has been the soul of generosity, Thad."

"Oh, I know that, but here's the thing. The long knives are out for me in that ethics investigation. We need the problem gone. Drew's solution is elegant."

"But contrary to domestic and international law," Copeland explains deliberately, his eyes pressed shut in exasperation.

"Howard, I'm open to a more elegant suggestion."

Copeland tries to clear his mind. The first thought to fill it is, "The Navy could buy her."

Drew clears his throat. "The ethics panel was not born yesterday."

Howard is clutching at straws. "Suppose the *El Caballo* goes into layup in some backwater cove. No one on board when she sinks. Maybe piracy is involved. No clear facts."

Drew says calmly, "The market is hot. No way does it make any sense to go into layup in a hot market. Honshu Lines would never do that. And no one seems to be able to control them or even talk to them."

Copeland cannot believe his ears. "Hey, guys, has anyone talked to the Japanese Self-Defense Force? They'll howl with laughter."

"Not yet," says Drew. "We're counting on you for that as well as the logistics."

Howard hangs his head. He needs time to think. To pray, even. "I'm making no commitment—I want everyone to know this. Where is the ship now?"

All eyes turn to Thad.

"Hell if I know," Thad whispers. "You're the admiral here."

Thad heads to the House floor after waving goodbye on the Capitol steps to Sec. Def. Copeland. A familiar figure catches up to him and walks with him. This is Ray Lion, a new addition to the government affairs office of Total Carbon Corporation, which is the most dominant player in America's fossil fuel industry. Twenty-eight-year-old Ray Lion II, the great-nephew of Walt Lion, the sole surviving founder of Total

Carbon Corporation, has failed in a critical test of managerial merit in his family's company. His family ties and his attendance at TCC University did not help Ray when his project for Canadian coal sputtered and failed. Ray Lion II is a fresh-faced, aw-shucks kind of fella with curly brown hair and a physique that shows his good taste in fine dining. He is a steady, faithful husband in his hometown of Saint Joseph, Missouri, also the headquarters of TCC, but decidedly unfaithful when he's on business travel status. He made an ass of himself trying to bed June Elgar in Tokyo a couple of years ago. After the coal debacle, he's been assigned to Washington to talk nonsense to the senators. Like all other male Lions at TCC, he speaks in the second person imperative, but warmly and never harshly. As in, "You're going to be the lead sponsor on this rare earth elements bill, Speaker Maxwell."

Young Ray comes from the family of Lions that founded TCC back in the Depression. He was pretty disappointed to land in Washington after his release from executive duties at the family's privately held industrial conglomerate. Ray knows from his studies and brief career as a frontline executive at TCC that the TCC business creed is not to make things, but to make money. Just as music "don't mean a thing if it ain't got that swing," business don't mean a thing if it don't spew money quarterly in a straight-line upward trajectory.

TCC has views on practically all legislative initiatives because it has business units in practically every sector of the economy. A TCC lobbyist has to be supple and nimble. TCC hedges not only its commodity risks, but also its climate change positions through counter-investments in both fossil fuels and green, clean alternatives. Most of its political spending is to prop up TCC's legacy holdings in petroleum and coal. But if an appropriation would help the renewable energy units of TCC, the lobbyist will champion climate change legislation. The wind blows in all directions within TCC, and money is always in the air—just as topsoil was always in the wind on the family's Oklahoma farmstead in the thirties.

Ray is all smiles, saying, "Mr. Speaker, you surely don't need reminding that with new stimulus to the rare earth industry, there will be new sources of cargo business for dry-bulk vessels of a certain class."

Thad continues to stump his way over the tiled floors to return to his office. "You certainly needn't do that, Mr. Lion," he mutters, testily. "Especially under the Capitol dome with TV reporters and microphones hovering in the shadows. Confine your observations on that to Evelyn Hutton. As to the merits of these strategic materials, a lot is riding on the Congressional Research study. You're preaching to the choir when you talk to me. You need to be getting your message to them."

"Then you'll want to hear me out on this unconstitutional attempt to slander assault weapons."

"You guys are in that one too?"

"As you know, TCC has investments in many sectors."

"Well, in that line of business, I get my daily lobbying bread from N2AR, the New Second Amendment Righters. I'm not sure you can add much weight to that."

"Mr. Speaker, you need to know TCC is in lockstep with N2AR folks in strong opposition to that resolution. You should also know that the rare earth elements bill is vital to our interests. In fact, to push this one over the line, you're going to dispense with the August recess and continue working on our business."

"Now, Ray, have you ever seen four hundred thirty-five members of Congress when told they will have no August recess? That there will therefore be no time to stump in their districts? No time to take their families on overseas field hearings? Can you even imagine a force of nature as apocalyptic as the pushback force that would create? The sudden, awesome unification of so many opposing elements would rival nuclear fusion. As always, I will take your company's interests to heart. But now, I need to go do the people's business. Thanks for stopping by. My door is always open."

Amaya rewakens to the doorbell of their room. It is the room service breakfast Brad has ordered for her. Along with the corn muffins, poached eggs, hash, and coffee he knew she would want, the trolley carries a floral arrangement from the arcade florist. She smiles and feels happy to be back in Tokyo, her dear city, with Brad, her very dear husband. Only she has no idea what will be in store for her at the prime minister's office at noon.

The Kantei building, which houses both the residence and the formal offices of the prime minister, is just minutes by taxi from the hotel. There, she clears security and follows Yuko's chief of staff to Yuko's office. Two years ago, Amaya had longed to be able to redecorate the drab vestibule and office. Today, though, the décor looks fresh and inviting. She approves the simple earthenware of Japan's earliest times displayed alongside modern works which incorporate the earlier motifs in contemporary designs. The effect demonstrates Japan's cultural hallmark of assimilating traditional ways with new ones.

And Amaya is very impressed with Yuko's new, slimmer look.

"Aya-chan! You are beyond loyal to drop everything to see me today." Yuko's face is bright and alive. "I shall be even more deeply indebted to you now."

"Yuko, you always flatter. So, in return, let me compliment you on the new décor in your office, and, oh my, the new you! You look amazing."

"Thank you, Amaya. Well, I'm just following doctor's orders."

Amaya assesses Yuko's sparkling eyes and graceful movements. "Doctor? Are you sure there isn't something else in your life besides government and doctors? You look positively girlish."

"You might think so, Amaya, but unfortunately, this is not the time for that kind of intriguing chat. I need your help. Please, let me explain what is going on."

"Yes, of course, provided there will come a time for an intriguing chat later."

"No promises, although some things in life should be remain mysterious."

"Ah," says Amaya, "I thought so. There is a man in your life."

They both laugh.

"Amaya, I am on the brink of a breakthrough in the Korean abduction tragedy."

Amaya immediately drops her playful demeanor and bows her head deeply. When Amaya and Yuko were last together, Yuko said that she'd begun negotiations with North Korea to finally clear the air on its abductions of Japanese people starting some forty years ago.

North Korea forced the abductees to give Japanese language instruction to its military officers. Prior Japanese governments never publicly admitted the sheer size of the abduction problem. Yuko took a personal interest in the issue and had made blunt declarations against the inaction of previous administrations over the abductees. She had pledged that as prime minister, she would reopen the issue. She devoted enormous energy into trying to gain trust and cooperation with the North Koreans to help relocate surviving abductees, or at least give their families some closure with information about their fate. Reports indicated that they had received harsh treatment and deprivations.

Amaya was painfully close to the problem. When she married Brad in 2020 and moved to America, she had hired Emiko Sugawara, then thirty-five, to manage her two galleries in Tokyo. It wasn't until two years later, when Emiko was injured in the confrontation with a North Korean criminal, that they learned that Emiko's mother was one such abductee. Emiko had been five when her mother was abducted by North Korea, presumably to teach their spies to speak Japanese. Her mother had been living in a coastal village in northern Japan, within easy reach of raids by North Korean boatmen. Afterwards, Emiko went to live with an aunt in Kyushu. Emiko had not heard anything from or about her mother in the ensuing years. Emiko would be forty-two now. Her mother, if still alive, would be sixty-two. The prospects of recovering her alive were not good, though it was possible. Emiko had been assaulted in the arcade of the Palace Hotel. The injuries had been caused by a garrote wire tightened around her throat by a North Korean. Emiko was being blackmailed by the North Korean. He intimidated her into giving up information about Brad and Amaya, even their room number, as part of a larger scheme involving an attempt to destroy, and then rebuild, Japan's power infrastructure.

Amaya, now solemn, looks up and says, "Yuko, I am eager to learn of your breakthrough and to help in any way you think I can."

Yuko stands and begins to pace. "The first thing I learned is that I could get nowhere by making a public issue out of this mess. Sure, I could whip up outrage, but that would have no effect on the North Korean government except defiance and denial. When you were here two years ago, you were in this office when I told my brother, Iseo, not to go off on his tangent to negotiate with North Koreans about maritime passage of our oil supply. I told him that I might be able to achieve more from them by addressing their growing agricultural crisis. That crisis has not abated. Their food production has suffered from droughts, then floods, then typhoons—and that's in addition to the harsh sanction regime enforced by Western nations. We are abiding by the sanction regime, of course, but the situation in North Korea has become intolerable even to its odious leadership. So, I decided to seize an opportunity. But I could not do so out in the open, and I have to fudge a bit, sanction-wise. That is why I, and you, must maintain secrecy."

Amaya smiles and says, "I am in awe of your resourcefulness, Yuko. How well you are doing when others were incapable of even admitting the extent of the problem."

Yuko approaches and takes Amaya's hand with a tight squeeze. "I have had help—enormous help, from an unobvious source. The government of Switzerland is in a unique position to play a role in this. I have been dealing with North Korea in secret through their ambassador, Marcel Bourquin."

Amaya withdraws her hand to make a note of his name.

"Please, Amaya, no notes of this conversation. There will come a time I will be able to introduce you to him."

Amaya puts away her notebook and looks up to apologize. It is then that she sees her friend blushing like a schoolgirl. "Oh. Oh, my. Oh, I see. Yes, Yuko, I will certainly look forward to that."

Yuko winks. "OK, enough on that for now. So, Amaya, I'll give you the gist of the mission we are on and then tell you how you fit in, if you agree to do so."

Amaya nods. "Of course. I will listen, make no notes, and try my best to help if I can. And to keep my mind off 'intriguing chat about more on that.'"

Yuko resumes pacing. "North Korea needs foodstuffs badly. Through Swiss emissaries, I have agreed to provide supplies of grain, and they have agreed to return a few of our people who are desperately sick and the remains of others who have died. This exchange would be considered by the West to be not only a breach of sanction commitments but also negotiating with hostage-takers. So, I am limiting my use of our government people to a bare minimum, mostly Japan Self-Defense Force personnel. The grain is coming from Australia on a Swiss-flagged vessel. Under their law, the Swiss government may commandeer the vessel when they need it, and they have given me official papers that put the ship at my disposal."

Amaya clasps her hands and raises them as a cheer. "As I say, you are resourceful. But where do I fit in?"

"I have needed the services of a reliable trading company to negotiate the purchase of grain and related commercial services. I have chosen your family's Sunrise Trading for this work. I know your long association with the company, including your position as director emeritus."

"I am honored you have chosen my company; I was unaware of it."

Yuko settles behind her desk, all business now. "But I now call upon you for a private service, and it is a deeply personal request. I have not notified Emiko or any other family members about the possible return of anyone. We have asked for identifications, of course, but without success. I am calling upon people I trust to go to families and prepare them as best as possible for what happens next. I would like you to go to Kyushu. Besides Emiko Sugawara, there are other families there who may be involved. Preparing them will take skill and tact. We have to manage hopes and inevitable disappointments. And there is a risk of premature disclosure. The point here is that if, say, Emiko's mother is not in the first group to be returned, she may be in a later group, and we don't want public disclosures to jeopardize that. Sadly, we cannot assure her that her mother will ever return or be accounted for."

Amaya frowns. Her throat catches. "Yuko, my daughter is just starting school. I came here without knowing I might be asked to make a long stay. I'm worried about how to manage both."

Yuko stands and walks around the desk to sit next to Amaya. "I understand. Look, let me ask you about a possibility. If you were to explain the situation to Emiko, is she the sort of person who could deal with the other families?"

Amaya is silent while she thinks. "I have been away from her too long to be able to say. I knew her when she was a manager of my store, and she exceeded my expectations. The attack was extremely hard on her. After the attack, she went back to Arita to work at the Kyushu Ceramic Museum, where she had worked before I knew her. I have not seen her for five years. I don't know her state of mind. I can only go there and talk to her to find out."

Yuko mulls over the possibilities. "Well, best case for me would be to know you will handle the entire Kyushu aspect of the plan. However, next best is for you to bring Emiko Sugawara into the picture if you feel she would be right. I would say, then, that you should leave for Fukuoka this afternoon, Amaya, and talk to Emiko as soon as possible."

Amaya sighs. "So soon? Am I to leave a goodbye note for my husband at the desk of the hotel? When is this grain boat supposed to arrive in North Korea?"

"Probably next week, I'm not sure. I am meeting with the people who know more about that part of it tonight. When I find that out, I'll contact you in Fukuoka. I can arrange for a car to take you to the airport."

Amaya stands and bows her head. "I appreciate the gesture. Please, I would rather be taken to Shinagawa Station. I prefer to travel on the train. It will get me there in good time, and I will be only five inches off the ground."

CHAPTER 18

Tuesday afternoon, Brad and Alden ride in a taxi to a skyscraper over-looking the southern part of Tokyo Bay, located in the Minato (harbor) district not far from Tokyo Tower. Dense with the tallest buildings in Tokyo, the area reaches from the edge of Tokyo Bay to leafy hills holding fifty embassies and two dozen universities. The air is sultry when they step from the taxi to the plaza, in front of one of the newest of the sky-scrapers built by Japan's second-largest steel company, KNN. Brad and Alden are old hands at visiting Tokyo, but they still crane their necks to gawk at the modern, super-tall buildings that dwarf the Tokyo Tower, which once was the spectacle of the Tokyo skyline.

They arrive comfortably early for their meeting with Iseo Kanawa, CEO of the pipe-making affiliate of KNN. Brad and Alden know Kanawa very well. He is a colorful throwback to the sixteenth century culture of warrior elites. This does not mean he lives in a simple samu-rai abode. It is a seaside, restored wooden resort hotel, repurposed with modern amenities, where he changes into a brown-and-black *montsuki* (a man's kimono with family crest). There are wall displays of *katana* swords and a collection of Noh masks from Japan's classical theater. Brad first came to know Kanawa when he, Alden, and Amaya were in Tokyo to untangle a nasty kink in Japan's supply chain of liquefied nat-ural gas in 2022.

Iseo could be a mean drunk, or at least a mean-speaking one. It was he who gave voice to pretty much all of the ugly biases that Amaya had ever faced in Japan: a childless woman in her forties, raised as an adopted only child, and fathered by an American who cheated on his American wife. He flung wounding words in Amaya's face after way too much sake at the Tokyo American Club. In so doing, he profoundly lost his face among the Japanese guests.

At that occasion, Alden, Brad, and Amaya were to meet the Russian ambassador to Japan. The purpose of that meeting was to introduce a commercial idea to the Russian. It would be an enormous economic sweetener for finally reaching "Yes" to a treaty between Russia and Japan, formally ending World War II some seventy-five years after the shooting had stopped.

Iseo Kanawa's sister was also at that reception, Yuko Kagono. She moved much more graciously among foreign dignitaries. She had just become prime minister.

So, Brad and Alden both know Kanawa's quirky personality. He is polite (until he is drunkenly rude), proud, and vain, and his mind moves so quickly that his words sputter at a pace barely able to keep up.

Since that rude incident five years ago, however, Iseo has mellowed. Just a few days after insulting Amaya, he was in the mood to insult a red-haired engineer from America named Cynthia Atherton, who was working as a consultant for Brad on the LNG problem. His mood suddenly and admiringly changed when, in his own home and with his sister at his side, Cindy unveiled her brainstorm on how to sequester carbon dioxide emissions from Japan's coal-fueled power plants. The idea warmed Iseo's heart of hearts because it would use exactly the sort of steel pipes that his company could make. He needed the new business.

Iseo struck up a friendship with Atherton, which later developed into a romantic liaison carried out through frequent visits from Cindy from her day job in Texas. When Cindy pushed the inevitable question (fish or cut bait, Iseo-san, where the hell is this going?), Iseo shed generations of prejudice and married the foreigner.

Two years ago, Brad turned to Iseo for an entrée to Kanawa's parent company, KNN. Brad had the coal mine problem on his hands and proposed to offer common stock of Elgar Steel to induce Japanese partners into jointly developing the project. He was dangling quite an attractive offer before KNN and Shin Steel on equal terms. He offered to each the option to buy a fifteen-percent stake in Elgar Steel, which at that point had become the owner of the Canadian coal mine with unproven reserves. The option would be open long enough for all parties to assess a proper reserve study. Eventually, the picture emerged that the mine held at least fifty years' reserves of high-quality metallurgical coal, the type used in steelmaking. Both Japanese companies jumped at the chance to pick up equity in that kind of mine and avoid the vagaries of market pricing for their coal.

Brad has rehearsed his pitch to Iseo for the *El Caballo*. He is convinced it is a sound proposition. He is absolutely convinced Iseo can get this through KNN's procurement and investment departments. Alden is just along for the ride. It sounds good to him, but he is jet-lagged.

Iseo is in his early fifties, about Brad's height, black hair combed straight back, and athletic. His open face is quick to smile. His wrists extend a bit too far from the cuffs of his black suit jacket. Conspicuous today, though, are the hand-tooled cowboy boots presented to him on a trip to the Elgars' Napa estate a couple of years ago on coal mine business. He keeps the boots in his office as a badge of honor and often wears them to board meetings and drinking parties where his stories of his familiarity with American business seem to grow year by year.

He is effusive in his welcoming of Brad and Alden. They exchange photos of Amaya and Kozue and Cindy. Brad briefs Iseo on the mine and on his fabricated steel business. Iseo asks Alden about Sarah Jane, and reveals his plan to present Sarah Jane with a surprise commission for a sculpture to rest at the entrance of the KNN skyscraper. He exacts pledges of secrecy so that it will be Iseo himself who will present the project to her. Brad and Alden solemnly clamp their lips shut and nod in agreement.

"So, by the way," Brad says casually in his windup, "may I speak to you about a business opportunity for KNN?"

Iseo brings a cordial but impassive look to his face and gives Brad a simple nod. Brad launches into his pitch. This is no time to talk about American politicians or torpedoes. Brad frames the pitch entirely as a straightforward business plan for reducing the ocean transportation costs of the coal to be delivered to KNN under the new long-term contracts.

Iseo folds his hands on the desk in front of him. In his rapid-staccato voice, Iseo asks, "This vessel. Please give me her particulars."

Brad does.

Iseo says, "When and where built?"

"In Japan, 1999."

"What shipyard?"

"Kobe."

Iseo looks down at his desk for a silent moment. He then looks to his left and the full-length windows facing Tokyo Bay. He reaches into a lower drawer of his desk and takes out powerful binoculars, which he hands to Brad.

With a patient smile, Iseo says, "Please, Brad-san, look out that window. The sky is hazy this time of year; I apologize for that."

"OK. What am I looking for, exactly?"

Iseo stands and moves to Brad's side. He points and says, "You see the giant Ferris wheel? That is in Yokohama. It turns slowly and carries foreign-exchange college students into sultry air that stings their eyes. They are told that in better weather, they would have a spectacular view of Mount Fuji. Most of them are not looking anyway because they are with their new Japanese girlfriends."

"So, Iseo-san, I am to be a voyeur into their private time together?"

Iseo laughs heartily. "Look, please, to the left, to ground level. What do you see?"

Brad tries. He really does. "I'm sorry, it is all industrial flatlands. What am I missing?"

"You see the cranes?"

"Yes."

"Those cranes are in the KNN shipbuilding works. They launch a new vessel every sixteen weeks there. KNN takes enormous pride in its naval architects and skilled builders. Kobe is our chief competitor."

Alden gets it immediately. He feels his hopes sink. If the coal partners don't pitch in on Lydia's ship, then there is little likelihood Elgar Steel will buy it alone.

Iseo fires an excited salvo, "Brad, if you are going into the shipping business, let me arrange a meeting with our North American sales department in a day or so, when I can also introduce you to the chairman of KNN. They will be eager to discuss a new-build for you. This will be true reciprocity, the mother's milk of Japanese business." He beams. Brad would rather be somewhere else.

Twice, Brad attempts to change the subject, to no avail. Iseo is beginning to gain momentum. He has had a dry summer of pipe sales, and he now envisions claiming a new cargo vessel as his sale. Brad begins to panic. When Iseo offers sake, Brad and Alden recognize it is time to go. With profuse apologies, the two men bow and back away toward the door.

Just as they turn to leave, Iseo booms, "Brad-san!"

"Yes?"

"I need a Stetson to go with the boots!"

CHAPTER 19

The 2:48 Shinkansen Nozomi bullet train, bound for Fukuoka on Tuesday afternoon, seems motionless when it first begins its whispered departure from the platform at Shinagawa Station. It appears to Amaya, looking from her Green Car reserved seat window, as if the platform slides slowly backward while she is sitting still. The odd sensation seems new again. She is deeply familiar with bullet trains, but since the last time she rode one was two years ago, she tingles as if she were perched on a magic carpet in Persia.

Beside her rests a thin, supple shoulder case, made in flat, woven, thin strips of leather dyed the color of pomegranates, containing the personal information of four Japanese individuals missing for more than thirty years. On the rack above her sits her overnight case. She gave over her large luggage—packed for the Seattle trip—to the bell captain at the Grand Palace hotel, to be shipped directly to the Okura Hotel in the Hakata district of Fukuoka; it will be delivered to her room in the morning. In her hands on her lap, she holds a small *bento* box, wooden, the size of a schoolgirl's notebook, filled with Gruyere-infused rice cakes, crisp vegetable slices, and broiled *weisswurst* lathered in dark, rich miso syrup. She would not have bought a *bento* for this trip, especially after Brad's sumptuous breakfast, but she could not refuse it from the prime minister, especially since she had prepared it with her own hands.

The train gathers speed immediately after clearing the station, and the sensation of motion becomes distinct but not distracting. The car's quiet is occasionally broken when tuneful chimes precede station announcements. Since this is Shinkansen service, stops are infrequent and no more than two minutes each. Before opening the files in the leather case, Amaya tries Brad's phone again. It is switched off. Well, she left him that note at the desk. She'll call back later.

She chose a seat on the right so that her window would face Mount Fuji as the train reached its top speed of 185 miles per hour. Her views frequently disappear suddenly in a black whoosh when the train goes through tunnels. At those times, Amaya sees her own shimmering image in her window, blackened in the tunnel's interior, as has just happened.

At such times, Amaya reflects on her personal journey since the fall of 2019, when an American steel executive appeared in her life with an offer of ten million dollars to buy her recent inheritance of one-third of Elgar Steel. Up to that time, Amaya had constructed a careful and near-perfect life of art and sophistication in Tokyo. Her Mori Art Gallery in the Ginza shopping district occupied most of her time, and her position as a director on the board of Sunrise Trading Company filled the rest. But as filled as her life was with culture and business, an emptiness gnawed within her. She had lived with such emptiness since her mother died—which then deepened when her foster parents died. So pervasive was this emptiness that she could no longer identify its feeling, any more than she could feel her heart or other organs. Feelings did return with the welcome attentions of Brad Oaks, but still she could not put her finger on another vital part missing from her life. A close family friend, Parker Wright, had given her the missing puzzle piece—it was commitment. With its discovery, Amaya became complete. She knew her love for Brad was also a commitment to the frightening prospect of leaving her Ginza world, where successful women are rare, for a new life in a foreign world.

Whoosh: the train shoots from the tunnel back into the afternoon glare of summer again. The window image disappears. Her ruminations end just as abruptly. Then new thoughts appear.

Emptiness didn't just magically vanish with her marriage. The feeling always reemerged when Brad left for Canada or Japan or somewhere else, always with a profound sadness. Each time, she had to call on her rationality to regain balance—everything was solid between them, and Kozue added another layer of glue attaching them. *It's the job he's in, nothing else. Still.*

And now, the irony of it! She is the one who has separated herself from Brad and Kozue, and they don't know for how long. She is on a mercy mission which she probably will not be able to even explain to them until it is in some yet-unwritten history book. Did that turn of events dispel the emptiness? No, the separation is the same, the sadness the same. She will say to Brad and Kozue she went to Kyushu on art and ceramics business. It is a stretch but with a scant bit of truth in it, since she will visit Arita town, birthplace of Japanese porcelain.

Shaking off dreary thoughts, she reaches into the portfolio of files. She picks Emiko Sugawara's file to review first. She's reminded of the resume she studied before hiring her to manage her art galleries. Emiko had been raised by an aunt in southwestern Japan. For four hundred years, the region had produced Japan's unique porcelain ceramics, known everywhere simply as "Imari." She had studied in the local prefecture's ceramics technical school. She added an art history layer to her technical knowledge by working at the prestigious Kyushu Ceramic Museum in Arita town. Amaya saw that the woman's background fit well in her galleries and hired her. The dossier then mentions the time the North Korean threatened Emiko with harm to her mother, captive in North Korea. Emiko was beside herself.

The dossier could not, of course, describe the woman's fright in that moment, or her horrific recollections of it.

Nor, of course, would it have information about something else uniquely private between Amaya and Emiko. After Amaya had married and moved to San Francisco, Emiko had started writing her distinctly amorous emails. Amaya had been flustered, flattered, and disturbed all at once about their pointed contents. In 2022, when she and Brad returned to Tokyo at Yuko's request, Amaya had to confront Emiko. She would have fired her except for Emiko's unique predicament.

Now, Amaya and Emiko are about to be reunited. And, thereafter, Emiko might be reunited with her mother. But that picture is so uncertain.

CHAPTER 20

Back in his room in the evening from Iseo's office, Brad senses the presence of Amaya from the early morning, but it is quite empty of her now. Not even her luggage remains. There is, of course, the floral arrangement, and beside it Amaya's own note paper, folded, with a snip of black hair taped on the inside and a hand-drawn drop of water clinging beneath it. It symbolizes their play after lovemaking, when she startles him with damp hair. She considers it a helpful reminder to her husband while they are apart.

He can't even find any sumo on the TV. He could use some sleep, but he's restless. He is still stunned by developments with Iseo. He came to Japan on an hour's notice to convince his Japanese partners to buy the *El Caballo*. Three days later, he faces a pitch to buy a new freighter from one of them. The room phone rings.

"Hello, Brad Oaks speaking."

"Just a moment please." The hold music is a Mendelssohn piano sextet. He is puzzled. A woman's voice breaks in.

"Brad Oaks! You are full of surprises. Yuko Kagono here. Did you bring my favorite teenager, your Tree? How tall is she now?"

Brad instinctively stands. "Madam Prime Minister, it's good to hear your voice. No, I came very suddenly; you seem to have more current news on my wife than I. Alden Knight is also here."

Yuko's tone becomes more solemn. "My Self-Defense Force has just briefed me on so bizarre a story that I could not believe it. I call you to tell me I should not believe it and that someone is pulling my foot."

Leg, thinks Brad. He does not correct her but tries for time to think. "You mean about the *El Caballo*?"

"That's right, Brad, unless there are other merchant vessels in the South China Sea we should target. I was hoping for a 'ha-ha-ha.' Hearing none, I must ask you to join me at the Kantei residence. Yesterday would have been preferable, but thirty minutes from now would suit us very well. I'll see you then. Bring an explanation that displays your impeccable logic. Also, you should bring Ambassador Knight; you will need all the help you can get. And bring photos of Kozue."

Brad and Alden clear the security checkpoint inside the prime minister's household. In the room next to the prime minister's sleeping quarters, where she met Ambassador Bourquin, wait Yuko, Masako Daigo, and Bourquin. Their faces are stern, their postures rigid.

Alden reaches to pump Bourquin's hand. "Marcel, what a surprise. Great to see you." He looks around at startled faces and explains, "We know each other from Washington, DC days. We played squash, he better than I."

After other introductions and exchanges of *meishi*, Yuko says, "Ambassador Knight, I decided not to call in people from your embassy, so you are the US envoy senior afloat at this meeting. I'm not sure of the proper protocol since I am still not sure whether we are allies or belligerents at the moment. Help yourself to tea."

She's redecorated in here. She's looking pretty svelte herself, Brad thinks. He should instead train his mind on torpedo spreads.

Alden ventures, "Madam Prime Minister, I assure you we had no intention of going behind your back. It is just that the situation is so fast-developing, we did not have a complete grasp of enough facts to bring you a complete picture."

"Breathe easily, Alden-san; we are all aware of this fun-house drama. Masako here has filled me in on your meetings at Honshu Lines today, and we have a private copy of her draft *ringisho,* which lacks any definitive conclusion. I was her Doshisha alumnae mentor, and we have stayed in touch."

Yuko moves closer to Brad, her dark eyes fixed on his shiny blues. In her actor's voice, she says, "I'll also tell you that my minister of defense received an encrypted email from your secretary of defense that says they want to organize an unscheduled joint submarine exercise with our submarine group in the South China Sea. It seems he wants a mock attack on the *El Caballo* after she clears Philippine territorial waters. More precisely, he wants two hunter-killer class submarines from each country. This is like no other training excursion I've heard of, gentlemen."

Alden and Brad look at each other in panic. Yuko goes on in the same tone, "That's not the half of it. Masako, tell us about the ship's current voyage."

Masako steps to Yuko's side. She, too, looks directly into Brad's eyes. She does not refer to notes. She is in a light wool suit with blue pinstripes and pearl earrings. "The *El Caballo* is making twelve knots, as I told you this afternoon. The weather system is intensifying. She is rolling on gathering seas because she is lightly loaded. The direction of the storm has forced the skipper to alter his course so as to pass close to Taiwan, where we think this submarine armada will engage her."

Brad closes his eyelids. Alden utters one word, "China."

Yuko fairly chants, "I fear that is the first word that will come to mind in Taipei, Australia, and perhaps your own navy if a torpedo is fired. You now know all that we know. Please tell us everything that you know. Ambassador Knight, Masako has said that the political troubles of Speaker Maxwell are at the bottom of all this. Say it isn't so."

Alden stands. He is accustomed to situation-room-intel assessments of government intentions. The difference today is that he is in a foreign situation room, and the assessment is of his own government's intention.

When Knight concludes his summary of Speaker Maxwell's hot-water dilemma, Prime Minister Kagono simply sighs. She is no stranger to scandals within the Diet, the top echelons of Japanese corporations, and even school districts from time to time.

Yuko turns and settles herself in her armchair. Her tone softens. "What Ambassador Knight has just said complicates matters for me and for Marcel," she says. "So, now I need to tell you gentlemen in strict confidence that the governments of Japan and Switzerland are engaged in a profoundly secret mission involving the good ship *El Caballo*."

Brad and Alden look at one another. Brad is pale.

Brad asks, "Why this ship? Why not some other one?"

Yuko blinks. She doesn't ask what she thinks, *Who are you to ask me that?* "Well, Brad, I'm going to let Masako comment on that question. And maybe the Ambassador from Switzerland can add something if he feels like it."

Masako says, "I'll answer the second question first. Brad, this mission is distinctly Japanese and needs to be carried out by the Japanese. The prime minister came to us looking for a vessel. We have only one vessel flagged in Switzerland, a holdover from earlier days. If this scheme is discovered, Switzerland is prepared to take the heat for political repercussions."

Masako plants one fist on her hip and leans forward. "As to your first question, I suppose you mean: How does it happen that your mission coincides with the prime minister's mission at the same time? I'm afraid that is a deeper philosophical question than I care to speculate on. Life is full of odd entanglements."

Alden is frowning. He breaks in, "Madam Prime Minister, I am now utterly dismayed to think that our government is hatching a plan that could result in disaster for your mission, whatever it is. It's a bad dream. I'll get right on to the embassy here, and we'll put a stop to it."

With a tight smile, she says, "Good of you to offer, Alden, but I've got it covered. Our submarine service people and their counterparts at the Pentagon have already talked. Wiser heads have prevailed. Your Navy will stand far clear."

Brad turns to Yuko. "You knew this all along. You knew this when you brought Alden and me to this meeting, quaking in our boots."

Yuko stifles a giggle. "Your boot is an apt reference, Brad-san. I was just pulling your foot. But you and Alden absolutely have a need to know this much of the picture. When I can release it, I'll tell you the rest."

Alden says, "Madam Prime Minister, levity is always a welcome break in tense situations. The military found a gratifying solution to the tactical issue. But what is your idea on calming nerves in Washington? Right now, they have only silence from Honshu. Because of that, they plan to handle the thing like a Wild West shootout."

Yuko straightens and turns to Alden. "You are right. My style has always been one of openness at times like this. But for the same reason, I cannot tell you about my specific mission; I don't want to have to explain it to the world. So, what would you advise?"

Alden stands and moves to the black-lacquered Chinese chest holding beverages. He turns. "Madam Prime Minister, may I fix something for you?" Yuko bows her head quickly. "No, thank you, Alden, but please help yourself."

Holding a tumbler of mineral water and ice, Alden says, "I always prefer openness, but I hesitate in this instance. The risk remains that Speaker Maxwell is determined to make this vessel go away. If he is thwarted and he knows it, he and his staff will simply cook something else up, and they cannot be relied upon to cook up something rational. We should hold off doing anything public."

Brad has gathered his thoughts. "Let me say that I like that suggestion for an even more specific reason. The military tactical decision certainly defuses the main problem. Alden's approach would give us more time to figure out how to take this ship off Maxwell's hands. Until then, I want him to believe that he and his staff have solved that problem. I say, let them continue to believe what they want."

Masako nods vigorously. "That is the straightforward way. Mr. Oaks, why has everyone assumed that Honshu Lines wouldn't just buy Mrs. Maxwell's interest in the vessel?"

Brad is uncomfortable. He is thinking about those phantom cargos but would rather not say so here. "The assumption has been that the vessel enjoys profitable and continuous employment because of Maxwell's prestige. We all assume that Honshu has no commercial reason to change that. If there is a change, the vessel's earnings would drop."

Masako looks at Yuko. "The hour is late. I suggest we adjourn this meeting to allow the prime minister to tend to more important business, or simply retire. You and I can continue this discussion somewhere else, Brad-san. I may be able to shed some light on that assumption of yours. I suggest that you, Ambassador Knight, and I break off from this meeting and continue somewhere else. I have a car and driver waiting."

Yuko Kagono stands. She has known Masako for years and knows her to be incautiously flirtatious. Many times, she has had to help Masako squirm out of distinctly inappropriate situations when she was at the university. Her years in New Orleans did nothing to subdue those urges. Yuko is fiercely loyal to Amaya. An evening with Masako might end up with a disastrous temptation to her friend's husband. She decides to fire a warning shot across Masako's bow.

She looks directly into Masako's eyes when she says, with a slight frown, "Brad-san, when you have a chance to speak with your good wife, please give her my love. The same goes for your delightful daughter, whom I also adore."

Puzzled, Brad shakes his head. "But Yuko, didn't you just see Amaya earlier today …?"

Before Brad can finish his question, Yuko interrupts, "It was pleasant seeing her. I believe she has porcelain ceramics business somewhere. She did not stay long. I'm sure you'll hear from her. I'm also sure you and I can talk in greater detail about current events when they become a thing of the past. Please excuse me, I need to retire."

Alden tries a different tack. "Marcel, is there a chance you and I can have a squash game now that we're in the same town together?"

Bourquin glances at Yuko, who frowns. "Oh, Alden, I'm not ready to accept your challenge on such short notice. Another time, then."

After an awkward beat, Yuko adds, "I'll tell you this much: this *El Caballo* saga beats anything I can find on TV."

In the parking circle of the prime minister's residence, Masako gestures for Alden to take the front seat of the black sedan with Honshu Lines decals on the rear doors. She sits close to Brad in the rear seat.

"Where do you boys suggest we have a drink? You must have a favorite haunt."

Alden is wary. Brad is uncomfortable. They say nothing. They have now been left in the dark by the chairman of Honshu, the prime minister of Japan, the ambassador from Switzerland, and Amaya. Is it all part of the same thing? Is Amaya caught up in this covert mission?

Masako breaks the awkward silence. "Right, then let's go to my favorite club. A lot of Honshu Lines people go there after work. The night is still young. Shall we?"

"I think maybe another time to visit your club, if you don't mind," says Brad. "What about this? Our hotel has a lounge on the ground floor. We can kick things around there." Alden grunts approval from the front seat.

Masako presses a playful elbow against Brad's arm. "Fine. We'll go to your hotel for a quickie."

Some eighty or ninety people mill about in the Grand Palace reception area and elevator aisle. They are members of the Austrian Philharmonic Orchestra who have just arrived on buses from Narita airport, laden with their instrument cases as they check in. Alden has excused himself from Brad and Masako to turn in for the night. Brad steers Masako around the edge of the herd and into the restaurant area, where the bar is serving late diners at the buffet. One entire half of the ground-level reception area is raised, accessible by a set of four steps that lead to the general dining room. Raised beds of ferns and cut flowers separate the restaurant from view from the lobby. In this space is served breakfast, lunch, and dinner buffets, with a small bar. Sunday mornings, the space is packed with families living in the vicinity who make the buffet a special occasion.

Masako bats her eyelashes and teases, "I was thinking more of a snug little dark bar with classic rock, Brad-san. *Kanpai*."

Brad lifts his Rittenhouse on the rocks, returning the toast. He tilts his head toward the milling musicians. "Well, maybe we could organize part of that orchestra for an impromptu quartet. In the meantime, I'd rather make this a short chat about that assumption I've been under."

Masako settles into her seat. "You were partially right today in that Honshu considers *El Caballo*'s earnings better than normal, but that has created a unique problem for Honshu. We want Lydia Maxwell to remain as co-owner of the ship, and we want her gone, both at the same time." Brad frowns.

"Let me explain," she goes on. "For nearly a year now, Honshu Lines has been planning to issue stock in the American market. We are very serious about this. We have worked with First Patriot financial services and a prestigious New York law firm. We are set for an initial public offering on Monday, October 18 this year." She adds with a wink, "We will help open the New York Stock Exchange for trading that day. Save the date."

Brad jots an entry on his pocket calendar.

Masako continues, "We have reshuffled half our global assets into our new American subsidiary, including our shares in Honshu Hull 33, Limited. Mrs. Maxwell would still own her shares, of course. You see, in our filings with your Securities Exchange Commission, we had to make full disclosure of the fact that she is half owner of that ship. We wanted that arrangement to continue, as you assumed, not so much because of the freight revenues, but because the relationship would add prestige to our stock. After what you've told us today, I'm not so sure it would."

Brad chuckles. Such ripples in the pond.

"But more than that, we want her gone," she says. "Under a long-standing operating agreement, Mrs. Maxwell controls hiring and firing of key employees and makes decisions about charter and cargo contracts. We want that control. She has been able to keep that agreement going because of her unique relationship with your unique Speaker of the House."

Masako pauses for a sip of her Rittenhouse rye on the rocks. She smiles as she sees Brad's confused look. "However, we do not want to be tainted by her husband's cloud of ethical charges. That would be a poor time to issue a Honshu stock prospectus. Just the investigation and publicity would stain our name and good standing. It would scuttle our IPO for now and for the foreseeable future."

Brad puts his glass down and shakes his head slowly. "And I thought I had problems."

Masako reaches as if to touch Brad's wrist, but holds her hand just above it. "You do, Brad-san. But they are ordinary, commercial ones. The kind of problems reasonable businesspeople solve every day. On this trip, you are carrying someone else's problems on your back: Speaker Maxwell's. Those are political ones skirting on the criminal. You may be out of your league."

Brad stiffens and turns. "Thanks."

Masako withdraws her hand and straightens. In a chilly tone, she continues, "Just saying, Brad-san. It's out of our league too. Washington is in a different league from the rest of us mortals. We have sleazebags in our own government. Yuko Kagono excepted, of course. She is exceptional in every good way."

Brad leans back and gives her an appraising look. "You are full of surprises, Masako. I'm impressed with your grasp. How much time did you spend in America?"

Masako relaxes. "After college in Kyoto, I went to New Orleans to study maritime law at Tulane University. I got my JD there and stayed on two more years for a master's. New Orleans is a great mixing bowl."

"Why the California Bar exam?"

Masako laughs. "It was on a dare. Three of us took it. Two of us passed it the first time."

Brad stands. "Masako, thank you for your candor in telling me about the Honshu dilemma. I'm off to bed, if you don't mind."

"So, Brad-san, again do you leave this girl waiting, hoping for a better next time?"

CHAPTER 21

Amaya checks into the Okura hotel in Fukuoka's Hakata district just before eight in the evening. Hakata was formerly a separate city with a long history. Once inside her room, she immediately calls Brad, only to reach his voice mail again. She leaves a longish message and enjoys her *bento* from the prime minister of Japan. She then falls into a deep catch-up sleep.

Her limited-express train to Arita is distinctly different from the bullet train. It is much slower and makes frequent stops along the way, including a short one in Kohoku, where Mariko and Aiko grew up.

Two tracks run past the small, one-room Arita train station, a northbound and a southbound. Amaya steps off the train on the southbound track at ten. Standing in the doorway is Emiko, holding a single long-stemmed rose. They clasp each other excitedly and quickly sit on the round, backless wooden bench. Amaya shows Emiko photos of Kozue, and she clucks approvingly. Emiko has chosen a blue cotton scarf with dove-gray streaks to cover her neck. Emiko is much more subdued than Amaya remembers. Gone are the quick, animated flashes of warm smiles and twinkling eyes. She wears a gray cotton skirt and a lighter gray short-sleeved blouse. Her eyes are dull. Her shoulders slump. She has put on weight. She has acquired the pale look of someone who spends long hours in a windowless workroom cataloguing antiquities, far from the admiring crowds of museum visitors.

"Will you have lunch with me today?" asks Emiko. "I have taken a personal day off from the museum, but if you wish to visit there, we could tour the exhibits and have lunch at their restaurant. Everything is served on period dishware made in Arita. It is a step back in time."

"Um, I wonder, Emiko. I want to speak with you privately about a confidential matter. Might we have a quieter day just for ourselves?"

Emiko frowns and looks at the circular fan above them. She turns back.

"Have you ever been to Okawachiyama?" she asks. "I'm sure you must have, but in case not, then you definitely should. We would be very private. It is only half an hour's drive. I have my car."

Amaya has only read about the place. It is called the "village of the secret kilns." It is a mecca for those who prize the history of Japanese porcelain. That history began with the discovery of the particular clay, kaolin, used to make it. Potters of China and Korea used the clay on the mainland and exported their products to the Japanese. Then, in the sixteen hundreds, a Japanese warlord attempted an invasion of Korea, hoping to conquer China. He was repelled. But as he returned, he rounded up a group of Korean potters as either captives or willing labor recruits, the real story having been lost in time. Each version has its adherents. It was a Korean potter who discovered kaolin near Arita. From that discovery, the entire industry grew in Japan, including the legendary rival kilns of Kakiemon and Nabeshima.

Lord Nabeshima, who ruled this domain, established the village of secret kilns to guard his production techniques and artisans. His blue-and-white products were made only for Japanese aristocracy as gifts and not for any commercial market. Many of his potters were descended from the original Koreans brought there as a war prize. Once in Okawa-chiyama, there was little hope of escaping past Nabeshima sentinels. They even had a special burial spot there. Its kilns have not been fired since 1870. The village of cobblestone streets surrounded by mountains was restored in 1984 with shops, restaurants, and museums.

Emiko drives out of Arita and onto a mountain road. Amaya relates to her the outlines of the mission to return those like Emiko's mother who were kidnapped and taken from northwestern Japan to Korea. Amaya has been apprehensive over how Emiko might react to news of finally having closure on her mother. Emiko is surprisingly passive.

Emiko pulls into the parking lot next to the bridge with a hand-painted blue-and-white porcelain façade that arches over a narrow mountain stream. The women sit a moment before starting their walk.

Emiko points out the irony that some 350 years after Korean potters were forced (or enticed) to go to Japan for their artistic skills, North Koreans abducted her mother for her language skills. She shrugs. "Mori-sensei, this discussion picks at a scab on my mind."

"Oh, my. I had hoped for a more positive response."

"But think about it, Mori-sensei: What do you remember from your age five? I can remember bad feelings, but I cannot remember my mother. I remember feelings of great upset and pain and separation. The photographs I have of her were given to me by relatives. I have no belongings or mementos or actual memories of her as a person, just as a nightmare story, like a ghost that seems slightly familiar. And I have a real scar encircling my neck that is forever a price for her I pay daily. It is noticeable to all who look at me and to me when I see myself in a mirror. I wear a tightly tied scarf there even in July and August and in an overheated museum in winter. It is my badge, of what? Honor? I think not."

Amaya listens in stunned silence.

Emiko continues, "And now, you come with news of a possible reunion, or perhaps the return of her remains, or perhaps none of that until a future trip, and possibly never. What you say is full of new responsibilities for Emiko. If she is returned to me, I owe her my life, and I will devote myself to giving her comfortable final years. If she has expired, I shall do my filial duty to honor her with proper services. Either way, I will have to find strength I'm afraid I do not possess."

Amaya leans against her friend's shoulder. "When you managed my shop in the Palace Hotel, you took the responsibility to protect your mother from personal threats and intimidation. Don't you feel something beyond duty?"

"Well, yes, Mori-sensei, as I just said, I feel the returning shock and loss from my childhood, as if it were the burglary of an intimate toy. If you ask if my heart jumps for a lost person, then I must in all honesty disappoint you. I feel only honor, duty, and dread."

Amaya places her hand on Emiko's arm. "Well, I am not quite finished. There is more. And I fear it will mean more responsibility."

Emiko turns her head with a slight smile. "In that case, let us walk to a restaurant in this historic place where you can tell me over sake."

They walk arm in arm across the bridge into the serene country charm of the village. A steep hillside rises to their left about fifty meters away. The slope facing them holds markers of Korean villagers who were buried there through the generations. Annually, Korean tourists come to this hillside to tend and decorate graves of their ancestors. One such family stands there now, heads bowed and hands pressed prayerfully.

Emiko leads the way to the right and up a steep cobblestone street, past remnants of kilns built to rise along the slope, containing as much heat as possible from the wood fires at the lower end. She takes them to a small noodle shop on a sunny street corner. The shop holds a tiny room, the kitchen, and a patio. A teenaged girl welcomes the women with excited and warm greetings. They carry bowls of steaming ramen and a small bottle of sake to sit alone on the shop's trellised patio.

"There, that's better," says Emiko. "Please continue explaining my further duties, Mori-sensei."

Amaya is uncomfortable with Emiko's response to her visit. She had hoped for something cheerier. But at this point, she can only press on.

"Emiko, I bring no more to you than information about a confidential mission and about what is needed. I ask nothing of you. What you choose to do is entirely up to you."

Emiko sips sake. "Mori-sensei, I owe you much. You entrusted your two Tokyo shops to me as a young manager. That alone was unusual for a high-end art gallery in the Ginza area. You treated me with understanding when I made foolish overtures toward you. You saw to it that high officials from the Tokyo police and national government supported my recovery from an attack by someone I had given personal information about you and your husband. Even the prime minister knows about the sorrows of Emiko. Of course, I shall carry out whatever duty may be required. Continue, please."

Amaya bows her head in respect. "There are other families from this area who may be affected by this mission. I am here to inform and prepare them as I have you."

Emiko straightens in surprise. "But this is a Japanese matter. You have become American with an American husband and daughter. You should not have to disrupt your life over this issue."

Amaya's brow tightens. "I am as Japanese as I ever was. But more to the point, the prime minister must avoid a public show. She wants the entire reunion to be unseen except by the families themselves. They will all be asked to keep the matter as quiet as possible. She fears consequences if the plan is exposed too soon. This first exchange will be followed by others. She wants it to be as secret as possible until it is completed. The ship will return to Australia to pick up more grain and then exchange it for others the North Koreans release. I do not know how many trips that will involve or how many will be returned. I can only conclude that future success depends on the success and secrecy of the first, and then the next, and so on."

Emiko says, "How many others like me do you mean to see in Kyushu?"

"I have three other files."

"Where are the families located?"

"One is in Takeo, the others in Fukuoka."

"Takeo is only twenty minutes from Arita by train. I am happy to inform those people in person. If you return this afternoon, you will be able to inform the other families, and possibly return to America from Kansai airport tomorrow or the next day."

"Here is the file."

Emiko studies the papers slowly. "I know that apartment building. These names—perhaps I also know. I'm not sure. I will see to it this afternoon. But what are we supposed to do next?"

Amaya now has mixed feelings about asking Emiko to take on new responsibilities, but she continues, "I have been told to invite you to go to the port of Hakata/Fukuoka one week from this coming Saturday, in the afternoon. A young marine by the name of Kimoto will meet everyone at the terminal building and take you from there. Here is a photo of him so you will recognize him. He will only recognize you by a password. You must say to him, in English, 'swords.' He will say, 'ploughshares.' Please do not tell the others the passwords. He will accept your group; you will all be permitted to proceed."

Emiko squints and whispers the words. "These are words from a Christian expression, aren't they?"

Amaya says levelly, "The prime minister is very well read in many fields and philosophies."

"Mori-sensei, you have brought me something better than news. Since the attack on my throat, and leaving your shops and Tokyo, my life has been a sort of sickly sadness. Even in the museum, I rarely look up from my work. I go through motions of my life amid historical artifacts. You have brought me a purpose. Will you be in Hakata for the reunion?"

"I honestly don't know, Emiko."

"Please do not be offended when I say, I earnestly hope you are home with your American family before then, not in a Japanese port to receive human wreckage. I also hope you understand I meant no offense about becoming American now. I didn't mean you had stopped being Japanese. I know who you are, Mori-sensei. You are a woman of beauty and culture. Now, you add to that a woman of compassion and honor. Japan is too small a place for you."

CHAPTER 22

Nancy Booth rarely smirks. This is one of those days. She loves that she can wear a smart summer-weight suit and pearls on her way to work with Drew, rather than the usual compromises she would make if riding crowded Metro trains and squirming through madhouse transfers at the Metro Center hub. These days, her stiletto heels click along the floors of the Capitol Building, and her every hair is in place. Facing Speaker Maxwell this morning, she has the air of a very secure, happy person.

Thad Maxwell also rarely smirks. It's only when stars align to heighten his well-nourished self-esteem. This definitely is not one of those days. His brows are deeply furrowed and moist with the exertion of coping with unhappy news.

"Nancy, shouldn't we be hearing some kind of report by now about the you-know-what event in the South China Sea? I mean, I'm delighted we're not fending off reporters, but still, I expected something in the news. What's the situation?"

Nancy is gravely disappointed that it falls to her to report the situation rather than the boy-lawyer who thought all this up in the first place. She folds her hands; it's her chief gesture of stalling. "Shall I call Drew to come by?"

Maxwell bats the suggestion away like a summer mosquito. "No, Nancy, I'm sure you're up to date. Besides, I hate to take him away from his vital work with spreadsheets."

Nancy stiffens, hands now clenched. "Sir, my contact at Sec. Def. reported late yesterday. There's been a news release about the submarine exercise, but nothing was said about the sinking. When I asked him about that, he told me that the misfire had misfired."

Maxwell starts to lift off like a missile. "Meaning?" he roars.

She flinches but remains seated. "Meaning, I believe, that the joint exercise stood down without a shot being fired. The Japanese Self-Defense Force broke off because the *El Caballo* is in the Taiwan Strait, and they don't want to create an incident in those waters. The Chinese navy patrols there regularly, and Taiwan is always on alert. It wouldn't take much to set off that tinderbox. So, without the Japanese, it's not much of a joint exercise."

Maxwell brings the palm of his hand down with the sound of an air-to-ground missile. "What a bunch of chickens. Who did you get that report from?" He is perspiring fully now, and deeply unhappy.

"Secretary Copeland himself. He hasn't dared to bring anyone else in on this at the Defense Department."

"Tell Howard how important this is to me personally."

Nancy sighs. Tension leaves her shoulders. "I already did, Mr. Speaker. He was rude to me. He went off on a tangent about unintended consequences and a pretext for war like the Gulf of Tonkin back in the last century."

"Dammit, Nancy," Thad says in another explosive launch. "We had two things going for us in this ethics investigation: Drew's sink-her plan and Drew's spreadsheets. Drew finally had to shred all the spreadsheets. And now the *El Caballo* didn't sink. Both of the things going for us— both of them—GONE. This is unbelievable. I smell a lily-livered rat."

Nancy remains quiet to allow the energy in the room to disperse. "It is a mystery, Mr. Speaker. Do you want me to have Secretary Copeland come to the office?"

Maxwell is quieter now. He mops his brow. He looks away into the middle distance. "That won't help either me or him. Bring me the name of one of ours in his chain of command. We're going to have to have the White House appoint an emergency replacement defense secretary in the August recess. No need for Senate dithering over it."

While distinctly not on the subject, Nancy seizes the chance to change it. "On that subject, Ray Lion is pulling out all the stops for continuing the session to pass his rare earth bill, canceling August recess if need be."

"Not going to happen." Maxwell allows himself the first chuckle of the day. "I told him that myself. Delay is all we have left in the inquiry without the spreadsheets and the torpedoes. I need that recess more than ever now."

"Yes, sir. Still, he persists."

"Not against me he won't." Maxwell now paces the length of the table. He stops near the ship model on the pedestal at the far end. "The *El Caballo* is off Taiwan, you say? Find out where exactly. And find out who we know at the Chinese Embassy. I've got a fallback plan." Maxwell taps the side of his head with his index finger. "Always thinking, thinking, thinking."

CHAPTER 23

In the second-floor private dining room of the Chinese Embassy near Tokyo Tower, Brad and Alden have just arrived after clearing security. The room is long, with windows on one wall facing the red-and-white sectioned Tokyo Tower landmark in the middle distance; the tower was built after World War II and serves as both a symbol and a communications beacon. The wallpaper is a plumb-colored plush fabric, hung with black-framed calligraphy and brush paintings of mist-covered, jagged mountain peaks of China. There is a raised stage at one end of the room where musicians frequently play traditional music from China. One of those musicians is the ambassador's daughter, Chu Hua. The long, black-lacquered table is set with Western silverware, lacquered chopsticks, lacquered lidded soup bowls, and porcelain plates. However, no food will be served at this occasion.

The men are not surprised to see the people they met five years ago at a reception in the Tokyo American Club. Chinese ambassador Shuai is tall and sallow-faced with sleepy eyes. For the most part polite, his manner can be brusque at times. Chu Hua, now twenty-eight, stands at his side in a bespoke light yellow shirtdress tailored in London. She still wears her long black hair coiled atop her head. Beside them stands Marilyn Trihey, the perky blonde deputy chief of mission at the American embassy. Marilyn seemingly reads the minds of others, even if their thoughts are in another language. Alden and Brad worked with her five years ago.

Brad and Alden are very surprised to see standing apart from them, and in a corner of the room, Masako Daigo and a uniformed Japanese naval serviceman. Both look uncomfortable.

After reintroductions, Marilyn Trihey clears her throat. "Alden, you and Mr. Oaks need to know of some developments. Unpleasant ones. Not because of you, but related to your business in Japan this trip. Ambassador Shuai, would you like to explain?"

Shuai looks at Marilyn. He'd rather not, but he does. "I cannot explain insanity. I can only report it. It seems that the American Speaker of the House called an official at our Washington embassy. If I didn't know the person, I would consider it dangerous slander. But I do know him, and I trust him to report honestly. Speaker Maxwell called to invite the Chinese government to commit an act of war in the Taiwan Strait. Whether the waters are international or territorial to China is not the real point. It seems the Speaker of the House has some animosity toward a certain vessel you know very well. The ship will pass the west coast of Taiwan, a rare routing into the Strait to put her clear of the typhoon moving up the island's east coast. Prime Minister Kagono informs me that the same Speaker Maxwell had the malign idea for American and Japanese submarines to sink the vessel. Wiser heads prevailed. But when the Speaker learned that there would be no such sinking, he pleaded with our embassy for the Chinese to consider the ship, which is unarmed, to be a rogue intruder hostile to China and to sink her ourselves. We are often baffled by American reasoning, but this one takes the cake."

Alden shuts his eyes, rolls his head back, and barks, "Idiocy!"

Chu Hua flashes a dark look and asks, "Chinese idiocy?"

"Of course not."

Marilyn Trihey, always one for unambiguous communication at times like this, declares, "And not Japanese idiocy."

"Is our ship still afloat?" Masako asks quietly in all seriousness.

"Yes. She labors through heavy seas at eight knots but is very much on course and under her own power."

"Thank you, Mr. Ambassador. Do you want us to order the ship to change course?" Masako asks.

Shuai nods in appreciation. He makes a dismissive wave of his hand. "No, there is no need from the standpoint of Chinese interests. Let her skipper follow the safest course he has plotted. We stand ready to assist in rescue efforts if the storm imperils the ship further. We shall certainly not imperil her."

He turns to face Alden Knight. "We have long observed that irrationality infects many of your politicians. To be fair, we see such strains in Europe as well. We are wary, but we show restraint, as we must."

Alden straightens and says, "Thank you for your restraint in this instance, Ambassador Shuai."

"You are most welcome, Mr. Ambassador." Shuai walks to one of the windows and studies the Tokyo Tower. He turns back. He sounds like a college lecturer. "This is not entirely gentlemanly restraint. We are creditors here. We hold over 1 trillion US dollars' worth of treasury debt. We also hold the debt of the government of Australia, where the grain has been lifted. We have no reason to harm its recipient. China paid for that debt fair and square, and expects returns of and on our capital. So, we have no cause to put our thumb on the scale involving this vessel. The Taiwan Strait makes people jumpy, of course, but Taiwan is a special case. Taiwan took that territory from China in 1950 without paying for it. We own that island; its twenty-four million residents are our citizens. When the war of unification eventually comes to that theater, it will not be over a shipload of grain. It will be to pull a hundred-year-old snag in the three-thousand-year-old fabric of China's history. It will certainly not be started at the behest of the distempered gentleman from Tennessee. Are you a friend of Speaker Maxwell?"

"Not a close friend," Alden replies. "He was a student of mine in law school. His thinking has strayed. I feel a duty to help him regain his footing."

"Admirable, Ambassador Knight." Shuai pauses and smiles, his eyes narrowed. "To aid you in that, I must tell you that we recorded his call."

Alden nods gravely. He and Brad exchange glances. Alden has begun a polite exit address to Shuai when Chu Hua appears at Brad's side and tugs his sleeve. She motions for him to follow her to the empty far end of the table, where she says,

"Did your wife accompany you to Tokyo this trip?"

Brad chuckles. "Well, yes and no. I arrived first, and then she arrived, then left suddenly before the day ended."

The ambassador's daughter searches his eyes. "Well, of course, you must know where she is now, and why …?"

Brad is embarrassed to say, "Well, you might suppose so, but in fact, I really don't know the details of her sudden trip. She took a train to Kyushu, but that's all I know."

Chu Hua is quiet for a long moment. Then, unexpectedly, she makes a very low bow and holds it. Brad returns it with a nod, but he is puzzled by her unexpected gesture.

Chu Hua's eyebrows are gathered in a worried pinch as she says softly, "I hope her trip is a safe one and that you will be reunited very soon. Oh, look, here is Ambassador Knight."

"Are you ready, Brad? I think we need to go."

Brad shakes Chu Hua's extended hand. "Thank you for your courteous sentiment. I'm sure she is safe and happy as she can be, gathering additions to her porcelain collection."

She smiles. "Ah, her porcelains. Yes, of course. So exquisite. So fragile. So at risk. Perhaps that is part of their charm."

Brad demurs, "I'm not sure I completely understand, but will give it thought."

The Americans make their way to the dining room's door, aiming to hail a taxi downstairs at the front entrance. But Brad hesitates. Something about Chu Hua's final conversation haunts him. He stops and turns to her again.

Chu Hua stands tall in front of the window which overlooks Tokyo Tower. In fact, her figure and that of the tower seem to Brad's eye to be of almost the same height as she stands just at that spot. The illusion adds to his unsure feelings of the moment.

As Brad looks, she immediately presses her hands prayerfully in front of her chest and bows again. When she stands, she turns her head to look away from Brad. Brad thinks immediately of Amaya, in part because the gesture reminds him of her, and in part because of his sense of unease. *This is the oddest sensation—this tingle of what? Anxiety? At least uncertainty, of not knowing something I should. Oh well, what I don't know about the Chinese would fill a big book; I've never even been there.* He nods again, and the men depart.

CHAPTER 24

Nancy Booth is washing her hands in the ladies' room on the House side of the Capitol. They felt slimy after a brief, unpleasant encounter with Ray Lion in the vestibule of the Speaker's office. She thought she had seen it all. It takes experience and a level head to run the staff of a Congressional office, especially that of the Speaker of the House. She prides herself on having grace under pressure. Brash Ray Lion has just turned on a fire hose of pressure to get his damned rare earth elements bill passed.

Lion has just said, through an insincere attempt at a boyish, engaging grin, "What part of critical national security don't you fully understand, Nancy?"

To which she replied, "What part of representative democracy don't you even slightly understand?" She knew it was a mistake as soon as she said it, the proverbial rock and hard place confrontation. She momentarily lost her cool. She is better than this and knows it.

"Look, the Speaker has given you assurances that he will get this passed," she continued in a more conciliatory tone. "He has the track record to back that up. He has promised this bill, and he will deliver. So what if it's after the August recess? What's another four or six weeks, or whatever?"

"Money, Nancy. Duh. Every day, our new processing facilities stand idle while money runs out like effluent into a mountain river!"

Nancy snapped, "That's a bad analogy, but I get your point. The problem is that your opponents want it to happen never, and you want it to happen tomorrow. In Congress, sometime is better than never, and hurry up only counts when members' own reelections are at stake. This rare earth bill is not earth-shattering with constituents and therefore not with their members."

She stopped walking. She controlled her impatience and explained, "Ray, we have two problems. That means you have two problems. The first one is that the Speaker can only spend political capital in short, successive bursts. The pending business today, as it was yesterday, is this assault weapon resolution. The Speaker's caucus is divided on it. The measure is wildly popular in the polls. The White House is following this one and leaning with the wind, as usual. In this case, the wind is against guns. POTUS is sitting on the sidelines, saying vague nothings and that it is up to Congress. The only thing that will bring this to quick closure, one way or another, is if the White House gives it a shove. You should take a couple of 'nice' pills and go down there to get them to unblock the logjam on that resolution. Only if that happens will the Speaker be able to bring the rare earth bill to a vote. And save your breath about canceling August recess. It'd be easier to stop the sun from rising."

Now more intrigued than bitter, Ray asked, "What kind of push?" Push is something Ray can arrange if he needs to.

Nancy turned and started toward her office again. Ray moved to her side. She said, "A strong one in either direction, it doesn't matter which. That's how close the balance of votes is. You guys are strong on guns, so I guess that's the direction you want."

Ray raised his voice. "We are neither pro-guns nor anti-guns. We are pro-money, Nancy. You're a slow learner."

Fed up, Nancy said, "I'm sorry, Ray, I'm going to have to break this off. I need to phone the Speaker. He's on the golf course at the Army-Navy club with the secretary of defense. Great talking to you. Our door is always open."

Brad is in the hotel's main-floor restaurant early on Thursday morning. Alden tucks into an omelet with actual yokes, not the all-whites ones Sarah Jane thoughtfully serves him.

"Did you run this morning, Brad?"

Brad chuckles. "No. Not in the summer here." The fact is, Brad runs a lot less these days than he once did. Noticing that Alden has finished his breakfast, Brad looks at his watch. "We have our family call in a few minutes. I have nothing else on after that this morning, so you've got time to go to the embassy if you need to."

Alden starts to gather his things, but Brad puts his hand on his arm. "Before you go, there's something else on my mind. It's more personal. I woke up with it early this morning, and as long as it's on my mind, I'd like to hash it out with you."

"OK. That sounds kind of ominous."

"Well, it's not ominous, but it is definitely serious. It's about something I've been thinking about after helping Kozue prepare her speech in Seattle."

Alden sits back down. "OK, that's interesting. She made a big impact on everyone with that speech. I'm glad I could listen to her. We've got a bit of time before the call. What's the gist of your idea?"

Brad leans forward. His words tumble out. "This idea is not very well developed, but let me spell it out, and tell me what you think about it. Gun safety advocates usually go about the thing by pushing for legislation that prohibits this or that, or requires gun owners to comply with this thing or that. That just hits a brick wall. It's not like with other industries where there's a gradual negotiation. Five or six years ago, we passed a law requiring automakers to come up with a technology to prevent a car from being driven if the driver is drunk. The auto industry was part of the negotiation and helped craft a law they could live with."

Alden nods. "I hear you. But the gun lobby has risen from the ashes of their bankruptcy. It's now the New Second Amendment Righters. N2AR won't play that game."

Brad nods quickly. "But assault weapons make for a special case. Those weapons are made for one purpose, military combat. So that means that there is only one buyer, the United States government."

Alden tilts his head in acknowledgment. "Well, Brad, there is a big market for those things in police forces, and then an aftermarket in the general public."

Brad's voice picks up steam again. "Exactly. But the first production run is for the military. It's the military who starts the ball rolling. The manufacturers even give a different designation for what they call their civilian market. Can you believe that? They call it a civilian market for a weapon like that?"

"Yes, the Department of Defense makes the market."

In haste, Brad replies, "Right. And the Department of Defense can only make their purchases under contracts having hundreds of pages of rules baked in."

"Oh, I know that. It's all laid out in the Federal Acquisition Regulations." Alden glances at his watch again.

"The FAR, exactly. And every contract issued under the FAR has precise specifications for whatever it is the government is buying. We bid on government work all the time."

"I know," Alden says patiently.

Brad leans in and taps the table. "So, you also know the FAR contract clauses go beyond the absolutely necessary commercial terms of a purchase contract. For example, there are a lot of social objectives built into the FAR. There are provisions in there about paying prevailing wages in construction contracts, and that means union scale. There are provisions meant to help small businesses, minority-owned businesses, buy America clauses, and all kinds of things." Brad takes a gulp of water.

He continues. "We're an innovative country. We can come up with all kinds of technological innovation when we're motivated. And the biggest motivator is commerce, the desire by manufacturers to satisfy their customers. What if instead of making assault weapons illegal, the government specifies it will only buy them if they have certain built-in safety features?"

"What kind of safety features?"

Brad pushes back. "I really don't know. But let's suppose there are ways to make these weapons only functional under certain conditions. Either the government specifies the technology, or it invites the bidder to submit its own. Then, the market does its work. For this particular weapon, the US military buys only the so-called safe ones. So, the government is not imposing restrictions on people, it is offering the big contracts for a new kind of assault weapon. A carrot instead of a stick."

Alden goes quiet. He's getting the drift. "You have been busy this morning. There's a lot to like about that. And maybe there'd be a clause in there that they can't sell work-arounds or noncomplying models to the public."

Brad grins. "Sure. So, how do we go about changing the FAR?"

Alden exhales. "Oh, that's a long, drawn-out process, but it is executive branch rule making. There will be tons of opposition, and the opponents have a chance to make their objections before the new regs become final. There is always a public comment period, and before that, the agencies circulate an exposure draft to all the organizations that have an interest."

Brad leans in again, nodding. "There has to be some connection to a law passed by Congress, Alden."

Alden puts up one hand. "Yes, yes, I know, but it can be something simple and palatable, maybe just a resolution calling for safe assault weapons. Implementation would be delegated to the executive branch. They do so through a change in the way they purchase the things."

Brad tips his chair back and looks out the window facing the hotel's garden waterfall. He sighs. "My Tree has to be able to understand all this."

"You know she can, Brad. Kids' toys and sports all have rules. They'd rather do something with rules than be told they can't do it at all. Try it out on her."

Brad looks at his watch. It's coming on to ten thirty. "Uncle Alden, I'm going to ask you a favor in return for coming over here for you. I'd like you to help Kozue understand this, and I'd like you to help sell the idea in Washington. It seems to me it fits into your new mission to straighten out your party."

Alden beams. "That's certainly fair, Brad. It's getting me fired up, actually."

"OK, then. I'm going to my room to email Kozue. I'll knock on your door in twenty-five minutes for our call. Finally, I'll find out what my wife is doing on her own somewhere in Japan."

CHAPTER 25

Sarah Jane and Kozue are just finishing supper at the apartment. They have picked up the kitchen and now wait at the dining room table for the call they're expecting as arranged by email: Brad and Alden from Alden's hotel room, and Amaya from her room at the Okura in Fukuoka.

"So, I want to pin Alden down on when he's coming back," offers Sarah Jane as they jot down a hasty agenda.

"And I want to find out why they are helping Speaker Maxwell, who is blocking our assault gun resolution," says Kozue. "Tennessee has nine Congressional districts. How does one man out of four hundred thirty-five members of the House, who represents one ninth of one state, get to hold up a law the majority of the people want?"

Aunt Sarah hums a line-dance country tune before saying, "Ask your father, dear."

The phone chimes.

Brad has always given full, informative reports to home and office from Tokyo. Over the years, he has polished his craft of brevity without loss of nuance, coloration, and intent. Throughout his trips, his running accounts leave everyone with the same understanding as he has. When crunch time inevitably comes, decisions rest on good foundations. At least that's how it goes in the business he is most familiar with. This trip breaks new ground.

Brad's agenda for this call is foremost in his mind, and he needs no notes for it. "My dear Amaya, I hope the country air wherever you are agrees with you, and especially that you are able to tell me and the rest of your family how it's going."

The phone is quiet. Amaya says, "I must ask you all to be understanding. I have agreed not to talk about what I am doing. You know that I am not a secretive person. But this time, I must be."

Brad nods and says, "OK, hon. I didn't mean to pry. We're going to respect that, of course. I just hope you are not going out on a limb of some sort. Not going into anything risky."

"Not at all, Brad. Do not give any thought to that."

Kozue pipes up, "How are the flowers there?" Sarah Jane looks over at her in surprise. Kozue winks.

Amaya, flustered, says, "The late bloomers are beautiful this time of year. There is one kind especially at the edge of the rice fields. It has a purple blossom."

Kozue says, "Lovely. That sounds like an orchid petal."

Amaya says quickly, "So, Brad, how is it going for you? Have you bought a company sailing vessel?"

After the chuckles subside, Sarah Jane says, "Brad, you may be the CEO, but as chair of the board and shareholder of Elgar, you haven't convinced me we need to buy a cargo ship, even if you do get a green light from the steel mills."

"I know, S. J., and I'm not pushing it."

"Well," says Alden, "don't beat up on Brad about buying a boat. I was the one who put this idea into Brad's head, but for a political purpose, to help Thad Maxwell save face and exit gracefully instead of in humiliation."

"That's really great, Alden," says Sarah Jane. "But does that mean your political party will put up their money on this, or are we Elgars the only ones to foot the bill?"

"Sarah Jane, I don't expect Elgar to do something like this unless there is a solid business reason," says Alden.

"OK," Sarah Jane continues. "So, Brad, have you talked to Shin and KNN? What do they say?"

"Heh, it didn't go all that well with Iseo. He wants us to buy a new one from them, Sarah Jane."

"You're sounding like a stand-up comedian now, Brad."

"Yeah, I wish. So, it's not going all that well for us over here. At least I'm getting to know people at the top at Honshu Lines."

"May I ask a question?" says Amaya quietly.

"Sure."

"You still believe that this ship is owned by Honshu Lines and Mrs. Lydia Maxwell, am I right?"

"Right," says Brad.

Amaya continues, "Has anyone talked to Mrs. Lydia Maxwell? Are you sure you know whether she wants to sell?"

The phone is quiet. Sarah Jane grins, and Kozue makes a finger-thumb OK circle in the air.

"Alden," says Brad, "I guess that is for you to answer. You were back there when this thing started."

"I only talked to Thad and some staffers. I just assumed Thad is talking for her. Why wouldn't she want what he does?"

Sarah Jane breaks the second silence. "Alden, her husband seems to think he doesn't need anyone's consent. He's just going to shoot the thing to hell. No one's told him that won't happen. You boys can't make a move until you know absolutely where Lydia Maxwell stands on this. Can you email her, Alden? Phone her?"

"Yes, I guess so."

"That's not the same," says Brad, "as a face-to-face. There is no substitute for one of us meeting with her, alone. I nominate you, Alden."

Sarah Jane groans.

Kozue says, "Can I go with you? I need to talk to Mr. Maxwell about something."

Brad says, "Come on, Kozue, why in the world would you need to do that?"

Kozue repeats her earlier question to her father.

Brad says, "Alden, that's for you again. You know more about Washington than any of us does."

Alden clears his throat. "I would have to look up the particulars. It's a House parliamentary rule."

"Not a rule in our house, Uncle Alden. So, can I go with you?"

Kozue hears nothing convincing in the multiple exchanges among the adults. The adults come to recognize there is no good reason she should not go to Washington, with Alden or anyone who'll take her. With that policy settled, they turn to the implementing details. Brad says he has decided to hang out in Tokyo's sweltering heat for a day or so, in case something develops for which he's needed here after all. Amaya cannot give a date she will be able to return. Brad ends by saying he wants to have time together with Amaya and Kozue at home before any of them goes off again. They'll plan their Washington trip with Kozue later.

So, Kozue is not to accompany Alden. As often happens, a good idea, this time Kozue's, languishes because people can't get their schedules together.

CHAPTER 26

On Thursday morning in the Cannon building, Drew Wallace stares into his desktop computer screen full of spreadsheets that display with remarkable clarity the realities of the revenue history of the *El Caballo*. Drew has set up a program that can display outcomes for different values and for certain variables. He can adjust length of voyage, number of voyages per year, cost of bunker fuel, freight rates for various cargos, and other cost inputs. But the vessel's capacity is fixed, and other variables have limits based on public data. Though fanciful, the only helpful spreadsheets assume unbelievable cruising speeds and unlikely cargos at unreal ports of call. But he likes a challenge.

He also likes his new office. Nancy Booth helped him pick out new furniture and tasteful wall décor for it. He likes the new car-and-driver perk. He likes his new apartment in northwest Washington. Nancy helped him decorate that as well. He likes that on Tuesday, she moved into it with him. At thirty-six, Nancy suits Drew's image of an older woman.

Assuring Thad Maxwell's smooth sailing in the ethics investigation gives them both a single-minded purpose. It has moved to the top of the agenda for his staff. On their way to work this morning, Drew and Nancy listened to a telephone briefing from the Pentagon on the position of the units tasked with underwater naval exercises with Japan in the South China Sea. *Man! This is the big time*, Drew thought.

This morning's report did not reveal, of course, that the ultimate tactical objective of the joint exercises has changed to more peaceful ends. Drew and Nancy therefore consider the phantom-cargo matter to be more of a circumstantial sidebar of history that Drew aims to mitigate by spreadsheet, or keep in the shadowy (but irrelevant) past and off the record entirely. The *El Caballo* is not a live issue; they are about to sink her.

"Where are we on the rare earth bill?" he asks as he stretches his legs in the spacious back seat and takes Nancy's hand.

"The tree huggers and supply-chain deniers are intractable. We're going to have to approve some bridges." Nancy playfully tugs the hem of her skirt a little higher.

"Bridges where?"

"That's for the Vermont delegation to decide." She shrugs. "They are looking for possible waterways."

"And the assault weapon resolution?" Drew absently looks at cramped, frustrated commuters in traffic as they navigate comfortably through the leafy Reno Road neighborhoods of Northwest Washington.

Nancy rolls her eyes. "It's stuck in bickering in the other caucus, whether to leave it toothless or do something we'd have to push back on."

After they arrive at the Capitol steps, Nancy goes to the front desk of the office to collect the morning's mail from Evelyn. As she sorts through for letters that need Maxwell's attention, she comes to a thin, blue airmail envelope addressed to "Mrs. Lydia c/o The Speaker of the House, H-232, the Capitol, Washington DC, Personal and Confidential."

Nancy holds it … hefts its slight weight, and thinks, *I need to hold on to this one and think about how to handle it.*

Evelyn says, "We do get weird ones sometimes, don't we? Shall I put the teakettle on?"

"It's hotter'n hell. No thanks, I'm not up to tea right now."

"I was thinking of the steam. You know—" She flicks the corner of the envelope. Without waiting for a reply, Evelyn heads to the break room to fill a teakettle and turn on the hot plate.

Dear Aiko-chan,

I cannot believe twenty-two years since we said goodbye. Every day I think of you with love. We are one. How can we be separated? Perhaps you think of me as well. Any sort of greeting from you would improve my heart. If you cannot, I understand.

I am not writing just about sentimental days, however. I break my vow of silence with this letter to tell you that I cannot keep on through my life without you being a part of it. We are bound by pledge of loyalty forever, and my emotions run even deeper than that. Would you please consent to seeing me? This seems such a simple request, but it may be a turning point for you and me. Either our lives have a future beyond old memories or not. Memories may not survive our approaching years. I cannot bear to think of that.

You know that I keep a post office box for only one purpose, to receive something, anything, from you. Please send something to me there. Let it be welcome news, but above all, let it be news of some kind.

I have good businesses here, and have a comfortable life, but I am so lonely without you. I beg you to send something to the place we agreed upon.

Love,
Mariko

Nancy puts Mariko's letter gently on the desk and reseals it. It feels ominous somehow. She dials Lydia's number.

"Hello, this is Lydia … Is this Nancy?"

"Yes, hello, I'm sorry to disturb you."

"Not at all, Nancy, how can I help you?"

"Well, a letter just arrived at the Speaker's office addressed to you."

"How odd. Did you open it? Who is it from?"

"That's what I thought, too. I certainly did not open it; it's marked personal." Nancy's been on Capitol Hill for fifteen years. She is untroubled by this lie. The first lie was the hardest.

"There is no sender's name or return address on the envelope. But the postmark is Guam. Shall I give it to the Speaker to bring home?"

"No, Nancy, I have a better idea. Could you possibly have lunch with me today? I need to come into Georgetown anyway. If you are able, I suggest we meet at Washington Harbour, and you can bring it to me then."

Now Nancy is even more intrigued. It's clear to her that the letter is significant to Lydia but that she does not want the Speaker to know anything about it. Nancy smiles. She could use a little soap opera in her life this summer.

"Of course, Lydia, I will like that very much. Shall we say one o'clock? Just the two of us."

Washington Harbour is a complex of offices, residences, and pier-side restaurants at the foot of Georgetown, on the north bank of the Potomac River. *Just the two of us?* Lydia had sounded nervous.

Lydia Maxwell wears a willow-green sleeveless cotton sheath to the knees and white pumps. She is tidy and quiet behind a shy smile. Her straight henna hair is gathered at the back and secured by a red hair stick. She stands when Nancy arrives and waves. Nancy may have been cool and composed when she arrived in the chauffeured car at the Capitol earlier, but the gritty, granular office demands had mussed her hair and deepened her worry lines. She arrives at Washington Harbour a bit streaked and caked with cosmetics hastily applied in the same car at the last minute.

Nancy has always enjoyed Lydia's company and recognizes her deep waters. Nancy's loyalty to Thad comes from her instinct for survival. Her fondness for Lydia comes from admiration.

Cob salads ordered, the women lean back at the sunlit window table and smile at one another appraisingly. Lydia looks five years younger than Nancy, even though she is older by three years. *How in the world does she do it?* Nancy wonders.

Lydia studies Nancy and says in a teasing tone, "Nancy, there is a new look about you on this hot day. Is there something—someone—new in your life? Perhaps that Mr. Wallace that Thad hired?"

Nancy says in haste, on top of an exhale, "No, nothing of the sort," and vigorously waves away the very idea.

Lydia lowers her head a moment with a smile. She straightens and says, "I want to discuss something with you before saying anything to Thad. We will all need your good judgment about it."

Nancy sips her white wine spritzer. "I'm happy you feel you can share it with me. Please let me know what's on your mind and how I may help."

Lydia leans on her elbows. Her tone is earnest. "I have received information from the man who manages the ship, Thad's Uncle Earl. It seems that the other owner, Honshu Lines, has taken over the vessel and is not reporting in to Earl. I am concerned about the ship's past and future. We worry that it might somehow ruin Thad. I don't know what to do. That's why I'm here with you."

Nancy fights a smile as she thinks, *Is that all? We're about to blow that ship to smithereens.* She says, "Well, Lydia, why don't you simply sell your interest in the ship? Get it out of your family's bright future?"

Lydia pales. She explains, "The ship came from the man who liberated me and my best childhood friend. She still lives in Guam, and that is her handwriting on the letter you brought to me. Long ago, I told Mariko that I will love her always, but that I have a new life with Thad. Thad decided he could not accept the true history of how we met. He decided that we met in Palo Alto, California, where he attended law school. He invented a past for me. He invented that I was an undergraduate when he was a third-year law student. He tries to avoid that he is fifteen years older than me. It is always vague and uncomfortable. He insisted that I break all ties to Guam and Japan, and that included breaking with Mariko. I have never spoken of Mariko to anyone except Thad and his uncle. Now this new letter arrives."

Pretty soon, it won't be the ship she'll own, it'll be the insurance money. Lydia should be glad to put some of that money into the scarred hands of her bestie. Maybe I can soften Thad up a bit about letting them get together somewhere.

Nancy pats the top of Lydia's hand. "Take your time. I can see this is crucial to you. But, if I may ask, have you in fact been keeping in touch with Mako?"

"Mariko. No, I have done as Thad insists. It broke my heart. Mariko is still in my heart." Lydia turns her hand over, palm up. "This scar is our friendship wound. We pressed blood. She can never be taken from my heart."

Lydia withdraws her hand when the cob salads arrive. Nancy is eager for lunch. Lydia looks out the window at the muddy river. Nancy feels an uncomfortable conflict of loyalties welling up. Her mind calculates faster than any spreadsheet. She measures this meeting in the metrics of her survival. After all, Thad has ambitions for the White House. There is no question about it. She will say comforting words to Lydia. She will see to Thad's and her own survival above all else.

Lydia sighs. "I don't know what to do."

"Dear Lydia, you should go back home and try to calm your mind. I feel sure something will come along to explode … to stop … this worry over the ship."

Lydia sniffs against her handkerchief. "And thank you for this welcome letter from Mariko. We are forever joined, even though I can never see her again. It is a pain beyond maddening."

"I'll bet." Nancy is getting itchy with all this melancholy talk. "I should be getting back."

"Nancy, you and Drew must work very hard on this. So much is riding on your skills. You have much at stake yourself. Personally, I mean."

"I understand, Lydia. I will turn my attention to this as soon as I return to the office."

"Oh, and Nancy?"

"Yes, Lydia?"

Lydia says flatly and with a squint, "I assume you do not want me to inform the Speaker that you are sleeping with his ethics lawyer."

After Nancy leaves, Lydia reads Mariko's poignant letter. She returns to where she has parked in the Watergate Hotel garage. It is a short walk along a sidewalk at the river's edge and then past the Thompson boathouse. She crosses a busy intersection and takes the escalator from the ground level of the Watergate complex to the plaza below, and then enters a large chain drugstore, where she buys an inexpensive flip-top phone and a one-year data contact. She asks a few basic questions on how to operate it. She buys a blank friendship greeting card. She ascends the same escalator and walks to the post office in the complex. Inside, she writes the ten-digit number of her new phone in the greeting card and signs it with her unique Chinese character for Aiko. She seals the envelope and addresses it to M. Isaemon in care of the post office box number Mariko has said she will maintain if ever Lydia needs her. This is the first time Lydia has used it. After mailing the letter, Lydia drives up the circular Watergate garage ramp, feeling exhilarated.

CHAPTER 27

Friday morning, Brad and Alden get together at the ground-floor restaurant's breakfast buffet one more time before Alden flies home. Brad feels pretty empty about the whole trip. Even when he goes home from his other trips without accomplishing much, he still feels himself embedded somewhere in a continuum of Elgar Steel business. Success is hard to point to at times, but rarely has he felt the abject failure that he does this morning.

"Alden, you asked me for a favor by coming here to get information from Honshu Lines on Maxwell's ship. I came and pulled some strings and got to the top of Honshu for a briefing. They stopped short of telling me what the current voyage is all about. Then, you and I had a rare audience with the prime minister, who gave us some comfort that the ship wouldn't be blown out of the water, but said that it was engaged in something she refused to open up about. Even your old squash buddy, Marcel, was evasive. I don't envy you. You're walking a tightrope here. This is going to take all your brainpower. But I need to get back to my job. I don't see anything in this picture involving Elgar Steel. I'm thinking I've done about all there is for me to do on this venture of yours."

Alden nods. "Yeah, I couldn't agree more. You have gone above and beyond. When are you thinking of returning?"

Brad tilts his head in the confusion that has welled up in him. "I'd go in a heartbeat, Alden, but not until I have a good idea what Amaya is doing or at least how long she's expecting to stay. I'm hoping she and I can have a weekend here together at least, maybe even come home together."

"Yeah, I wish you luck with that." Alden is quiet a moment. "But before I go, I want to say something about USTR."

Brad groans. "Alden, I have quite enough on my plate at the moment. This trip is turning out to be a complete bust. No one is talking about that ship with us, and Iseo has no appetite for a change in delivery terms. I'm ready to bag it."

Alden has been listening with half an ear only. He is visualizing Brad as part of the new blood bringing new life to his terminal political party. He hunches his shoulders and leans closer to Brad.

Alden raises his voice in enthusiasm. "That's really great, but I'm talking about something in the big picture, the world picture, and the revival of a two-party system in our republic. You have all the right ingredients and credentials to be the United States trade representative."

Brad looks away. "Alden, come down to earth."

Alden drops his hand on Brad's wrist with a firm grip. "No, Brad, you need to look up into the sky. You need to visualize launching from terra firma into a rarer atmosphere. It's just around the corner for you, I have a feeling. Don't tell me you haven't thought about it already."

Brad relaxes a bit and reflects. "I have, of course, Alden. Long before we met, I knew of the good you were able to do for American industry in that job. But face it: jobs like that are doled out to big donors or those with considerable political muscle."

Alden waves the suggestion away. "Not really, although it has been that way in the past. But there's no reason you can't join those ranks as well. Just open up that CEO wallet. Think generously, Brad: the party can use it and can use you." He chuckles.

"Alden, I am not one to attach to a political party. I never have in the past. That's something I really don't relish as a purpose in my life."

"Well, Brad, I'm not saying you'd have to. You are suited for USTR on merits alone. You told me earlier that the idea was your sweet spot. Just give me a nod or a whisper that you'd be interested."

Brad calms himself. It has been a sweet spot, but not today. He begins to reminisce. "At one point in my life, I would have been. After deep immersion in the legal work at Elgar, and a few trips to Japan on Elgar business, I would have jumped at the chance. But I was single then. I could picture myself in far-flung trade negotiations and Washington-insider intrigue. All that changed with Amaya. After all, you were a widower when you had that job. As for some sudden launch into the stratosphere, I'm at my best with my feet planted on the ground."

After an awkward silence, Alden says, "So, Brad, are you saying you wouldn't even consider it? That it is out of the question?"

Brad leans forward, his eyes fixed on Alden's. "I'm saying my mind is already jam-packed with other present and future purposes. When I thought about USTR work before, I didn't have family or prospects of family. So, even though the idea is still intoxicating, I don't dare touch the stuff. I like what I have way too much."

Alden is bitterly disappointed. He says quietly, "OK, Brad, I hear you. So, if not the USTR, where do you see yourself in five years?"

"I never have had a good answer to that question. I suppose I see myself thinking about an Elgar Steel future. Maybe even that merger with Shin we've always talked about."

Alden stands and shakes Brad's hand. "Well, that's an even bigger mystery that keeps Sarah Jane guessing but is never solved."

Brad nods. "It's all a part of the Elgar lifestyle. You must have figured that out by now, Mr. Ambassador. Have a good trip and soft landings. Say hey to S. J. And to her niece."

<hr>

"Iseo? It's Brad. I'm calling to say I'm about to leave Tokyo. I'm not in a position to meet with your shipbuilding people." Brad stands in his hotel room, looking out at the summer drizzle beginning to fall on the sidewalk leading to the subway station adjacent to the hotel. Clear plastic umbrellas have blossomed everywhere against the damp.

Iseo speaks at his noticeably fast rate. "I'm sorry to hear that, Brad. Cindy will be disappointed not to see you this trip. But I'm not surprised. I have consulted with the KNN raw materials section. They will not consent to changing the coal delivery point from the coal terminal in Vancouver. They are adamant that they must control shipping as is customary. Even the equity we have in the coal mine does not change that practice."

"OK, Iseo, I can't say I'm disappointed really. They just saved me a lot of money."

Iseo laughs. "But I would have gotten you a discount on the price of a new-build. Come back soon. I thought you knew better than to come here in summer. Where are you off to next?"

"Home for a few days, then to Washington, DC, I think."

"Washington is no better than Tokyo in summer. Stay in San Francisco with your wife. Best case, I think. I thought you could have figured that out without my help."

"There was a time you'd have been right. A touch of madness possessed me. Maybe I've been bitten by a fox-demon here."

"That could well be. I understand you have met Masako Daigo. She has a reputation for such bites."

How do these guys find out about stuff like that?

"It is a hazard of international business, Iseo. Speaking of hazards, please give my kind regards to Cynthia."

"I shall. She is assimilating very well to life in Japan. But she still won't wear a kimono. So, assimilation is gradual."

Brad hangs up with a broad smile. *Yeah, Iseo. You have a lot to handle.*

He dials another number.

CHAPTER 28

"My Man of Steel, I'm glad you persisted in phoning me. I just walked in the door."

"My Amaya. May I ask where your door leads, or is that a state secret?"

"You may ask. The Okura hotel in Hakata is very much out in the open."

"Yes, but what about behind its doors?"

Amaya turns her head downward and lowers her voice, "Behind a closed door, I keep nothing from you, Brad. I hope you will not hint and tease to learn what I cannot do, which is to talk about what I do here."

"No, Amaya, I do not want to talk about business, yours or mine. That would give over precious time of our own to the various things that keep us apart."

"You are a smooth talker, Mr. Oaks." Her smile is incandescent. "But your talk melts my heart. I can't believe we are in such a relish. Both of us in Japan at the same time, yet worlds apart."

"It is indeed a pickle. Has Kozue met her new little sister?"

She nods eagerly. "They met at the school. They got along well. Kozue says she 'over-giggles.' She wants to play baseball like Kozue, so there is much in common."

"Including excess giggles. Don't tell me Kozue thinks she has outgrown them?"

"Oh, Brad, she is outgrowing everyone. Sarah Jane said she can barely keep up with her. They are doing very well together. Kozue is deep in studies about how to prevent civilians from owning war weapons. It amazes me that that should be a problem, but since it is one, I'm glad to see that Kozue is working on it. Brad, Kozue has her heart set on going to Washington. Alden and Sarah Jane know people who will listen to her. We cannot stop her from going. It's a good trip for her to make. You and I should go as well."

"We'll see. First things first: Would it be possible for me to spend the weekend with you there?"

After a pause, a pain stings her. Slowly, she says, "I have duties. I cannot predict my movements."

"Amaya, I'd come just for lunch. So much to talk about—and none of it about business."

"My own dear Brad, business is always there because duty is always there, yours and now mine. Unspoken business never goes away. I think it would be best, for me at least, to complete my duties and return home as soon as I can."

"Do you have any idea …?"

With a catch in her throat, she replies, "No, my Brad. But surely you will be able to go to Kozue soon? Your mission must be winding up."

"Unwinding, actually. But, yes, I plan to return to San Francisco the first of the week."

"And this weekend? Could you see Jerry and Yoko? Or Iseo and Cindy?"

"I saw Iseo; he sends regards. I do need some more time with Jerry. I can't stand it that we can't even … but your judgment is good enough for me."

After a silence, Amaya squares her shoulders. "Brad, when I married you, I closed the door on all my business in Japan. I would never have guessed I would be the one taking time away from us for my duties here."

"Don't dwell on it, Amaya. It is important to you. And it is temporary. That's all I care about."

"Surely that is not all …?"

"This much more. I love you, Amaya, and we will have a few days together with Kozue before any of us goes off again."

Brightly, Amaya asks, "Could there be the canoe, Brad? We would love that."

He smiles. "Yes, of course, the canoe and birds and a lunch in Bolinas Bay."

After ending the call with Brad, Amaya stares out her hotel window. She knows she must call Orchid Petal.

"*Moshimoshi*? Amaya? I'm glad to hear from you."

"Yuko, I have been to Arita. I spent the entire day with Emiko. She has changed greatly. She wears gray, and it reflects her inner spirits exactly. I found her willing but not passionate to help us. She is meek and anemic. Her spirit is thin. She said she will inform the family in Takeo and be with the group a week later. I will have to check in with them to assure myself that Emiko has done even that. Tomorrow, I will try to see the Fukuoka families. And I will then continue through the week in the next phase until all is finished, Yuko. I can do no less, and I cannot recommend that Emiko do any more than I've asked of her. I am committed to seeing this through."

The line is quiet a moment. Softly, Yuko says, "You honor me, my forever-friend. You have never, ever settled for second best in your life. My plan will be the better for your decision. But I have not told you what lies ahead, Aya-chan."

Amaya looks startled. "Will you be able to tell me …?"

Yuko interrupts, "Not on this call. Tomorrow, please visit the Kyushu Defense Bureau headquarters. It is a short distance from the Hakata train station. Give your name at the security desk. They will direct you to a room where you may call me. Shall we say eight in the morning?"

"I shall call you then. That will give me a full day to meet with the people here."

"Aya-chan, sleep well tonight. Sleep will be a scarce commodity for you after that."

CHAPTER 29

The coastal ridge makes a steep rise just to the west of the adobe home the Elgar family has owned since the days of Prohibition. Sarah Jane and June have been going up and down a rutted, narrow trail on horseback for most of their years there. This Saturday morning, though, it is Alden Knight and Kozue who set out early with day packs of trail snacks and water. Kozue would have preferred her favorite of Sarah Jane's horses, but Alden insisted they walk. He needed to un-crimp his legs and swing his arms, he said. He has set a slow pace. The morning sun has cleared the crest of the ridge over on the east side of the valley, where the Elgar vineyards sprawl among acres of bright yellow wild mustard blossoms. The new light sweeps dewy shadows covering ripening grapes and leaves just beginning to show the colors of the fall harvest, which is a month away. Near the top of the rise, the two hikers sit leaning against a madrone trunk and watch the valley floor gradually illuminate as they open their snacks. Kozue always calls Alden "uncle," but he is much more to her. Alden is her stand-in for a grandfather, a wise patriarch. For example, Alden gave her purpose in grinding away at her Latin assignments. After all, he had been through years of it in Chicago Latin when he was a kid. He showed her how the logic and regularity of the language made English grammar comprehensible. He helped her locate online an old book he had used to unlock the texts of Caesar's accounts of the Gallic Wars. That book gave her a distinct advantage over others in her class. Alden never talks down to Kozue and simply assumes she will always understand serious adult conversations.

Alden hands Kozue a packet of trail mix. "So, your dad tells me he sent an email about his thinking on the assault weapon issue."

Between crunches, Kozue says, "Yes, a short one. It was about changing the military's purchase orders."

He picks up a fallen twig and clears the clay that clots the soles of his boots. "That's right. I don't think you'll get far trying to get the government to ban the ownership or use of those things." He frowns and growls, "There is too much scare-talk about taking away freedoms if you take away guns."

"Oh, Uncle Alden, I sure know about that. I hear about that all the time. Lots of the time, I hear about it in colorful language."

Alden laughs. Through a smile, he says, "Colorful meaning 'loaded.' That's the problem with language like that. It conveys emotions like hatred and fear rather than any useful ideas."

Kozue fixes her eyes on Alden's. "Uncle Alden, sometimes you have to hit that stuff head-on."

Alden tosses away the twig. In a more serious tone, he replies, "That's true, but think about your dad's idea. I'm not an expert on gun making, but there must be a way to make sure they fire only when in the proper hands."

Kozue hurries her words, "I know, Uncle Alden. I'm not sure I know exactly, but there are ways to do it. Fingerprint recognition, or even optical recognition. It's like passwords."

Alden hunches himself closer to her. Earnestly, he says, "What he and I are saying is that the people who know best how to do that need a business incentive to build it in. The biggest business incentive would be that the gun customer insists on it. I don't mean the general public. The first and most influential customer of assault weapons is the US government. What we're talking about is for the government to change its purchase orders to specify protections in when and how these guns fire bullets. They've got fail-safes for other stuff, why not those things?"

Equally earnest and nodding with enthusiasm, Kozue replies, "Yeah, I don't know why that wouldn't work. That's our problem. We don't know enough to tell the government what we want."

Alden spreads his arms. "Kozue, that's OK. I'm thinking it would be enough for Congress to tell the military to make it happen. So, instead of pushing for the resolution that's going nowhere because it really doesn't do anything, we should try to get the wording changed. It should say that the Congress will only pay for these particular guns if they have some sort of protection built in. If that is a condition tied to the money to buy the guns, I am confident that the gun makers can figure out exactly how to do it. And the government would pay a research and development incentive as well."

"I get that, Uncle Alden. I don't know what I can do about it though."

Alden goes quiet for a minute. Then, he says, "Kozue, I'm thinking this is an idea you can take to Washington. I'm going back there in a few days, and I'm taking Sarah Jane. I'd love it if you'd join us later. I can introduce you to some people in Congress, and you can tell them about it."

"Sure, if my folks say it's OK. Your friend is the Speaker of the House. Do you think he'd even listen to me?"

Alden knows he can't predict Maxwell's moods anymore. "Yeah, Kozue, I really hope he'd listen. I think others would listen. So, are you on board?"

"For sure. What about Mom and Daddy-Brad?"

"You'd go after they're home from Japan for a few days."

"I wouldn't want to leave before then. I'm glad you took the time to explain it to me. We should probably head back down the hill."

CHAPTER 30

That does it. Iseo won't support new delivery terms. Honshu won't discuss the vessel. As far as I'm concerned, that ship can go ahead and sink; it's out of my life now. The best part of that is that Masako is out of the picture too. I know where I'm needed, and I know when to fold 'em. There's nothing here in Tokyo that's doing Elgar Steel any good.

Brad is packing the new blazer, slacks, and yellow tie in his bag to check on the flight home. He'll carry on what he planned for the flight to Seattle. He has booked his return home on a noon flight from Narita tomorrow, Sunday. It's the right thing to do, what with Amaya's schedule being such a mystery. He's the one to hold the fort at home. But when he called to say goodbye, Jerry insisted on coming into town for dinner. He sounded like he wanted to tell him something.

He goes to the lobby and waits by the front entrance. Jerry walks up right on time. They head to the Wadakura restaurant in the hotel's lower lobby. Its cozy atmosphere is inviting to the men, and since most diners are in the French restaurant on the top floor, they have the place to themselves.

At times like this evening, their conversations can flow from granular details of steel specifications to philosophical puzzles, from there to occasional quotes from a novel or a play, and then back again. Two years ago, Brad brought Amaya and Kozue to Tokyo to try to help Jerry work out Shin Steel pipe sales to countries restricted by US export controls. Since Elgar Steel had designed and installed the expensive pipe mill for

Shin's steelmaking works in Tokyo, Brad and Jerry were in what could have been a conflict disastrous to their friendship. With Alden's help, the conflict was deflected.

Jerry eases into the subject of what Brad's doing in this city in the middle of summer on something that is none of his business. "Brad, I only skim the news about American politics. I know there are power grabs and scandals, but I can't even keep up with the ones in Japan. I am more than willing to help with your bad situation, but I have no idea how to do so."

"Just help with talking through it. You have always done that."

Jerry clicks open his ballpoint and sketches a triangle on a cocktail napkin. "Maybe it will help to show it this way. At this corner is Speaker Maxwell. His problem is not your problem, but you have a loyalty to Alden Knight. OK, so your obligation is to Knight. In Japan we call it an *on*, one of hundreds we accumulate in our lifetimes, beginning with filial duty to our parents. Much of our life decisions require discharging these duties, and the process is always complicated when there are directly competing duties. Second, at this angle, you have your responsibilities about operating your businesses, and whether you should invest in a ship because it would be good for business. Iseo has basically said no from the KNN viewpoint. You have not heard from me about Shin, although you know it would be very difficult. Honshu Lines and Iseo's company are out to sell you something you might not want to buy. Finally, at the third angle is your family, where the conflict is one of time and attention."

Brad slaps Jerry's back. "That is a succinct restatement, Jerry, but which point of the triangle should be at the top? Now, there is the possibility of a new job. Alden wants me to think about a high position in the government if we actually do solve Maxwell's problem. He is trying to salvage his political party from the ash heap. It is an existential problem. Some believe it is a lost cause. Alden has mentioned to me the position of United States trade representative. There was a time I would have been very interested, Jerry."

Jerry takes back the napkin. "Then should we change the diagram to include another corner, and call it Elgar Steel's future?"

Brad smiles. "No, leave it as you have it. My family includes Elgar Steel and the Elgar sisters. I can't consider separating the Elgar business from my own lifeblood."

Jerry pauses and purses his lips. "Frankly speaking, Brad, then you must rank your values. Are you really a candidate for the political job? You may be their candidate, but do you value that opportunity highly enough to give in to the temptation?"

Brad shakes his head. "I've decided that I do not at this point in my life. Still, there is another issue, a political one, and it is where family overlaps with the Maxwell corner of the diagram. Kozue has an *on* which she is deeply invested in. It is the assault gun issue, and it's connected to her trauma from the shooting that killed her parents. So, I cannot completely compartmentalize these triangle corners. They come together in too many ways."

Jerry frowns and gathers his thoughts. "In Japan, we have an expression: *chusei shin,* which means 'ultimate loyalty.' For the Japanese, such ultimate loyalty derives from the hierarchy of values, and of stations in society. We Japanese all learn the same hierarchy, unchanging through history, generation after generation. Western thinking reconsiders the matter of ultimate loyalty at significant periods in its history. It doesn't change often, but the changes are associated with the most significant eras of thought. The last great shift was the Enlightenment. One outgrowth of that era, its humanism, was the elevation of the individual to the top of the mountain from which to search for ultimate loyalty. No longer would wisdom be received or institutionally imposed. Every person was declared to have the right to find the ultimate loyalty for that person. Institutions might compete for that loyalty, and advocate for this or that doctrine, but the inherent freedom of each human left the decision to the individual—the ideal of self-determination."

Brad is listening. This is why he has been listening to Jerry for all these years.

Jerry goes on, "The Japanese did not experience the Enlightenment. We may study humanistic thinking academically, and may assimilate some part of it, but ultimate loyalty is not really a matter of local option. *Chusei shin* for the Japanese is societal, familial, and corporate before it is individualistic. The individual is subservient to it. This constant need to conform to culturally inherited loyalty goes hand in hand with being Japanese."

Jerry lets that sink in. He looks at his watch. His mind goes to his wife, Yoko. But he needs to raise the subject that brings him here.

"Brad, you are of the humanist tradition of Western thought. You are a deep thinker. I believe you have the necessary ingredients to find your priorities and 'to thine own self be true.' That's all I'm able to help you with tonight. But, speaking of families, I should leave soon and return to mine."

"My regards to Yoko, Jerry. And thanks for the diagram."

Jerry does not move. His eyes sparkle. He leans forward, his voice gathering energy. "I can't go just yet, Brad. I need to talk to you about something. The diagram is still incomplete. Please, may I?"

Brad hands it back. Jerry draws a circle on the right side connected by an arrow-line. In the circle, he prints, "Shin Steel Merger."

Brad releases a long exhale. It had always been Ernie Elgar's hope that the two steel companies could find a way to combine. Brad had picked up that hope and discussed it with Sarah Jane. They have taken two partial steps. The first was a joint venture to convert Shin's flat steel plates into the Wishbone project's tubular pipe at the Stockton plant. Then, a couple of years ago, Shin bought fifteen percent of Elgar's common stock. The partnership has been cordial and worthwhile. Now, with Sarah Jane just settling into her retirement, the subject of a full-scale merger is very ripe in Brad's interest.

Brad needs to calm a rising excitement. He draws out the words, "Jerry, is this just a placeholder, or do you have something in mind?"

With a quick nod, Jerry hurries his words, "I have something specific in mind. We had a board meeting last Tuesday, the day after our Honshu meetings. Not at the meeting, but at informal times before and after, I spoke to directors about possibly buying the met coal from your mine on a delivered basis. That would be contrary to the way we always do business. But one director made a startling suggestion to me. He asked as a theoretical question whether it would be in our best interest to merge with Elgar Steel. The significance is that this is the same director who vehemently opposed the idea before. He was against the Wishbone joint venture. He was against the equity purchase two years ago, even though it gave Shin a piece of a metallurgical coal mine. From the standpoint of momentum, his question was a breakthrough. He pointed out that if there were such a merger, it would make sense to consider delivery on those terms, and possibly invest in a coal cargo vessel."

Brad leans back, incredulous. "You waited until the end of all that philosophical conversation to tell me this?"

Jerry smiles. "First things first. But do you think the Elgar heirs might favor moving forward on it at this time?"

Now it is Brad whose voice gathers energy, "I think this is the time, Jerry. I assure you the Elgars would consider it a dream come true. Sarah Jane will need to see a detailed business plan. You would need much the same thing in your *ringisho*."

"Yes, Brad, I well know. This may not be why you came, but it is the reason to stay a little longer. Why not plan to stay in Tokyo, and we can work on it together?"

Brad groans and waves the idea away like a wasp. "There is too much else going on. My mind is on Amaya and Kozue. We are all on quick trips into separate worlds. The last thing I want to do is to start extending this trip of mine and have a longer separation. I'm going back tomorrow. My instinct is for Shin Steel to present us a business plan for the merger and especially the vision for the merged companies. Too often in our country, a large company acquires a smaller company, and the smaller one disappears. The culture and mission of the larger one take over. The smaller one is just a historical dot on the timeline of the other. It loses not only autonomy, it loses its identity. So, I would like to present the Elgars a proposal that expresses your intentions. Elgar Steel needs to know that it survives this merger with a purpose. You said, 'First things first,' and I think this should come first."

Jerry reaches to Brad's arm. "That makes good sense. There are many success stories of Japanese-owned manufacturing businesses in America. These offer good models. I think we can make a convincing case. But when it comes to what will appeal to the Elgar people, you can't expect me to figure that out on my own. The logical thing is for you to stay another week, and we'll work on it together."

Brad is silent. He clenches his jaws. He knows Jerry's right. He also knows he's right.

Jerry is more insistent now. "Brad, I'm talking about the broad overview. You and I can prepare a proposal for the three heirs of Elgar. It would serve as the foundation for a detailed plan for your board and mine, as well as the Japanese government. In fact, we should get a head start with the board and the government informally before you leave. Clear your mind tomorrow, and we'll jump on it Monday morning. What's another week in the big scheme of things?"

CHAPTER 31

Lydia again recoils from boisterous cheeseburger breath at the country club Saturday afternoon. Thad Maxwell, Earl King, and Drew Wallace give off low radiation from their skin after eighteen holes of golf in the full sun. At Lydia's insistence, Thad revised the guest list to keep Nancy away and sent her off to the Library of Congress to study the draft Congressional Research Service report on rare earth elements.

Lydia endures the irritating barbeque smoke and foul talk in order to spend quality time with Drew, her new favorite staff member from the office. Thad's face darkens, and he grows quiet. He then declares that he needs a few minutes with King and Drew in the part of the clubhouse reserved for cigars. Lydia might ordinarily roll her eyes at this. Instead, her eyes make instant contact with Drew's, which makes him blush.

Drew goes through the motions of lighting a cigar, uncertain exactly how far out to hold the match, and smacks his lips over the first sip of port. Maxwell and King are leaning their heads together, speaking in low tones. Occasionally, Maxwell glances at his ethics lawyer. Maxwell's mood is subdued.

"Drew," says Thad, "plan A is not going to happen. Earl tells me that the *El Caballo* has cleared the tip of Taiwan and makes for Nagasaki, Japan."

"Sir," Drew starts, "then we should no longer consider that strategy."

"Correct, Drew, or even talk about it. The topic at the moment is a new one."

Drew grimaces. He has been dreading this moment. He knew the time would come when he would be in the hot seat. "Well, Mr. Speaker, we may be out of good and less good options, but we are not entirely out of all options."

"Give me an example of a bad one that would work," Maxwell grumbles through cigar smoke.

"I guarantee you that it is both bad and would absolutely work."

Thad Maxwell breathes a sigh of relief. He hires the best, doesn't he? "I'm listening."

"Abandon ship, Mr. Speaker."

Thad reddens and sputters.

Drew continues, "Not as a member of Congress or your position. Divorce this ship. You are not on the title to the *El Caballo*; only Lydia is. I'm now recommending that you throw Mrs. Maxwell under the bus. No one will do more than raise an eyebrow over that. They certainly wouldn't intervene to stop it. Suppose that there have been, or might be, marital difficulties with Mrs. Maxwell. Suppose that such difficulties would be a drag on your progress to the White House. If you were to divorce Mrs. Maxwell, she takes the vessel out of your life, and you brush your hands of any distasteful implications of the phantom freight."

Earl King calculates to himself, *The ship stays afloat. I still have the management contract. The good times keep on rolling.*

Thad is quiet. *My Lydia? My island dream? But the White House. Within striking distance. Sacrifices must be endured.* "How?"

"In Virginia, for a no-fault divorce, there is a six-month waiting period," says Drew. "So, it'd have to be for cause. Adultery would do it. Could there be infidelity?"

"Mine or hers?"

"Hers, of course."

"Preposterous!"

Drew tilts his head, musing, "Something might be staged."

Thad lowers his voice, "This is vile thinking. I want no part of it. Besides, what you're suggesting takes a lot of planning, and I'm not sure we have the time for that. There's gotta be real high-stakes money involved in something like that."

Drew stands and puts his smoldering cigar on the ashtray alongside Speaker Maxwell's. "Is tonight soon enough, Mr. Speaker? To set the stage, I mean? Discovery and appropriate outrage would follow."

King and Maxwell stare at Drew's young, sunburned face. Maxwell thinks, *Tonight? No looking for accomplices or cash transfers? That can only mean one thing. But it really is tidy.*

"I didn't hear this," says Earl King.

"Neither did I." Maxwell places next to the ashtray a plastic key card to the front door of his condominium on the thirteenth fairway.

"Good," says his ethics lawyer, gathering the key card.

"Have her home by eleven, young man," says the Speaker of the House.

CHAPTER 32

At half past one on Sunday morning, Amaya huddles against a sharp breeze, her phone pressed to her ear. She stands outside the sleek, modern Nagasaki Minato ferry terminal on a pier in Nagasaki. A restored, three-mast-tall ship creaks as it rides nearby at anchor in the choppy waters of Nagasaki's long natural harbor, a UNESCO World Heritage Site, surrounded by high hills and the city rebuilt on their steep slopes after the war-ending second bomb. The ferry building is a gleaming aluminum, concrete, and glass structure, elliptical in cross-section like a slightly flattened steel pipe from the Elgar steel mill. Amaya leans against the enormous anchor sculpture at the end of the pier, reminded of works of steel sculpted by Sarah Jane Elgar.

She wears a navy camouflage uniform provided by the Japan Coast Guard. The wind has cleared away low clouds so that the skies are starry even through the competing lights from the Mitsubishi Heavy Industries shipyards. *Brad would enjoy these stars. I would enjoy Brad enjoying them.* The waves slap and spray over the edge of the pier, and she steps away quickly. A ship at anchorage at the mouth of the channel gives two short horn blasts, signifying that the new complement of crew and officers aboard the *El Caballo* stands ready to sail. Eight hours earlier, the replacements, handpicked from the ranks of Honshu Lines, relieved the men who brought the ship from Australia and who now seek joy in Nagasaki's entertainment district.

"Till when?" Kozue shouts into the phone. "What is it this time?"

Amaya says, "I know. I am disappointed as well. You know who brought me to Japan, Kozue, but you do not know why. It is something I cannot talk about, maybe not even when I come home."

"Good to know you're thinking of coming home, Mom." Kozue bites her lip, regretting the sarcastic tone. Brightly, she asks, "So, a week?"

"A week or so."

Without the bite of sarcasm, but still needling, Kozue replies, "OK, Mom, I've met this neat couple from Napa named Sarah Jane and Alden. They might want to adopt me."

"That's because they have not spent a long time with you yet." Both giggle. "Do you like the new girl?"

"She's so young, Mom."

"A good four years younger. Oh, my. She will have a lot to learn from you."

"I'll take care of it, Mom."

"She can count on you."

"I'm proud of you, Mom. You were chosen. You are special in the orchid petal industry."

"Keep our secret, Tree."

Seriously now, Kozue asks, "And we will still go to Washington?"

"Yes, of course. This will give us time to shop for a new summer hat for you to have in Washington."

"Daddy-Brad called. He's having dinner with Uncle Jerry tonight, and then he's coming home Sunday."

"I haven't spoken to him. But, Kozue, I have had many calls from him like that in the past. It only counts if he calls from an actual departure lounge of an actual airport."

Kozue flattens her lips and shakes her head. "Good to know. He's doing what is important to him."

"I have to hang up, Kozue. It is time for me to go silent."

Amaya stands across from where the man-made island of Dejima was constructed in the sixteen thirties to isolate Portuguese traders, and especially missionaries, from the people of Japan. When Japan expelled the Portuguese, traders of the Dutch East India Company replaced them during two centuries of Japanese isolationism. From this confinement went Japanese porcelain creations into northern Europe and American homes under the generic label of "Imari." The island has been rejoined to the mainland by land reclamation, but historic warehouses and other remnants of the era remain, restored.

Amaya watches three figures approach along the pier from a black SUV. It is Chu Hua and two Chinese Embassy escorts. Amaya and Chu Hua grip each other's hands tightly in anticipation. She, too, wears the navy uniform of the Japan Self-Defense Force, her hair pinned in a braid coiled inside a long-billed black cap. The women met briefly before at a dressier Tokyo American Club reception. They liked each other immediately, but circumstances did not permit the follow-up rendezvous they wanted. They kept in touch through occasional emails and holiday greetings. Amaya and the daughter of China's ambassador to Japan are about to embark on the prime minister's covert mission of mercy, each with a specific role.

Chu Hua has been quietly working behind the scenes with Yuko Kagono on the intractable problem of Japanese abductees in North Korea. China refused to exert overt pressure in the public eye on North Korea. But unofficially, they were keen to reduce unnecessary frictions between the two countries. So, when China was on the hunt for a fat contract to supply natural gas to Japan five years ago, it sweetened its offer by promising to intervene on the abductee issue. Chu Hua's humanitarian instincts propelled her to pour her own energy into the project. She had the right positioning to convey unofficial persuasion to the North Korean unofficial presence in a small diaspora in Tokyo.

The two women step from the pier to the deck of a Japan Coast Guard buoy tender. They put on the flotation vests handed to them by a clean-shaven, uniformed deckhand. The tender moves off slowly into the ship channel and under the Megami suspension bridge. Amaya looks up as they pass under the bridge, reminded of the Golden Gate Bridge.

The tender makes its way to a Swiss-flagged dry-bulk carrier swinging at anchor near the mouth of the Nagasaki channel, at the southern tip of Kyushu. A few meters above the waterline of the looming, forty-foot-high hull, the pilot's hatch door stands open. A fixed ladder angles upward to the door from the waterline. The ship rides high with less than half a cargo of grain, so a steel extension dangles from the last rung of the ladder to lapping waves. The women gingerly mount both sections of the ladder and eagerly grasp the hands of seamen waiting just inside the pilot's hatch door. Last up the ladder is Chief Petty Officer Kimoto in camo face covering and combat gear. Two hours after she clears the light buoy off the Goto Islands, the ship makes a turn to starboard and glides north by northwest with minimum running lights.

Amaya is excited to the point of trembling to be aboard a ship the size of a hotel. Its interior of white-painted bulkheads is decorated only by utilitarian red-and-black-painted lettering and arrows. In her narrow cabin, where once slept a Tennessee-born apprentice master, she is too restless to sleep.

The skipper has set course for the North Korean port of Nampo, off-limits to sanction-abiding nations. An Oyashio-class training submarine of the Japan Self-Defense Force moves from its holding depth to twenty meters, directly below the *El Caballo*'s keel.

CHAPTER 33

Ray Lion has his mind on rare earth elements suspended in basic metal ore and salt deposits. The Saint Joseph headquarters of Total Carbon Corporation has grumbled about the slow pace of progress on the bill in Congress that would help lift them to dominance in their gathering, transportation, and conversion to computer and battery applications. So, although he still doesn't like meetings with staff of Congress members, he accepted one this morning with the chief of staff of the Speaker of the House. Besides, he has taken a liking to Nancy Booth, who sits at the center of the table in the Speaker's conference room. The wallpaper of the high-ceilinged room is new: ivory with regency-green-and-gold vertical stripes. The mahogany-paneled wainscoting remains in its original form, including the gashes suffered during the 2021 insurrection. Just this past weekend, Nancy bought this snappy Breton red skirt and crisply tailored tan long-sleeved top. She has improved her makeup skills. *She's different-looking somehow— new clothes, a more worldly look. Makeup, even. She looks, well, she looks a whole lot more appealing.*

Ray holds the high card. His rare earth elements bill is stuck in a rut. Ray has figured out how to pry it loose and quash the pesky gun resolution in the same stroke. He plans to strong-arm the Speaker into keeping the House's session going straight through August, in order to get the bill passed and the resolution voted down. He stands annoyingly close behind Nancy's left shoulder. She sits, rearranging a portfolio of papers and calculating how she can get away.

"Nancy, I should tell you that I have spent a lot of time over at the N2AR shop. They aren't much interested in rare earth, but they don't like the way the assault weapon resolution is stacking up."

"You know the Speaker's mind on both of those proposals," she says without looking up.

"I do." Ray moves deliberately to sit opposite Nancy and catch her eye. "The next thing to put in his mind is what I'm about to tell you, Nancy. TCC is a strong financial supporter of N2AR's agenda. So, here's what TCC and N2AR have worked out as a cooperative coalition. We want the Speaker to bring both proposals for a vote at the same time, one right after the other. The N2AR folks are in the process of compiling their scores on House members."

Nancy swallows. She folds her hands and closes her eyes. Of things that matter in her world, the topmost priority for the Speaker's caucus is how the gun lobby "scores" its individual members. A low score, say, a D, issued by the N2AR can easily end a member's career. His funding dries up, and his primary opponent is given a winning ticket that no lottery could match. The score is a nonviolent means of political extortion that no one has been able to change.

Now Nancy fixes her eyes on Ray's. "Well, Ray, I'm sure the Speaker has no reason to be concerned that his long-running A score is not about to change anytime soon, is it?"

Ray waggles his finger in front of Nancy's face. "Allow me to finish, and then you can assess that for yourself. This time, the scoring is going to be a little different. It is not going to be on the gun resolution alone. With TCC's encouragement, the N2AR folks are going to score based on a two-vote system. Favorable scores are earned only by correctly voting on both measures, as if in the same bill. So, any member who splits his or her vote is scored down. We're breaking new ground here, but I think it's real progress, don't you agree? And all scores are going to be delayed until the two measures are voted on by the House, back-to-back. You'll take me to see Thad now, Nancy."

Nancy returns the now-stacked pages to the leather portfolio. She makes to leave. "The Speaker is tied up on personal business right now, but I'll convey your ideas to him as soon as I see him."

"Nancy, let's not quibble over words. These are not 'ideas'; these are the facts of life." Ray Lion leans back in his chair and touches his fingertips together. He is about to change tack.

"Nancy," he continues, "this may be a little off the subject, but I'd like you to listen to another idea I'm working on. This one is more personal to you. I can tell you have been thinking more about your future, just from the way you've taken on a brighter look. The Second Amendment folks need a shot in the arm, funding-wise. I have figured out just what they need, which is a women's auxiliary. This isn't going to be a bridge club; it is going to be a powerhouse group of very competitive women with distinctly aggressive personal agendas. They are going to raise funds in the hundreds of thousands, not small grassroots donations."

Nancy grimaces. "That sounds ambitious, Ray, but I'm uncomfortable talking about it in this room."

"I'm looking for a woman capable of raising breathtaking amounts of money. If I can onboard the right chairwoman of the new auxiliary, she's going to need a whip-smart Hill expert as her executive director, and I can think of no one more qualified than you for that job. As I see things, that new executive director would also be in charge of scoring members of Congress for the N2AR."

Nancy squirms. She knows she should leave right now. But something about Ray's urgency keeps her seated. Oh, yes, to be sure, her own ambitions have risen a bit since the *El Caballo* unpleasantness came into the forefront of the Speaker's personal quest for the White House. She relaxes her tense shoulders.

"Well, Ray, you have been busy thinking great thoughts. We probably should be talking about this somewhere else. Perhaps over lunch?"

Ray beams. *Oh, yeah.*

CHAPTER 34

The *El Caballo* and its unusual escort cruise the Yellow Sea three days and two nights from its Nagasaki bay anchorage to the Nampo container terminal on the west coast of North Korea. At mid-morning the first day at sea, Amaya and Chu Hua practice lifeboat drills with the vessel's fresh crew, a standard practice. Out of the ordinary during this morning's drills, however, are the wheelchairs that they must be able to load efficiently if need be on the return voyage with the new passengers.

At noon following the drills, they sit on the deck just outside the superstructure in the stern. Amaya is ready to try getting some sleep in her small cabin. Chu Hua is having none of it. She is feeling chatty. She hands Amaya a *bento* box.

"I was with your husband a few nights ago. He and Ambassador Knight came to our embassy for a briefing on the fate of this very vessel," Chu Hua says brightly. "How would he feel about you going on this mission? It is not without its risks. When I left him, he did not know you would be here. If he did, I'm sure he would be concerned."

Amaya frowns. "No, Brad does not know I am here. Well, he knows I came to Japan but not to be with him. At Yuko's request, I have not told him what I am doing."

Chu Hua is quiet. She looks away. "That must be difficult for you both. If I may ask, why are you here?"

Amaya smiles and shrugs. "Because Yuko asked me. And you?"

Laughing, Chu Hua answers, "Because Yuko asked me!"

Amaya continues, "It is always difficult when Brad and I are separated. It has become a part of our way of life. We do what we can. For example, I gave up my gallery shops in Tokyo after the time when we met at that reception. It helped. Then our daughter came into our lives. That makes separations even more difficult."

Chu Hua nudges her elbow against Amaya's arm. "Oh, yes. Kozue. Tell me about her."

Amaya breaks into a wide smile. "So energetic. Her aunt Sarah says she is 'like a match trying to strike itself.' But she's not that way always. We have a long journey together. I shall tell you more along the way. Do you miss being away from your home in China?"

"Oh, I'm an embassy brat," she says, clutching her billed cap to protect it from a sudden gust. "I have lived all around. We were in Paris for a while. This discussion reminds me of a phrase the French are fond of: *l'art de vivre*, meaning the art of a full life, enriched with work as well as relaxation, fine art and fine food. The British expression would be, 'All work and no play make Jack a dull boy.' I believe the French phrase is deeper, though. It is something they live, not just say, unlike the British."

"Or the Americans, or especially the Japanese," Amaya adds.

They both laugh. "But yes, in answer to your question, I do miss China. Given your interest in art, surely you have been," Chu Hua says, her eyes asking.

"No, although you would think I have. I have studied its arts, of course. I have especially studied the history of porcelain developed in Jingdezhen four hundred years before Japan's Arita ware."

Chu Hua looks up and around her. "That way is northwest, right?" she asks, pointing forward. "So, Jingdezhen is that way, inland," she continues, bringing her arm to the southwest. "I have been there. It is compulsory for you, Amaya." She clasps her hand. "I will take you."

"Another trip."

"One with your family along as well."

The next day, Kimoto briefs the women on tactical details. Amaya will receive the abductees and their papers. They expect the returnees to be wheelchair-bound. Amaya and Chu Hua will see to their comfort in the ship's staterooms. Officers and crew of the vessel's manifest will make temporary quarters on and below deck during the return voyage to the port of Hakata/Fukuoka. The empty ship's draft will just be able to clear bottom in the Fukuoka channel and tie up at a pier to disembark the passengers.

In the late evening of the third day, the *El Caballo* drops anchor forty kilometers off the rogue nation's port of Nampo. The submarine escort breaks away, surfaces, and stands two hundred meters off at decks awash, deck guns manned. The submarine's crew will be on armed and watchful alert for surprises. At near-surface depth, the Japanese sub will be clearly observable. They are in the hands of the good faith and influence of DRNK diplomats and a jumpy detail of the DRNK military throughout this operation.

At dawn, the *El Caballo*'s onboard conveyers begin to unload her gift of Australian grain onto large, floating transshipment platforms, brought alongside by sea tugs. The platforms are designed to move commodities between vessels at sea in a risky operation known as ship-to-ship transfer. STS transfer is the method of choice among DRNK sanction-busters, and for coal exports from meager, hazardous mines. Unloading the grain will be slow and require skill aboard both the vessel and the platforms.

Chu Hua plays another unique part in this operation. Before the returnees are brought to the platform barges, during and after discharge of the grain, she will stand between two North Korean soldiers as a human token of the good faith of the mission. She will be the last to reboard the *El Caballo*.

CHAPTER 35

In the equestrian countryside of Loudoun County, Virginia, Drew Wallace has just awakened from another night of special duty in his new mission to separate the *El Caballo* from Thad Maxwell's life by giving something for the Speaker to complain about in his for-cause divorce complaint. Lydia Maxwell, in a mini-length, thin cotton blue-and-white *yukata* after-bath wrap, sets a tray of English breakfast tea and cranberry scones on the small, round table by the bedroom's sliding doors. The doors lead to the edge of the thirteenth fairway of the Speaker's country club. Despite the early morning heat, the course whirs with the sounds of electric golf carts doing the heavy lifting.

With a sparkle in her eye, Lydia says, "Yes, Drew-chan, I like your idea to call me Aiko. I'm flattered you remember my Japanese name. The 'Lydia' name has bad associations for me. I also like it better than Okan; you should keep thoughts about me as 'motherly' to yourself. It does not seem gracious in conversation. You, of course, are always my Drew-chan, home early from school." She was well trained in Guam to play roles fancied by young men.

"Aiko, my moments with you are beyond anything I may have imagined." Drew swings his legs over the edge of the bed and tightens the belt of his terrycloth bathrobe with the club's embroidered badge. "I did not circulate much in school. I kept focused on my studies. I'd rather you not mention school choir, though. I hear enough about choirboy from your husband. I like 'Drew-chan,' or at other times the other one you say."

Aiko looks up, surprised. "Um, remind me."

"You know: 'feral-wilderness-naughty-beast.' I am entitled to small vanities."

"You have oversized vanity, Drew-chan." She butters a scone.

Drew joins her and yawns. "When all this comes out in the open, as you know it will, I shall be 'toast-san.' It's fine. I no longer enjoy the work I do. It has no significance beyond the Capitol grounds."

In mock astonishment, she says, "You have tired of Ms. Booth?"

"She is an icicle by comparison." His smile fills the bedroom.

She scolds, "Don't think harshly of Nancy. She has taken vows of devotion to political life. Heat is rare in that environment except in debate." She sits closer to him. "If you have decided to leave that sphere yourself, where will you go?"

Drew yawns and stretches in the warm sunlight. "I am clear-eyed about my future. As soon as your husband tasked me with making his ethics problems go away, I knew I could not succeed or even survive. My desperate torpedo plan might have salvaged my career had it worked, but then what? An arms war against ethics? I am not cut out for that kind of work permanently."

Aiko stares out the sliding glass doors to a middle distance. She muses, "Could you manage the *El Caballo*? If I go to the trouble of shedding my husband, I might as well shed his uncle as well."

Drew blinks. He warms to this suggestion. It would be a way to cash in on his recent spreadsheet labors. "I am a quick study. I could not book freight at a hundred fifty percent of capacity, but after study and tutorial training, I could indeed manage the vessel's operations. That could be done from anywhere, Aiko, so neither of us would have a tie to Washington or northern Virginia. Full partners. I like the sound of that."

In a lowered tone, she says, "I cannot be seen to be happy about my divorce."

"I understand. But would you be?"

She squeezes his arm. In a burst of joy, she tells him, "I would be ecstatic, Drew-chan. I heard from my childhood friend in Guam, and she is coming to see me. You will like her. So much to look forward to. Please help me out of my robe."

"We do need more photos." Drew loosens the belt of his robe. The warm sunshine brings out sparkles of mica in the condo bedroom's pebbled walls. Aiko thoughtfully draws the heavy curtains, easing the glare considerably. His eyelids grow heavy. "How is the weather in Guam?"

"It is a tropical South Pacific island. Daytime temperatures are mid-eighties, year- round."

Drew's breathing calms. He slurs, "So, now say it … the long version."

"I cannot. Um. Feral … it's too much. The microphone makes me nervous."

"Concentrate. It's in there. You'll get it."

"Feral-wilderness … what?"

"Naughty-beast. It'll do. As you say, Okan, so much to look forward to."

CHAPTER 36

June Elgar had to sell her condominium in the renovated flour mill over-looking Lake Ontario in Toronto. She nearly lost all her money and that of her two sisters in her brief encounter with a disreputable mining engineer. She took up a less ostentatious lifestyle in a Toronto suburb. It's a comfortable life, based on the income from just her tiny holding of Elgar Steel stock and a meager pension from the environmental nonprofit that she founded twelve years ago. For example, in earlier times, her visit to Seattle to be with Kozue would have been in first class, but she made the round trip in coach and was at peace with her reduced circumstances.

She does miss the old political scraps from her days as an environmental activist. The only semblance of that in this suburban pasture is contention over noisy leaf blowers. She also misses the company of men—men of real daring and substance, unlike the lawn-lords of suburbia. June has always played with fire when it comes to men. Since the Seattle trip, the summer idleness and annoying sounds of mowers and trimmers have made her mind stir adventurously.

So, as Drew and Lydia indulge in fantasies and scones, she gives in to an urge and dials Nancy Booth, who left her at the airport with a warm invitation to come visit the capital any time. Nancy is surprised and delighted to hear from June, a woman she finds intriguing. She is even more surprised by June's blunt request. "So, Nancy, you need to understand another thing about a spur-of-the-moment visit. I need you to put me in touch with an adventurous younger man in Washington.

Not a political nerd, but someone with vigor, if you catch my drift. Who knows, it might turn into many happy returns."

Nancy chortles, "Well, yes, I think it's a theoretical possibility. Thanks for clarifying the purpose of the trip."

"To clarify further, Nancy, I fancy late twenties to early thirties."

Nancy is not often flustered. She thinks of a couple of names, and then suddenly, one rises quickly in her mind. She says she'll give it some thought and should have a plan when June gets there. "And when are you thinking about making the trip?"

"Tomorrow morning, Nancy. I'll book myself into the Jefferson. If you're free, why don't you meet me in the Quill Lounge at six tomorrow night. If that organizing mind can work fast enough, you are welcome to bring anyone fun."

Now she's packing. *June, this is mad … no, stupid. Washington in the heat. My heat. Ughhhhhhhhhhhhhh. Take this chiffon? Dammit, June, act your age.*

The Jefferson Hotel, within sight of the White House at Fifteenth and M Streets, is expecting June Elgar, and reception staff have asked if she is related to the Sarah Jane Elgar who stayed with them in 2019. The hotel's unpretentious elegance features décor of antiques and artifacts from the days of the American Revolution.

The Quill Lounge on the ground floor is nearly empty when June arrives—in the chiffon, ivory with peppermint streaks, scooped in front and gathered by a black patent narrow belt. The Quill's sidewalk tables are crammed with the after-hour cocktail crowd. June allows as little sunlight as possible to fall on her pale skin, so she carries her kir royale to a table in the corner where she can survey comings and goings. *There they are. She is. They? Who the hell is that with her? Help! It's Ray Lion!*

Ray Lion II plants a breathy kiss on each cheek as June politely thrusts her chin forward, her eyes drilling in on Nancy Booth, who looks away. Nancy has changed at the office into a sleeveless A-line almost to the knees with red-white-and-blue flag stripes. Ray's faded polo shirt is untucked over light blue golf slacks. He carries a tan safari jacket over one arm.

Ray asserts himself. "June Elgar, this truly is fate. When Nancy called me to suggest drinks with an out-of-town friend, and when she said your name, I couldn't believe my good fortune. I'm looking to fill a job that you will be perfect for."

"I don't need a job-job, Ray. I see that you found a new one," June sniffs.

"It's a calling, June. Don't you ever hear a call you need to answer? Hmm? Be honest here."

Ray shifts into throaty persuasion. "June, this is absolute karma. I only just told Nancy about my plans to revitalize an amazing public interest group, and she brings me to you. And you have come from, where? Canada, right? Looking for some summer heat here?" His wink is disgusting.

Without pausing, he shifts into high gear. "You are top executive material, June. I'm organizing a powerhouse new group to waken the restless spirit of patriots in this republic. It'll consist of smart, strong, influential women. It will have deep resources to move mountains in American liberties. It must be led by someone with proven experience in unpopular but righteous causes, like the environmental causes you moved mountains for in Canada. This is the big show, June. It's America! I need—the country needs—a woman of your influence to be the new chairwoman of the auxiliary I'm forming. You'll be new to Washington but not new to money, and that's the best experience there is. Nancy, here is your executive director. She is the insider's insider on the Hill. Just let her work her magic, and give her your full support."

The women lock eyes. Without altering her gaze, June says, "Ray, why don't you work your magic and get us each a kir royale. After you bring us those, you can go back to the bar and order us all some crab cakes. We'll be happy to see you again when the food arrives." Nancy smiles approval. Ray can't think of a better plan. He retreats to the bar.

"June, I …" Nancy begins.

June holds out her hand, palm facing Nancy. "Before you start. Before we start. It all starts with this one question: *Did he tell you about Tokyo?*"

"No, June, he didn't." Nancy's eyes widen.

June clenches her teeth, eyes probing for any sign of mendacity from Nancy. June's an expert at that. "Then, that's for another evening, Nancy. Please tell me what the hell he's on about with a women's auxiliary, which is way, way out of his wheelhouse?"

Nancy clasps June's hand, her brow furrowed. "I didn't bring him here to interview you for a job, June. You said 'young,' and I thought, well, for short notice, at least he's young."

"I know quite a bit about young Mr. Ray Lion II. But, as I say, that's for another evening." June winks. "Business first. Auxiliary to what, exactly? Where's this money supposed to go?"

Nancy leans closer. "Ray Lion is trying to revive the shambles of the gun lobby that went bankrupt. He plans to prop up the N2AR group with new money so they can prop up the special interests of Total Carbon Corporation."

"Whoa, Nancy," June blurts. "You heard my goddaughter's speech."

"I see that, June. I just figured to bring him along to make a pass at you, not a job proposition. I haven't even talked to him about the job offer he threw at me. I don't know where Ray Lion gets his presumptions. They must grow along the median strips of western Missouri."

"Here you go, girls, two kir royales. I'll be right back with my Tennessee whisky and branch water."

June says levelly without turning around, "Ray, be a dear, and enjoy your first one at the bar. We're getting along very well here. Nancy is a gem. We can all chat over crab cakes."

"How do you do that?" Nancy asks. "He's like a ten-year-old with you."

"Yes, he is. As I said, Tokyo is another story for another night. Go on about this lobbying group. Who are they again?"

Nancy lowers her voice. "It's only a gleam in his eye right now. The New Second Amendment Righters are the new gun lobby. I suppose you know that, given your family's involvement in gun reform laws. They sort of rose out of the ashes of the long-standing group that went belly-up five years ago. They have the same policy issues, but the old leadership went to pot and skimmed millions of reserves. It went into bankruptcy, and what that meant is that whatever was left or could be clawed back went to the bankruptcy trustee and the lawyers. Plenty of lawyers in that one, for sure. Anyway, they are still a major force on the Hill. Lion sees a chance to get into it and rake in some of that for himself."

"Guns? Nancy, you know I'm into environmental issues, and if you were in Seattle, you certainly heard Kozue on the matter of assault rifles. How does anyone expect me to raise money on the side of guns?"

"I get that now, June. I didn't know he would go after you that way about an auxiliary. Hell, I didn't even know he was thinking to put me in it, too, before he blurted it out the other day. We were just going to meet here for drinks. Once again, that's Lion being crafty, not putting his cards on the table up front. Yes, I heard that girl's speech, and I still react to it. My problem is that my boss is on the gun rights side, not Kozue's side."

"Well, in that case, Nancy, what the hell are you going to do? Support your boss or your conscience?"

Ray appears, a waiter behind him with Maryland crab cakes and the Jefferson's signature sauce. "Here we go, girls, something to chew on while I tell you about your future in the political world."

"Yes, Ray, by all means, sit down and let's talk shop," says June. "Nancy has just cleared up pretty much all of the mystery in your new venture. Now, Ray, as you enjoy your seafood, let me give you an earful about assault weapons. Nancy, feel free to chime in whenever you feel like it. My thirteen-year-old goddaughter lost both her parents to an AR-15 church shooting in Canada. She was eight at the time. Ray, don't look so unhappy, there's more. Let me scoop some more of this hot sauce on your patties."

Ray gathers himself. He looks for an ally. "Nancy, you know me by now. You know I am not a heartless, unfeeling person. You know that gun violence is the work of mental cases. Some so mental they can't even stand trial. The New Second Amendment Righters put incarceration and mental treatment at the top of its agenda. I don't see any conflict here."

Nancy says quietly, "I was in Seattle at a convention where June's goddaughter made an outstanding presentation. June's right, the job you want this auxiliary to do is diametrically opposed to her family's prime objective. You can go around splitting hairs like that if you want to, but don't expect someone like June to do it."

Ray leans back. "Then tell me, Nancy, are you saying you won't do it either? Would you turn your back on the chance to help the only boss you've had in your career into the White House? Are you going to walk away from Maxwell over a thing like this? Am I going to have to sit down with Thad Maxwell and have a heart-to-heart talk about who on his staff is loyal and who isn't?"

Nancy glares. "Ray, I think I know the man who's been my only boss better than you do. You can pour your heart out to the Speaker if you can find him. I happen to know he is unreachable on personal business for the next few days. I also happen to know that this goddaughter of June's and her family are coming here sometime this week, precisely to talk to the Speaker and others on the Hill about assault weapons and the pending resolution. I'm going to have a heart-to-heart with him myself about it."

"Does that mean you think the resolution is about to pick up steam?"

"I don't know, Ray. What I mean is that I think the Speaker needs to listen to someone other than professional lobbyists on this. He needs to hear from ordinary people whose lives are forever affected in these incidents. Are your people going to score him down for that?"

"Yeah, Nancy, it always comes down to the score, doesn't it? The score matters most. Well, we can talk about scoring if you want. It seems like two great friendships in my life are hinging on how we score votes on this namby-pamby resolution. If I put scoring on the table, will you two come to your senses and talk about this auxiliary?"

Nancy looks at June. "Let's at least listen to this one."

June shrugs. She's heard Ray Lion squirm and struggle before. "Might as well."

Ray smiles before he serves himself the last of the crab cakes. His hand shakes. The sauce decorates the front of his trousers. "Sometimes, a man has to accept the good instead of the better. Total Carbon needs the rare earth bill because it's a money machine for TCC. I need the N2AR because it is a money machine for me. You can see my dilemma, can't you? Suppose I can get the score for votes to pass the gun resolution to a C? It's still linked to a pass vote on rare earth though. Without that, the score's a D."

Nancy looks at June again. "You see this 'score' we keep talking about …"

"I know the score, Nancy. A gentlemen's 'C' doesn't cut it for me, I'm afraid."

Nancy looks back at Ray. "She's right. We need a 'no-score' on this. Both matters come up together, and N2AR takes a pass—no score on either one. That means the members can vote their consciences, such as they may be, and the gun score is unaffected. Whatever score they had going into the vote stays the same no matter how they vote. Then the House goes into August recess."

"Very neat, Nancy, but you're overlooking the 'money-machine-for-me' part. Do I get you two for the auxiliary?"

June says firmly, "Nancy and I need to talk. I also need to talk to my family. Do I assume that if I do take on this auxiliary for the money, I also get a say in the policy for N2AR? On an issue-by-issue basis? And control how the auxiliary spends its money?"

Ray pushes his chair back. "You're getting out of your lane here, June. I'll be frank: this has been a deeply disappointing meeting with you. Nancy, I'm leaving, and I'll drop you off at the office or your place, whatever you want."

"I think June and I aren't finished just yet. You go on, Ray; I'll stay on and take care of myself the rest of the night. What about the 'no-score'?"

"We're still talking, aren't we?"

CHAPTER 37

Emiko Sugawara has sat in the modern Chuofuto Cruise Center at the port of Hakata/Fukuoka expectantly for three hours after the hulking *El Caballo* eased against the pier, aided by two harbor tugs. She watched the gangplank lower from a hatch door in the superstructure over the stern. Then, after an hour, a young JSDF marine strode down the ramp and along the full length of the vessel before turning to enter the building. There were no cruise ships in port or expected. The building was mostly empty except for city police and the crews of four ambulances parked at the rear of the building. Emiko recognized the marine from the photo Amaya had given her. She gathered her group of twelve middle-aged individuals who had arrived there about the same time Emiko did. Emiko wears a gray shirtdress, black pumps, and a turquoise silk scarf tied tightly around her neck.

"Swords," she whispers to Kimoto.

"Ploughshares," he whispers in answer.

He then leads the group to an area behind a plain cloth screen with folding chairs in three rows, where they sit to wait. They wait for two hours. Then, two merchant seamen in dress whites emerge from the doorway of the ship's superstructure and slowly guide a rolling table holding two, fifteen-inch-square boxes covered in coarse black cloth, gathered and tied at the top. The seamen push the table along the pier, through the waterside sliding doors, and beneath a standing flag of Japan. One by one, merchant officers in dress blue uniforms carefully guide two wheelchairs down the ramp, along the pier, and toward the doors.

Amaya follows one of the chair-bound returnees, and Chu Hua follows the other. They wear the same uniforms they wore when they boarded the vessel a week ago. The returnees, in their sixties, emaciated and in critical health, gaze around the gleaming terminal building as if they have been transported to a castle in the sky. Their gray faces are wrinkled, but their eyes enliven when they spot a crowd of vaguely familiar family faces.

Emiko strains to look at the faces of the haggard women in wheelchairs. She then tries to catch Amaya's eye, but Amaya simply looks straight ahead. Kimoto holds four thin file folders. He calls a name. A cluster of four rush forward, bend, and greet their relative. Kimoto reads another name. The remaining greeters welcome their relative.

Emiko stands alone, stoic, and resigned. She moves a few steps closer to the other one who has not yet been reunited. They grip hands.

Amaya gathers one of the boxes and holds it easily in her forearms. She walks toward Emiko. Emiko's wait is over.

<hr>

"Mom!"

"Yes, Tree, I'm back in the Okura hotel in Fukuoka."

"Are you OK?"

"Yes, my Treetop, very OK. Exhausted. Emotionally drained. I will sleep well, that's for sure. But tomorrow, I fly out of Fukuoka to Kansai International, and then to San Francisco. I'll have you in my arms soon. Can you put Daddy on the phone?"

Kozue is quiet—puzzled. "But, Mom, no. He's still in Tokyo, working with Uncle Jerry on something big. Didn't you talk to him?"

"Oh, Kozue, no, I had no telephone service at all. Well, I warned you though. You can't really count on the coming-home call unless it is at an actual airport."

Amaya has to hold the phone away from her ear as Kozue bellows, "Mom! You are only in an actual hotel. Does that mean …?"

"It means that I am coming tomorrow, and nothing can stop me. How is Aunt Sarah?"

"Oh, Mom, she is a ton of fun. More than I realized. Man, does she love foghorns! Wanna talk to her?"

"Later. I need to hear about your week."

"Yeah, well, I got new school clothes with Aunt Sarah, and I've been to baseball practice, and I've helped my new little sister. Stuff like that. Are we going canoeing?"

"Of course we are. I'm going to try reaching Daddy now. And then I'm dropping into bed."

But Amaya's call goes to Brad's voice mail, or would have except she's informed his voice mail is too full for her message. Too tired to sort it out, she turns the light off and falls fast asleep.

Brad's phone was powered off because he was sitting in the Suntory Hall performing arts center Saturday night. He had decided to hear the Austrian symphony's concert. Picking out familiar faces he'd seen all week in the hotel added to his enjoyment.

He returns to his room late Saturday night to find his message light blinking. He grabs a cold beer from the minibar and punches the message button.

"Do you dance, Brad?" asks Masako's recorded voice. "Call me back."

<hr>

The air-conditioning at the women's facility of the Hagatna Detention Center, Mangilao, Guam, broke down last Saturday. The deputy warden filled out the on-paper, numbered requisition form for repair or replacement of the compressor unit, installed in the late twentieth century. It's exactly one week since the thing stopped blasting spurts of less-hot air within the cells holding pretrial adult women detainees. Blossom Harvey hardly slept last night, her unhappy mind filled with regrets. She is an American massage therapist who came to Guam last year in response to an online job center ad. Her hair is blue, clipper-close on one half of her head and loose above her ear on the other. She is short and short-tempered. Her face has faded freckles, and her waist shows the effects of a constant diet of fast food. It is more with exhaustion than joy that she walks with her guard escort to the front of the facility, to be released on bail into the custody of her employer.

Mariko drives with the seat adjusted as far to the front as possible, and at that point, she has little room to spare between her waist and the wheel. She still colors her hair blonde. It is a stiff pouf shaping her round face. Mariko's lower lip is full and extends beyond the cupid bow of her upper one.

"Mariko-san, I was beginning to think I'd die in there."

"You probably would not die of stale air."

"The food, then."

"You don't know the meaning of bad food. You are soft. But that is your appeal. Make yourself ready for afternoon shift and for open house in the dance studio Monday."

"I need two days off before I can dance."

Mariko taps the brake of her 1997 Honda and pulls to the side of the road.

"So, now you push me out? To walk with sore feet in this heat if I do not dance with sore feet in your hot dance hall?"

Mariko says flatly, "Dancing is business. Massage is business. Business does not stop when you wander off the reservation. Besides, there will be new people on Monday, a woman from Japan who might have with her an American businessman. We serve a smorgasbord of dancers at the open house. I cannot allow one of your unique looks to be absent from the smorgasbord."

"I am not a pickled mackerel."

"Only a pickled massage therapist. You are not allowed freedom of choosing when you work. You have the freedom to choose between walking now or dancing Monday."

"I will gladly lose myself in this afternoon's rubs and Monday's music."

The Honda resumes speed.

Sunday morning, Brad finishes up an email to Jerry with last-minute thoughts for the *ringisho* proposing the merger. He looks at his watch. No sense in calling Kozue at this hour; she'll be asleep. He tries Amaya's phone on a hunch, but it goes to her voice mail. She is on an actual plane and actually going home, but he won't know that until later. He shrugs.

I have no business calling this woman back about dancing. But I did come here to get information about the El Caballo, *and so far, I've struck out. It seems to have dropped off the edge of the Earth.* But since Masako is the only possible source of information about the ship, he contacts her.

"Hi, Brad, I'm delighted you called. So, do you?"

"I used to, Masako. The last time was at my wedding, over at the Palace Hotel. Dancing shows off my two left feet. It's too hot to even think about dancing in Tokyo."

"I'm not thinking about Tokyo, Brad. Guam. I looked it up, and there are two dance studios near Anderson Air Force Base. One of them has open-house ballroom and quickstep nights. It's a four-hour flight in our Gulfstream, Brad. I figure we could meet out at general aviation at Haneda airport at eight in the morning. We'll arrive in Guam around two their time. We can take a spin on the dance floor after dinner. I'll have you back here the next day. Are you up for it?"

Hell, no, I'm not, he thinks. "I don't have any business in Guam. I'm not sure I'm doing my company much good in Tokyo. Why are you going to Guam?"

"I want to get you a mile high in our jet, Brad."

"Masako, the banter is fun, but I'm not here for fun."

"I get that, Brad. And I'm talking serious business here. I need to meet with an old friend of our partner, Lydia Maxwell. She still lives in Guam."

"What do you need to see her for?"

"That's Honshu business confidential. Maybe the time will come when I can tell you confidences, but I don't want to get ahead of myself."

"What do you want me there for, Masako?"

"Eye candy, Brad. You're the best I've seen."

"Masako, it's looking less and less like Elgar is in the market for a vessel. I don't have any need to go to Guam."

"Don't jump to conclusions about that, Brad. If not a sale, there could be a very favorable long-term charter in it for Elgar Steel. You need to spend some quality time with me on the Gulfstream so we can sort out bright ideas."

"I need to check …"

"With your wife, Brad? Really?"

"I need to check on things. I've got a business to run."

"And I want to talk to you about business. Honshu business. Remember, I told you we're floating the company's stock in America? Well, I need to talk to you seriously about things connected with that."

"Masako, I don't think …"

Her voice combines exasperation and hurt. "Hey! That first Monday you were here, a lot of people at Honshu dropped what they were doing to listen to you on the spur of the moment, including my father. I'm serious about wanting you to listen to what I have to say about something important to Honshu."

Brad closes his eyes. Reciprocity is the oxygen of Japanese business life. Brad stares at the room phone. The daughter of the CEO of Honshu Lines is on this thing like a dog with a bone. She's right: he did drop in out of the blue, and they did show him uncommon courtesies on short notice. *Business is business. I didn't choose this person to do business with. Why am I even hesitating?*

"Brad, I know I'm pressing pretty hard. But I have my reasons. When are you thinking to return home?"

"Well, there's not much to keep me here, frankly, and a whole lot I should be doing there. I was thinking of going back on the four p.m. flight tomorrow."

"Make it as a leg to Guam tomorrow on the Gulfstream, and then home commercial from there. Pack your bags. Pay your hotel bill. Wheels up at eight thirty, Brad. I'll have a car and driver at your hotel at half past seven. Breakfast aloft. Don't fade on me."

CHAPTER 39

Brad never wanted a corporate jet for Elgar Steel. There is no way to justify owning one of these things, and on the very rare occasions it might make any sense at all, it is easy to charter one out of Oakland. This one is nice, though, a Gulfstream G400 painted in Honshu Lines light blue with pale yellow tail insignia. *I suppose if you've got a fleet with as many ships as Honshu Lines, it could make sense,* he thinks as he climbs the steps into the caramel interior. Masako has stopped inside the doorway for a word with the cockpit crew. Brad takes a single seat over the wings. He can smell the coffee and scrambled eggs in the galley behind him. Masako walks to his seat, shrugs, and then steps on the pedals of the seat in front of him to swirl it around, facing him. She sits and smiles. Masako's white floral-on-cinnabar-patterned summer dress falls from a rolled neck collar straight down, leaving both shoulders bare, to a gathered waist, and then flares loosely to a couple of inches above her knees. It was tailored in Singapore.

"Buckle up, Brad."

Brad has done so, but something about her tone makes him cinch the buckle even tighter. The jet rolls slowly to a stop on the last runway before Haneda airport meets the choppy brown waters of Tokyo Bay. The engines whine, and then whine some more. The plane lurches ahead. Masako fixes her eyes on Brad's. Her lips move soundlessly as she counts.

"Rotate," she whispers.

And the G400 does. It tilts sharply upward and bursts into what fighter pilots call a "zoom climb." They, however, would be wearing parachutes. This morning's stunt breaks that regulation as well as every noise-reduction measure in effect at Haneda. There will be hell to pay later. Masako will see that it is paid.

"The steward will have to pick up in the galley and make some more eggs. The coffee survived, I think. How do you take yours? Or do you want to just skip that and get to the Rittenhouse rye on the rocks?"

"I'm real glad I skipped breakfast." Brad gulps. He looks down at the sight of Tokyo falling away straight underneath them. "I'll just have black coffee with the eggs. You can probably straighten up now."

Masako blushes, pulls her head back, fixes the hem of her skirt, and crosses her legs. "We have a long time to be alone together in the wild blue yonder."

"Love the banter, Masako." Brad points at the blue-and-yellow soft leather portfolio still slung around her shoulder. "You must have a ton of maritime law work you can be doing on this trip."

"I brought it; I don't have to do it." Masako leans back. She pushes her foot forward until her ankle rests against Brad's.

Brad's face darkens. It's going to be a long four hours before they touch down. He needs to clear the air.

"Masako, I'm going to have to complain about the banter. I don't understand why you keep it up. I'm a married man with a daughter, and we are as happy as a family can hope to be. I'm not the right target for your flirts. Nothing is going to come of it. I'd hoped you'd have seen that by now." He scrolls his phone's screen briefly, then holds it at arm's length for her to see. "This is …"

Without looking at the screen, Masako recites, "Amaya, married 2020, adopted Kozue a couple of years later. A family assembled from broken shards."

How the hell do they know these things?

Masako withdraws her foot. She folds her hands over the portfolio now resting on her lap. "Sure, Brad, that's fair. It's time I put it out in the open and on the table. I'm not really trying to seduce you. Not in the traditional meaning of that word. I'm interested in you, though. Very interested."

Brad slowly shakes his head. "So, you have an agenda after all. And you have me in an enclosed space thirty thousand feet above the Pacific Ocean. I guess I'm about to find out about that agenda. It's high time."

"That stock offering I told you about, the one in America by Honshu Lines? That is serious stuff, Brad. I brought along the draft prospectus. No one outside Honshu or its New York lawyers and investment banker has seen a draft. The copy I brought is for you if you'll take it. I'm hoping you'll take it to heart."

The steward brings trays of freshly scrambled eggs and sizzling ham, and a shiny canister of coffee. Brad welcomes the break nearly as much as the chance to fill a stomach still looking for a place to land.

Between bites, he says, "I'm fully invested; I don't think I'd want to buy into that stock."

She laughs. "I'm not hustling the stock. Just bear with me. The management section of the prospectus names me as the American managing director. That's just a placeholder until we find the right person. My father's looking, and I'm looking. We are a search committee of two. Sure, we have consultants and all that, but he and I are going to decide on this. I want to put you on the short list."

Brad is very quiet. "Masako, you hardly know me." *Is that right? She seems to know an uncanny amount about me.* "I have absolutely no background in shipping. I canoe flat-water shorelines to look at birds. I don't know the first thing about your business."

Masako stands and clears the trays herself. On her return with a basket of warm croissants, she says,

"My friend Yuko Kagono knows you very well. She and our art world know your wife, Amaya. The steel industry here knows you. You've been a lawyer in international business. You worked for a while in Washington and know that scene. You had the vision for the Wishbone project. You import raw steel for your plant, and you'll export coal from that new mine, so you know cargo from the customer's side of things. You have a way with words. You work well with the Japanese. That tells us that you are honest and authentic. You have what we call 'a good face.' I'm not talking about good looks. The trust and loyalty you have built up with Japanese executives over decades will be your strongest trait with Honshu, Brad. You have the respect of the prime minister of Japan, someone I admire more than words can express. The more I talk about it, the more I see that you are head and shoulders above anyone else on our short list. I want you to allow us to continue pursuing our interest in you. I want that in the worst way."

Brad stares out the window silently. First Alden, then Jerry, and now this. "Thank you for the compliments. You seem to have looked me over pretty closely. What are you after? It seems like you could put yourself at the top of that list."

"I have good bones, Brad, plus a privileged start in life. I embrace that. I've had high goals set for me, and I've been competitive. I am grateful for my upbringing, and I hope to prove myself worthy. Fate has given me a great deal. I have spent all my life examining my privileges and good fortune. I am not a victim, Brad. Not many women can say that. I am not going to try to disown my good fortune to become a victim or live like one. I am dedicated to my good fate. As you have seen, I am not like most Japanese women because I am outspoken, and do not automatically defer to men. I am independent. However, I am deeply Japanese in other ways, the ways that count the most. I owe my strongest loyalty to my father and this business. I will be at my father's side until I am called to take over his duties. It is the Japanese spiritual way of living. I do not need to conquer America. I have all I can handle here."

"Masako, what about the flirts? The suggestive come-ons? Hiking the hem of your skirt on this plane? That's how you go about hiring a managing director?"

She blushes and laughs. "That's how I whittle down the list."

"A test, then? All that was a test to see if I'd take the bait?"

"You can call it that. We all have ways of evaluating a person's character. That is one of mine."

"What if I'd taken the bait?"

"That would have put you on a different list. But off this list entirely."

"I have a family, Masako. I can't see enough of them as it is, and that's the largest issue on my mind these days. I simply cannot pull up stakes for a brand-new job that would eat me alive."

"Brad, Honshu is a proud family too. And there's no need to pull up any stakes. You live in San Francisco, and that can be our American headquarters. It's a great place for it, actually. Your family can be a Honshu family. You're a builder, Brad. Build our company; build Honshu Lines of America. The new company will have a new corporate jet. Given the size of America, this G400 would be less suitable than, say, the G800. No one is far from home with one of those things. By the way, are you a shareholder of Elgar Steel?"

"My wife is. She inherited one-third of the company when the founder died."

"That would be her separate property under California law. We would make you a shareholder of Honshu Lines America and put you on the board."

"Are you asking me to take this job?"

"Like any good lawyer, I never ask a question unless I know what the answer will be. I haven't asked you yet because I can't figure out what your answer is."

"I guess I should read that prospectus."

"There's always tonight. We are dancing tonight, right?"

The Gulfstream banks in its approach to Guam's international airport. Brad peers out his window. The island stretches thirty miles from its wide southern shore northeast to a narrow neck that turns north, and then to the northeast again into a more bulbous tip. From the air, Brad sees it as an abstract seahorse. He's reminded of his favorite name for any island—Aeaea, the island of Circe, who lured lost ships and transformed their crews to pigs. Well, she spared one, anyway, his favorite Homeric character: Odysseus. But the island's name has always fascinated him: Aeaea, a sigh of an island, a circle, a flow, a passion of vowels.

"Let's decide that later. I booked myself into Tsubaki Tower. Is that close to your hotel?"

"Nearby, Brad. On the bay. You have good taste. The dance studio is the Red Camelia—the one with the open house tonight. It looks shabby. Are we going dancing, Brad?"

"I dunno, Masako. Did you bring a shabby dress?"

Brad doesn't change for the evening. Masako does. She picks up black toreador pants and a seafoam sleeveless top from a shop in her hotel. When they arrive at the Red Camelia, Brad refuses to pin a printed number on his pants leg to enter the ballroom competition.

They sit as wallflowers under the rotating lights, watching contestants of every size glide and turn and snap their necks. Mariko approaches their table. She is forty and wears a garnet-colored velvet ankle-length skirt with black leather edging, and a platinum satin top. On her thick frame, it looks smart, not flashy, and right for the mood of the evening, although regulars recognize its years of familiarity. Her pearl necklace drapes a wrinkled, fleshy neck.

"I am Mariko. You are an unlikely pairing, stiff, not dancing, and definitely off-islanders. I can join you for a short or long chat, depending on what it is you are doing here. My girls will not hustle you the champagne and cold-cut sets while you are opening up to me. If the conversation does not go well, I assure you that you will be offered nothing but the most expensive."

Masako smiles and says, "A very effective extortion technique." She leans in and says, warmly, "All right, here's the deal. I'm here as a lawyer for the Honshu Lines, and I'm also a member of the family who runs that company. We are shifting ownership of our ships in a major reorganization. I have examined the title to the *El Caballo*. I want to clarify that as Fujio Isaemon's daughter, you do not claim any interest in that vessel and do not challenge the ownership of Mrs. Maxwell. I do not doubt the validity of her ownership, but we are dealing with major financial institutions, and they will go over things with a fine-tooth comb. Would you be willing to sign a paper for me tomorrow morning to that effect? If you want a lawyer to assist you, I would understand. This would not be a trick; I simply want to clarify for the legal record."

Mariko breaks into a wide smile. Her eyes soften. "Ms. Daigo, if you have the document with you, and if you can persuade Mr. Oaks to dance a waltz with you, I will look it over. I will not need a lawyer. Helping you with this piece of paper may enable me to make a dream come true; I will sign it immediately."

Both Masako and Brad exhale with relief. She nods. "The document is in my hotel room, Mariko. I did not want to bring it here to shove under your nose at your open house. I can return with it around nine tomorrow morning. I do not think Mr. Oaks could last through a complete waltz with me on the dance floor."

Mariko's face again breaks into a smile. "He seems to have much else going for him, so it doesn't matter to me whether he allows himself to dance. Perhaps, like many men, he dances inside."

In the bright morning light of the poolside patio of Brad's hotel, Masako sits with Brad at a table where he is poring over the document with Mariko's signature. It is the document Masako had the foresight to prepare before she left Tokyo. She went back to the Red Camelia early this morning, and Mariko signed it. It is what real estate lawyers would call a "quitclaim deed," but the object of this one is floating real estate, the *El Caballo*. It says, in effect, that Mariko has no claim to the ship, but if she ever does acquire some sort of ownership in it or its proceeds, she "quits" her claim and "deeds" it to Honshu Lines.

Masako frowns and speaks rapidly, "Brad, I want you to listen to me. Mariko Isaemon is frantic. Lydia Maxwell contacted her for the first time in twenty-two years. She is going to divorce her husband. I am calling on you to do something kind for the person who owns the other half of the *El Caballo*. Mariko is desperate to go to America to see Lydia. She holds a US passport, but she knows nothing about going to America or how to get to where Lydia lives. She wants to help Lydia, and if there is a divorce, to bring her back to Guam. Brad, would you consider helping her? Would you fly out with her? Would you take her with you? I know this is an imposition."

Brad looks at Masako in disbelief. "I'm not a divorce lawyer!"

She sets her jaw and continues, "Just escort Mariko to the mainland. Did you read the prospectus?"

"Yes, I did. I have formed no opinion on the matter you asked me to consider."

With this opening, Masako presses, "If that is the case, then you have not closed the door. For that reason alone, it will mean a great deal to our future relationship if you take on this inconvenience. There is a flight from Guam to San Francisco tomorrow, making one stop in Honolulu, arriving in San Francisco at five p.m. Honshu Lines has reserved two business class seats on it. Will you consider accepting this imposition?"

Brad looks away, his eyes on an unfocused middle distance. *I'm not thinking about imposition. I'm thinking opportunity. This might actually help. Alden needs to talk to Lydia Maxwell. Kozue has her heart set on making a ripple in the Congressional swamp on gun reform. We need every advantage we can muster. I hate to get into the Maxwell family mess, but this is a chance to do Lydia Maxwell a favor. We could use a favor in that camp. From there, who knows?*

"I'll do it, Masako. We're going to Washington anyway, and we can take her along. I'll have to postpone a canoeing weekend. Again."

CHAPTER 40

Thad Maxwell hasn't been to his office since the night Drew Wallace brought Lydia home late from the country club. His feelings have been distinctly up and down. He tries to look ahead to the day the ethics inquiry will end, clearing the way for a grueling campaign for the White House. He likes his prospects, mainly because the only people he talks to about it are eager to see him win—his uncle Earl, cronies in Tennessee, cronies on the Hill, a few of the dwindling local newspapers in Tennessee, and his staff. Thinking of staff brings him to thinking of Nancy Booth, Evelyn Hutton, and that damned Drew Wallace. He doesn't want to deal with Wallace anymore, or even see him for that matter, although it takes some careful planning not to cross paths with him in Northern Virginia these days. He hasn't known him all that long, but in these few short weeks, Wallace has made his head swim and his stomach sink. This latest brainstorm of his, this in-house, bespoke, adultery on demand, well, it just doesn't seem right. Rather than think much about how not right it is, he redirects his mind to his duty to country as the leader of the free world. Round and round it goes in his head, but he never takes himself away from his home office enclave and the putting green on the east lawn of his Virginia pied-à-terre.

He sees Lydia come and go, she with a lighter step than usual, but they take their meals separately and see their divorce lawyers on alternate days. He'd like to see Nancy, but she always has some reason not to come out to the place. She sends him a concise report by email every morning and afternoon. Every report is positive, but he wonders. *I should get to the Hill today,* he thinks every morning, and then *I should get to the Hill tomorrow* every afternoon.

Her report today brings additional good news: his old pal Alden Knight will be in town for a few days with his new wife and others in her family. Nancy says he should carve out at least a half day to listen to Alden and his niece, Kozue Oaks, on some breakthrough ideas for dealing with the gun issue.

He thinks, *So, if I bring that crowd out here and to the club, I can put off going into the Hill another few days. Gun ideas? There aren't any; there are only gun pressures. Ideas have no capital in gun issues. So, I'll listen to them, yada yada. But, the real problem is that Nancy's trying to get N2AR not to score that resolution. That means they also won't score the rare earth bill. Well, even so, I've got the votes on that one. Or do I? I need to lean hard on Mr. Ray Lion II about scores. The days ahead look to be muddy.*

Drew yawns and opens the drapes of his Cannon House Office Building corner office. Drew moved out of Nancy's condo when his new plan to save the Speaker by making him a cuckold came to light. It's fine. Drew can work his own hours, and when he needs to take a break from that, he can catch the Metro to take him to the end of the Orange Line in Vienna, Virginia, where Lydia picks him up for R and R in Loudoun County. Drew does miss staff meetings, but with Nancy running the meetings now that Thad is away, they are a thing of Drew Wallace's past.

Drew gets himself sponge-bathed and shaved in the men's room on his floor of the Cannon building, and folds his futon away for the next night. At his desk, he opens the familiar file, the only one in his work life now. With the help of Earl King, the de facto vessel operations manager, Drew has managed to shift all incoming current revenue from the vessel to new accounts in Switzerland owned solely by Aiko Watanabe. Some of the records of past accounts and transactions are reported on paper. Earl has sent boxes of those files to Drew, who has shredded them. Other records are digital, and this is a field Drew is extremely skilled at. Drew has deleted all references to Lydia Maxwell and substituted Aiko Watanabe wherever he can without running afoul of banking and tax laws. He has decided it is far too risky to tamper with those laws. But those records are sparse and pertain only to money movements up to the date Drew started on the task. It's the best he can do. It's not complete by a long shot, but it leaves a sketchy history that has a clean-cut ending at the end of the calendar quarter, before the ethics inquiry was launched. It's not perfect, but it's better than a poke in the eye with a sharp stick. It's the sort of record upon which compromises can be reached. Sure, there's some residual smoke from the smoking gun, but it'll have to do.

Lydia's lawyer thinks the whole idea of her keeping half of the *El Caballo* as her separate property to be a lot better than she could have hoped for in a for-cause Virginia divorce, the first time she was shown those raunchy photos of her client with an ethics expert. So, as Drew tidies up the records from his computer in the Cannon building, Maxwell's case with the ethics panel looks a whole lot better than it did when Drew got into it.

But what has given Drew the biggest rush is the insight into the economics of modern oceangoing ship ownership. He really wants the same management contract she gave Earl King.

Drew has no trouble living out of his office, or going down the hall at night to the men's room. He can project his imagination to a future in Guam, where life is tropical and unhurried, and where he can begin to build a shipping empire for Aiko and himself.

As Drew daydreams of a quiet life on a tropical island, Nancy Booth has an office to run. With her in the conference room holding the ship model where Drew Wallace first saw the warts are Evelyn Hutton and her new friend from Canada, June Elgar. The subject is the N2AR and the proposed auxiliary. Evelyn is about as skilled a fundraiser as anyone on Capitol Hill. She also has eyes on Nancy's job if Nancy leaves.

"June," says Nancy, pitching like a telemarketer, "the world here turns on compromise and flexibility. What would it take for you to accept what Ray Lion is offering? I think we could work well together. I'd like to work with you as chairwoman and me as your executive director. Evelyn is the natural choice for succession in my job. The three of us could gain stature and influence and make some changes for the good."

June shakes her head adamantly. "I'd love working with both of you, but I don't believe for a moment that we could make much of a difference in N2AR policy."

"They have new leadership now that the kleptomaniacs are out and the group has a new leaf to turn over," says Nancy.

Again, June shakes her head. She is firm and her voice strong. "That all sounds good, and looks good on paper. But just because the organization is newish, and maybe it has different top staff, the underlying membership is the same. They have over five million members, Nancy, and they are not about to change stripes. Evelyn, you know that bunch. What do you think?"

Evelyn nods quickly and says, "June's right about that. You are talking about 'reform,' Nancy, but these people have no interest in reform. June could never deliver on a promise of change on gun issues to her goddaughter. There's no chance in hell of passing even that flimsy resolution."

Nancy draws this out for emphasis, "Not so fast. Ray Lion may be able to get N2AR not to score a vote on the gun resolution. That's what he has put on the table to get us to take on the auxiliary work."

Evelyn smiles. "Even if he comes through on that promise, which is a big assumption, that resolution is toothless. As soon as it passes the House, it drops into obscurity."

June stands. With finality, she says, "I agree with Evelyn. I've lived in Canada most of my adult life. I've seen a lot of fool's gold. The resolution you're talking about is fool's gold. It won't take Kozue long to figure that out. No, I can't take on this auxiliary thing. The money I could raise wouldn't change N2AR policy one bit. I like you two. I hope our paths cross again, but I am not going near the auxiliary job. Kozue and her folks arrive today, and I'm going to join them. I'll bring Kozue to the visitor's center and then on a tour of the Capitol Building. I'll bring her by here so you all can meet her."

PART III

MOORINGS

Their flight to San Francisco is delayed three hours for want of a certain hose coupling. Brad and Mariko sit facing each other in the Sagan Bisita Lounge in the west concourse of the airport. Mariko has relaxed a bit from her initial tenseness. The last time she was on an airplane was when Fujio Isaemon brought her to the island with Aiko. Of course, the sounds and smells of aircraft are constants in Guam, with operations in and out of the Navy base, the Air Force base, and this airport. Still, her life has been solidly on the ground. Her only glimpses of Japan and America are from TV and the homesick remembrances of her customers. She imagines she would fit into San Diego and Los Angeles, but has no real idea about the rest of America.

Mariko has been staring quietly into her teacup. She looks up and exhales. She seems burdened. "Brad-san, do you know the Japanese word *'on'*? It means obligation to another person for service. Not a money debt. I have *on* toward you but no idea how to repay or acknowledge it."

Brad looks up from the newspaper. He folds it and smiles. "Yes, I know the expression, and how deeply it affects Japanese people. You are kind to say, but coming here to bring you to America is a favor I do without any expectation of repayment. As it happens, your friend Aiko is in a position envied by many in the US. She can influence the Speaker of the House. I gather as much *on* from helping you just because of that. I might be able to speak with Mrs. Maxwell more easily than would ever be possible had I not helped you. Don't let such *on* be a worry to you."

Mariko bows her head, her face somewhat brighter. "I won't worry. I will be eager to help your introduction to Aiko if that is something you would want. I know the American expression, 'It's not what you know but who you know.' I remember Maxwell-san very well. When I met him here in Guam, he was very unimportant. Well, important to Aiko. It is breathtaking to realize the young man I knew then could rise to high government power. Another American dream story."

Brad looks up at the departures screen on the wall. "It's time to go to the boarding gate, Mariko. They'll call the flight soon."

Mariko stands quickly. "Yes, let's start. I want to buy a gift for your wife and one for your daughter."

"There's no need for that, Mariko."

"Oh, but there is. It goes with *on*."

Brad's not expecting anyone to meet them. He'll make sure Mariko gets her luggage after clearing Customs, go with her on the airport bus to the nearby hotel, and leave after she's been checked in. Since he's not looking around the arrivals hall, he overlooks completely two figures in dark chauffeur uniforms and billed hats, one holding a white sign reading "Mr. Oaks and party." He might have walked right past them had one of them not shouted for the entire hall to hear, "DADDY-BRAD!"

Brad is overwhelmed with hugs and laughter. Amaya turns around completely on his request; the uniform fits her perfectly. Kozue has organized a pushcart. After introductions, Mariko's luggage is on the cart and under Kozue's control. Amaya conducts her entire conversation with Mariko in Japanese.

Before they budge, however, Mariko places her hands above her knees and bows low. "*Gomen nasai (I'm sorry)*, Mrs. Oaks, for your trouble and keeping your husband for an extra day on my behalf."

Amaya returns and holds the bow. "It is nothing, Mariko-san. I am pleased to meet you. My daughter and I have nothing else to do, and this is a welcome break from boredom. We've hardly missed my husband."

Mariko breaks into a smile. "Oh, Mrs. Oaks, you must be extremely busy, and your husband has been away in Japan."

Amaya laughs lightly. "Kozue and I are accustomed to his trips. It gives us a chance to do all the things that are just personal to us. You must think we are a bit insane to wear these costumes, no?"

Mariko waves her hand vertically in front of her face. "Oh, those are costumes? I thought perhaps it was a family business, like the Uber I have read about. If I may burden you, please accept these last-minute and humble gifts for your hospitality." Mariko hands the wrapped scarves to each of them.

Amaya gasps. "Oh, how especially thoughtful of you on such short notice. We will treasure them. If there is any spare space in your bag, I have brought you this journal to record your special days in America." Amaya bows again and presents with both hands a hand-stitched blank diary from Japantown, its pages cream-colored *washi* paper made by hand in Japan in the traditional custom.

Amaya and Kozue carefully roll and tie around their necks the gold, royal blue, and turquoise silk memento-of-Guam scarves handed them by the grateful Mariko Isaemon. Then they look up and scurry to catch up with Brad, who has taken a few steps toward the doorway leading to the hotel bus.

After goodbyes at the front desk, and with Mariko on her way to her room, Brad and his chauffeurs step into the sunshine and onto the curb of the circle drive. Brad says, "OK, now what? Neither one of you can drive." Kozue opens the passenger-side front door of the first taxi waiting, and Amaya and Brad slide through the rear door. Kozue turns to the driver and says, "The corner of Larkin and Filbert, please, partner."

The driver looks at her with a grin. "Partner. Got it. But do you want me to 'step on it'? If you do, you have to say those exact words."

Kozue glances over her shoulder to the back seat. "Uh-uh, slow and steady, or else someone will chip a tooth."

CHAPTER 42

The foghorns of San Francisco Bay that so enchanted Sarah Jane continue through the nights of July and August because of the ever-present fog from the ocean. The summer heat east of San Francisco warms the air, which rises and creates low pressure that ocean air moves eastward to fill. The resultant draft condenses into the fog that air-conditions the whole city.

But it's not condensed fog that wakens Brad in the dark that night. It is droplets of shower water sliding down Amaya's long black hair, in a ritual she has visited on Brad since the first night they made love in a Tokyo hotel. In the ensuing eight years, it has never failed to surprise him. He makes a sound like a foghorn. She laughs, and dabs his face with the corner of a towel. They listen in contentment to the oddly intermittent sounds from the bay.

"You perhaps have not noticed," she says softly. "I have not asked you about the daughter of the chairman of Honshu Lines that Yuko was kind enough to telephone me about."

"I did notice that."

"Yuko sounded worried."

"There is much on her mind that is worrying."

"Should I be worried about the pretty lawyer-heir to a shipping fortune?"

"Yes, absolutely, you should be gravely worried."

"That is usually a good sign, your honest indifference."

"This time, however, you do have cause to worry. She made bold suggestions to me every time I was with her."

"Were you tempted?"

"Only by her last one."

Amaya shoves her palm against his chest.

"But obviously, you resisted temptation."

"It is so obvious?"

"Oh, Brad, your face is an open book. Everything about you is obvious."

"I see."

Amaya waits until she cannot wait any longer. "So, tell me about the temptations you rebuffed with indifference."

"Now?"

"Is there a better time?"

"I was thinking perhaps to tell you in the canoe after we return from Washington. There would be an exquisite irony in that."

"But Kozue will be with us in the canoe," Amaya points out. "Would it be appropriate?"

"I could never be otherwise. She is going on fourteen. She needs to be a part of adult issues."

"I know her mind, Brad. She can handle adult issues very well. But I am impatient."

"For that, you should put your *yukata* back on."

"I will wait until the canoe, my Man of Steel. I am not yet ready for the *yukata*."

As the sun streams into the bay-facing windows of their bedroom, Brad again feels moisture against his skin. It is different. Alarmed, he looks quickly. Amaya is weeping. He wraps his arms around her silently. She simply quakes with emotion. He waits—a long wait.

"How can I help?" he asks quietly.

"I cannot say."

Propped on his elbow, he says, "Take your time. Say it in meaningless fragments. We can put it together after that."

"I cannot even do that, Brad. I want to tell you where I have been, what I have seen, what I have experienced. But I cannot. It is impossible."

Brad searches his mind. He will not probe. But how else can he help?

Amaya dabs her eyes.

"Perhaps I can guess just a little part of it, Amaya. You were pulled into a long and unexpected task by a good friend you felt a duty toward. Your friend is in an uncommon position. She has asked you not to talk about where you have been and why. I accept that. You are not withholding from me; you are fulfilling your pledge to her."

"Ugh," she says. "You are too reasonable. It is not fair to you."

He fans his fingers through her tangled black hair. "However unfair 'it' may be, *you* are never unfair to me or the Tree. You are being faithful to a promise."

"We must find a way to be at home more," Amaya blurts. She is shaking. She raises her voice. "We must find a way to be less important to others so we can be more important to each other."

Brad is quiet, but his brain is not. He sifts through the developments in his Tokyo trip. *There's the USTR thing. Well, I've ruled that out. It's too iffy in the first place and too disruptive if it did happen. There's the merger thing. It is the Elgar dream. It is a majestic cap of my friendship with Jerry. But the thing with merger is that I'll be more deeply locked into the steel and coal businesses, and those businesses are even more tightly locked with Japan.*

Still on one elbow, Brad asks, "Amaya, what if I could convert two hours of business a day to two hours at home?"

Amaya sniffs. Her throat catches. "Do not be such a dreamer, Brad."

"Let's both try to imagine. What if we all had two hours a day of found time? Time I could be here?"

Amaya rolls onto her back. "You can manufacture pipes, but you cannot manufacture time. This is woolgathering."

There's a knock on the bedroom door.

Brad looks at his watch. "I cannot explain it in a few short minutes. There is a way, though. Will you listen to my thoughts when we have more time?"

Amaya shrugs. "If you are so good at manufacturing time, why not do so now? Why must we put off the conversation, oh, wizard of the time factory?"

Brad nudges her. She nudges back. He whispers, "Even wizards have certain limits. But I would not just casually toss out an impossibly idle fantasy for discussion. It is too important."

Another knock; Kozue says, "We pro'ly need to get moving, guys. We've got stuff to do today, and then we're off to Washington first thing in the morning."

Amaya flings herself back across Brad's chest. "Ugggh. WHEN?"

Brad kisses her and holds her face quietly. "I'm thinking when we're in the canoe. Come on, this trip's for the Tree."

CHAPTER 43

Lydia Maxwell does not consider herself greedy in the property settlement in the divorce. She does, however, insist on the title to the country club three-bedroom condo as well as her interest in the *El Caballo* as her sole and separate property. She might have been successful in clawing back some of the vessel's past earnings, but she does not want to prolong the process, and besides, Thad has already spent that money. She prefers this small, more manageable place with a view, access to the club's dining amenities, and having Thad fifteen miles away at the estate all by himself.

She busies herself this morning arranging flowers in the brightly sunlit open kitchen and dining area, in anticipation of the magical reunion with Mariko she has longed for. Her guest for the past two nights has been June Elgar, introduced to her by Nancy Booth as "good people." She and June await the arrivals of Brad, Amaya, Kozue, and Mariko from the West Coast, and Alden and Sarah Jane from the city, where they have spent the last three days in Alden's quest to reform his old political party. At two o'clock, June and Lydia decide to declare victory on the preparations and open a cold one.

June fans herself with a copy of *Wine & Country Life*, a self-styled magazine of "elevated living" in Northern Virginia. It's of little help against the heat and humidity, which even the condo's air-conditioning struggles to repel. She's very curious about this Mariko and Lydia friendship. It seems to her to be the linchpin in everything she's heard so far about the drama surrounding Lydia's marriage. "I'm sure it feels strange to be meeting your friend after all these years," says June. "I want you to know that I'll pack up and leave with the family today to give you more of a chance to catch up."

Lydia considers the statement the best news she has heard from June Elgar, whose drop-in presence is approaching the unwelcome. "That's thoughtful, June. Frankly, I think the only surprises will be that we have grown older. We know each other's interior spirit very well, and I do not expect that to have changed in twenty-two years. Are you sure you won't stay in Washington for the N2AR job? Thad always listens to them."

June drops the magazine on the glass-topped coffee table. She adopts a smile just bordering on condescension. "You'll meet Kozue Oaks soon. After you are around her for a while, you won't even have to ask me that question, but I'll answer you now. I can do the job they want, raise money from rich people. I have done that all my life for environmental issues. The N2AR gun issues are vile and hypocritical. I want no part of it."

"I'll be glad to be walking away from that bad energy myself," says Lydia. "I believe Nancy Booth may be tempted to fall under their influence."

"I can smell raw ambition a mile away, Lydia. Nancy reeks of it."

The doorbell rings. Lydia lets in Alden and Sarah Jane.

Lydia bows, her hands pressed to her thighs. "I'm so glad to finally meet you, Sarah Jane. I've heard so much about you. You are a corporate executive as well as a sculptor. You are a celebrity."

Sarah Jane's eyes sweep the condominium. It is as new and inviting as the famed Silver Trails golf resort at the edge of the Napa Valley. "Thank you, Lydia. I'm happy to meet you, but this must be an unhappy time for you. I'm sorry if your breakup is painful."

How rude, Lydia thinks. In all these years, she has not become used to such direct talk from Americans, especially on first meeting. "You are kind. It is distinctly unpainful. It is uplifting, in fact. And for me, it is a particularly happy day because I am meeting you and later the rest of your family."

"And," adds June, "you will be reunited with your Mariko."

Lydia bites her lip. *Yet more personal and intimate conversation by guests in my home.* "I am as giddy as a schoolchild. I have missed her so much for so many years. Please come in. May I offer you a beverage?"

Sarah Jane nods and says, "Mineral water on ice for me if you have it, as I'm sure for Alden …"

"A beer would be very welcome indeed," finishes Alden.

"June," Sarah Jane continues, "I haven't seen that chiffon on you in years. It suits you."

"Thanks, twin. I call it my hunter-gatherer outfit." Sarah Jane smiles in acknowledgment.

Sarah Jane asks, "Catch anything with it?" but just then the doorbell rings again.

There follows a bedlam of hugging, handshaking, introducing, and bowing back and forth, followed by more hugs. Kozue looks her Aunt June up and down and winks. Brad stands back as Mariko bows to the waist before Aiko. Aiko bows to her waist. These bows are not deferential but meant as dignified tributes to each other's souls.

The women rise but say nothing at first. Mariko is the first to move, extending her arms forward. Aiko walks slowly to her and takes her left hand. She turns it palm up and presses her lips to a scar. Mariko takes her hands back and kisses the same scar. Aiko's legs ache. They speak in rapid, low tones in Japanese as others make for the beverage counter. Amaya watches and gathers in their sense of great peace and supreme joy.

Aiko picks up Mariko's bag and pulls her to the bedroom she has prepared. Its windows face a grove of birch trees, not the fairway. On the small, round table in front of the window, Aiko has arranged a low, blue-and-white Imari rimmed platter from which rises an arrangement of wheat stalks and yellow jonquils. Once in the bedroom, they hold hands.

"I have never given up hope," Mariko says warmly. "But each year is harder."

Aiko leans closer. "We have much hope and time left for each other now. My time with Thad Maxwell has run out. I have no regrets of coming here, and no regrets of leaving him. Do you have someone, Mariko?"

"No. I have the businesses. They are less objectionable than when you lived in Guam. The bedroom houses are sold. I try to provide diversion and joy in a dance studio. There is always the massage parlor. There is no escaping the high returns from that. But you are in the upper class of society, Aiko. How can you think of leaving that?"

"I can think of it very easily. The fact is that in this part of the world, in Virginia's horse country, upper-class society is very selective. You must find that in Guam."

"It is better now, Aiko, but there is always a residual resentment that the Japanese occupied Guam during the war. The place is too small for those sentiments to carry on in a big way. But there are little ways."

They sit on the edge of the bed. Mariko says, "You still dye your hair! We both do. Perhaps we can change that now? Go back to the way we were?"

Aiko looks carefully at her. "I think that is a good idea. We can do it this week, actually. There is a good salon I know of in Tyson's Corner, an easy drive from here."

Nothing more is said. The women do not move. Finally, Mariko says, "You have other guests. We must not ignore them."

Aiko stands. "For the moment, yes. They will leave soon, I think. We have all the time in the world."

They return to the living room, where mineral water, beers, Coke Zero, and white wine spritzers have been distributed. Everyone has spread out around the large, open kitchen and dining area. The chatter drops to near-normal volumes.

"What will …" starts Aiko, only to be topped by June's, "How long has it been …" followed by silence and deferring nods.

"I know what," announces Ambassador Knight. "Let me propose a toast, and then we'll go around the room, starting on my left. Welcome to the mainland, Mariko Isaemon, welcome back to America, Brad and Amaya Oaks, and welcome all to Washington. Thank you, Aiko, for your hospitality. A toast to our hostess, and to the grand reunion with her childhood friend. *Kanpai.*"

Amaya, on Alden's left, says, "I feel wonderful energy between you two. It is the energy of *wa*, harmony, the highest state of contentment. I am so glad to sense it now, and I hope for you it continues."

Kozue says, "I'm trying to learn Japanese. I'm glad to experience a specific case of *wa*. I can actually feel it from everyone in the room. It is especially an honor to finally come to Washington. I hope to spread a little *wa* around Congress."

June chimes in next. "I can't wait to leave Washington this time. Life is not all harmony there. I hope you can prepare yourself for that fact of life, dear Tree."

"I'm optimistic," says Brad, "that Kozue will find her ideas welcome with at least some of the people we've come to see."

"I've done a bit of spadework along those lines," says Sarah Jane. "I have arranged meetings on the Hill tomorrow with the Napa and Stockton members of Congress."

"And I'll take you to meet the Speaker's chief of staff tomorrow afternoon," says June. "After that, you are all on your own. I'm going back to my personal suburban *wa*."

"I am just pinching myself," says Mariko. "It is overwhelming to travel so far, so fast, from my island in the Pacific. I will probably sleep all day tomorrow."

"And I am delighting in my brightest day in twenty-two years," says Aiko. "I wish you all success in your endeavors. I will be content to pamper my Mariko here tomorrow."

June stands to refill her white wine spritzer. "I urge you all to enjoy the glow of the moment. To my family, I say, be careful. You will hear very encouraging words when you are on the Hill. It's the words you don't hear you must be concerned about. There are always people in this town who talk out of both sides of their mouths. Joining them recently is our old nemesis, Ray Lion. Karma and Nancy Booth reconnected us, very unexpectedly. He could not be trusted when he was on the business side of Total Carbon, and a danger to our business, even when he was in their headquarters with senior management looking over his shoulder. In fact, he received way more oversight than he could handle. He is on his own here. He is a danger to more than business here; he is a danger to the republic. I hate to rain on today's sunshine, but for everyone's sake, especially Kozue's, I implore you to keep a skeptical eye on that gent."

"Well, June, on that sobering note, we should think about going to Middleburg to check into our rooms at the Red Fox," says Sarah Jane.

An hour later, the condo is quiet. Mariko and Aiko are alone. They have repeatedly pressed their hands together, scar to scar, and renewed pledges of lifelong loyalty.

"Aiko, would you consider coming back to Guam? To live with me?"

"I now have full access to the management and business of that ship. I do not want to continue to employ Mr. Earl King. I have in mind taking over ship management myself, if Honshu will permit it. I could move to Guam or anywhere. I no longer want to live in this area. There are too many politicians with selfish spirits. It reminds me of my childhood household and my father. Do you have any interest in returning to Japan?"

Mariko shakes her head violently. "No, never. Returning Japanese are not considered Japanese anymore, even though we are. People judge us as foreign. I think we would be happier in Guam."

"I suppose you're right. I will have money from the divorce and when I sell this condo. I think there is another young man who could take over ship management. I also think he would want to move to Guam."

Mariko stiffens. "A young man? Aiko, is he someone you are attached to romantically? I think that would be difficult for me. I always dream of you and me together. I have given up on men."

Aiko takes her hand. "No, there is no attachment. He is bright, but he has a sinister heart. I have gained all I can from him. I agree with your sentiments. We are just starting our forties, Mariko. We can begin a new life together."

"It is good, Aiko. We have harmony and trust. Why should we search elsewhere for what has been with us for our lifetimes? And I believe we could manage the ship ourselves. We are smart. We can learn special knowledge about ship management somewhere, perhaps here in America, or London, or maybe Norway. Or I am sure Honshu Lines would even buy you out. I met their lawyer. She is also smart and sincere. We are in a good place for a new beginning."

Aiko beams. "Mariko, just your being here is a blessing."

Mariko pokes her friend's ribs. "So, Aiko, who is this smart and sinister young man you have used?"

"He is Drew, a boy à la mode. He works for my husband as his ethics lawyer. He thinks like a snake. He has furnished me my divorce based on adultery. My lawyer calls him my unnamed correspondent, a droll expression. He wants to work for me, but I made no commitments to him. We are free to choose."

"Oh, my! You are even cleverer than I remembered. I'm sure a boyish, sinister ethics lawyer who cuckolds his client can easily find work in America's capital."

CHAPTER 44

As Aiko and Mariko rekindle their bond, the others have checked into their rooms and now sit in the tavern at the Red Fox Inn in Middleburg. Its walls are joined fieldstone and its floor broad, dark planks of oak. The tables and bow back chairs are reproductions of Colonial furniture. On the walls hang electrified tin sconces and maple-framed paintings of red-jacketed gentlemen riding at full gallop in pursuit of elusive red foxes. On this summer day, there is no fire in the wide fireplace and cooking hearth. The building has operated continuously since 1728.

Alden brings his frosty mug of lager to a space next to Amaya on the bench against the wall. Kozue sits between Amaya and Brad on the bench, which faces a tavern table filled with kettle potato chips and cream cheese from a local dairy. Kozue is quiet, her mind on what lies ahead in her first Hill lobbying visits. Alden thinks it's time to break the silence.

"Well, Amaya, Brad came back from his intel mission to Japan with absolutely no intel on the *El Caballo*. It turns out we really don't need it now, thanks to Thad Maxwell's ethics lawyer's resourceful thinking. Maybe you had more success when you were away. I'm eager to hear about it—just so long as there's no freighter with illicit cargo involved." He chuckles at his own dry humor.

Amaya looks downward and away. Kozue breaks in, "Mom was on a ninja secret mission. She can't talk about it. If she did, she'd have to poison your beer."

Amaya flashes a frown at Kozue and sips her white wine. "Hardly a ninja …"

Kozue picks up speed. "Really, she's always been a secret ninja. She knows all the ancient secrets of ninja spies in Japan. She can scale castle walls, wring someone's neck, and slip away without a sound."

"Tree!" Amaya scolds, smiling. "Alden, the thing is I might as well be a ninja because I have no permission to discuss why I was in Japan for such a long time. Please don't press me. The time may come when I can tell everyone, but now, may we talk about something else? May we hear about the gun reform measure?"

Alden looks into Amaya's dark, unblinking eyes. While no expert on ninjas, he understands keeping quiet about behind-the-scenes pursuits and diplomatic silence.

He looks around and grins. "Absolutely, I'm sorry if I made you uncomfortable. Well, while Sarah Jane was on the Hill yesterday and this morning, I've been making the rounds to try out this idea we're working on. Everyone I talk to likes the idea. To move it forward, there needs to be a legislative directive. The bare minimum would have to be language added to the pending resolution."

Sarah Jane has been watching Amaya's discomfort. She's eager to pick up on the new subject. "I can tell you the sentiment on the Hill. If there is an amendment to the resolution, it would rally the support of those who think it is too flabby in present form. However, the problem would be those who oppose any resolution in any form. Those people are intimidated by the gun lobby. What they are really worried about is how the N2AR will score them on their votes. June was told that the N2AR will not score the vote of a member favoring the gun resolution if that member supports the rare earth bill."

Brad leans closer to Kozue. "Tree, are you following that?"

Kozue shrugs. "Sure, it's easy to follow. It's just not easy to understand. N2AR is saying if you vote yes on the rare earth bill, we'll look the other way when you vote yes on the gun resolution."

"That's it in a nutshell, Tree," says Brad. "June, you've been talking to Ray Lion. How sure are you that N2AR will do it that way?"

"Brad, all I can tell you is what he told me. He said he would, but consider the source."

"Yeah," says Brad, "I guess that will have to do, for now." He reaches for Kozue's hand. "Tree, you have to watch it around here. Just when things look the brightest, that's when the situation may be at its worst. I moved to Washington for a few years to get the Wishbone project restarted. It was pretty much my sole lobbying issue. It was unpopular at first, and I was very alone on it. I was also living alone. Nothing is easy here, especially being alone. Good ideas in this town have a way of going nowhere. There are too many competing good ideas. And that's even before you get to all the bad ideas that pick up momentum. Don't get your hopes up."

The table falls quiet. As people drift into their own thoughts about the dueling resolutions, Alden clears his throat.

"I want to change the subject again, if Amaya's trip is off the table and if we've hit a stopping point on guns. Sarah Jane and I have an announcement to make." Heads turn. Startled glances shoot to Alden and then Sarah Jane. Alden continues, "In addition to working on the gun issue, I've been meeting with people about that matter I spoke to you about, Brad."

"You mean running for office?"

"Not exactly that. It's about putting some muscle together to try to salvage my party from self-destruction. This is something I believe in strongly. To me, it is more than repairing the party: it is restoring the two-party system. Maybe it would lead to a job in government, but that's not my objective. It's going to take a long time, maybe several election cycles. Sarah Jane and I have looked at condominiums out on Connecticut Avenue. We are going to move back here to work on this together."

Kozue is on her feet. "No way. Aunt Sarah, you can't give up Napa for this mess."

Sarah Jane reaches across the table to take Kozue's hand. "I wouldn't be giving up the winery or the steel plant for good. But this is something Alden is committed to, so I am committing to him. Remember, Brad, when we were back here working on Wishbone? I enjoyed myself immensely. We are determined to succeed at this, and when we do, we'll return to California. In the meantime, I can still go back and forth as often as I please."

Kozue goes quiet. In the time they spent together in bunk beds, listening to foghorns, Kozue has given more of her heart to Sarah Jane. Now, she clenches her fingers tightly against her palms. *She can't just be gone. She can't.*

Brad is caught off guard. He gets it about Alden, and he gets it about Sarah Jane's commitment to Alden. But it sure is a shock. He looks at Sarah Jane. "But if you're taking this on, you won't have much to do with the steel plant. I still depend on you for the big stuff."

Amaya feels the weight of the implication of added responsibilities for him. She deeply depends on Sarah Jane's companionship, and Kozue's bond with her has grown stronger just in the last month. Amaya simply lets her head fall to her hands, her shoulders quaking.

June says, "Sarah Jane, you are going to find the working conditions around here are not as magical as that White House dinner Alden took you to on your first date. What Alden's talking about is going to be messy, and it's going to take money. I know something about political fundraising, and it is every bit as exhausting as making a steel sculpture with your own hands, day in and day out."

"Want to help me, twin?"

"No, I do not. I've already turned down an invitation to raise money for Ray Lion. I like you a lot better than I like him, but I'm still not interested."

"You were playing with fire with Ray Lion," Sarah Jane points out.

June grimaces and picks up her purse. "Sarah, you'll be playing with fire and gunpowder. Look, let's not get too far ahead of ourselves. You have meetings on the Hill, three at my last count. I'm going home tomorrow night. I don't know about you, Brad, but three lobbying meetings in one day is one too many in my experience. I say we get to bed early."

Brad's arm is around Amaya's shoulder. Amaya looks up brightly, but her cheekbone is streaked. "Did you know this?"

"No, hon. But it's not that big a change."

"You don't know that," sobs Amaya.

"No, I don't. But if she is determined, we can't change it. We will adapt. We always do. Sarah Jane has paid her dues. She's entitled to do this."

"Then, Brad, will this mean you will spend less time traveling? Fewer trips to Japan?"

Brad clenches his jaw. He's thinking about the merger with Shin Steel on top of everything else. Negotiations on that cannot just be in California. He cannot make promises.

He pulls her closer to him. "I cannot see around corners, Amaya. Let's deal with the gun issue tomorrow and then go home. We should be in our canoe, the three of us, when we talk about it."

CHAPTER 45

It's a rare moment in the life of June Elgar that she thinks more about someone else's feelings and spirit than her own. She holds close the girl whose adoption into the family she orchestrated, in the conference room of Speaker Maxwell with the Regency period striped wallpaper and where the *El Caballo* sits atop its pedestal. Kozue's face is quiet and stunned. The teenager perspires from the exertion and Washington's oppressive August heat. She is limp in June's arms. Brad and Amaya look on, unable to do any better than June to restore pep in their daughter. Evelyn Hutton has left them to recover from the news she has just delivered.

Representative Joyce Gregor, as promised, introduced an amendment to the gun resolution which would lay the foundation for executive action on safe AR-15 gun design. Phil Perry from Stockton supported the amendment on the floor. Alden and Sarah Jane had talked to members of the Speaker's caucus whom Alden knew from his years as the USTR. They thought they had a shot at this thing. The rare earth bill was voted on and passed easily. The gun resolution came up next. Gregor's amendment was objected to on a point of order, but the Speaker had ruled it in order. The gun resolution as amended was voted on without any comment from the Speaker. By an overwhelming vote, the resolution failed.

"You see," Evelyn said before she left the conference room, "most members were avoiding a low score from the N2AR on the resolution."

"But ..." said Kozue.

"But ..." said Brad.

"But ..." said Amaya.

But Evelyn had left the room.

Finally, June speaks. "Obviously, Ray Lion reneged. It was all a setup. Maxwell brought them up for a back-to-back vote, but he knew the votes would be scored. He didn't tell his caucus to vote their consciences."

There's a knock on the door. They turn their heads. The door opens a crack, and a voice says, "*Sumimasen*" (Excuse me); it is Aiko.

"I am here to gather some of my Japanese mementos from Thad's office. I heard about the vote and that you are here. I wish to express my disappointment. You have experienced what I have been watching for sixteen years: betrayal and mendacity in politics."

Brad says, "Thank you for looking in. We're about to leave. I must say that this did catch us off guard, although I should have been more alert. I think I was hoping for too much for the sake of my daughter."

"Brad-san," says Aiko, "you can never reduce your hopes in that regard. I can also fill in other details for you. My ex-husband's staff is breaking up. Nancy Booth has taken a job with Ray Lion. She will be the chair of the women's auxiliary. Evelyn Hutton will be her executive director."

Brad grimaces. "It makes sense, I guess, in this world. And Mr. Wallace? Will he still work for the Speaker?"

Aiko displays a wry smile. "Yes and no, Brad-san. He will no longer work for him as an ethics lawyer or any other staff position. The ethics committee has closed its investigation. Drew-san is going with Nancy and Evelyn. He will be the new chief lobbyist for N2AR. So, in that sense, still working for the Speaker."

Brad shakes his head. "No, I believe more correctly it would be the other way around. And the Speaker is still the Speaker."

Aiko smiles again. "Yes, still the Speaker, but without the freight money from the *El Caballo*. That reminds me. Kozue, would you please come with me?"

She takes Kozue's hand, and they walk to the far end of the conference room. Aiko lifts the scale model from its pedestal and says, "Kozue, would you accept this as a gift from me? Mariko and I leave tomorrow, and I have nowhere else to put it. If you do not want it, I will throw it away."

Kozue looks it over and turns back to Amaya. Amaya approaches, then picks up her pace. She leans to examine the model and read the name on the prow.

She inhales sharply. She looks at Aiko. "*El Caballo*? Can it be?"

"Yes," says Aiko. "Kozue, is this something you'd want?"

Kozue is about to shrug with indifference.

"Yes! Absolutely," exclaims Amaya. She grips Kozue's hand and shakes it up and down.

Kozue says, "Yes, ma'am, I—we—would like that if …" She looks back to Brad, who nods in puzzlement. "I'll take good care of it."

Aiko says, "I'll give you a note to make it official, and to get you past Capitol security. You may repaint it, and even give it a new name if you want. It is yours now."

CHAPTER 46

The taxi carrying Brad in front, and Amaya, Kozue, and the *El Caballo* in the back, pulls away from the Capitol grounds and heads west on Independence Avenue. Brad is determined to lift spirits.

"Kozue, today was a setback. It was a long shot anyway because we were so rushed. It's not over. You understand that, don't you?"

"Yes, I do. I think you're right: it was short notice. But you had a brilliant idea about it. We can come back. Uncle Alden can help us."

"Absolutely, Tree, and you had quite a day as it is. You lobbied Joyce Gregor and Phil Perry, and met with staffers in the Speaker's office. I know guys who haven't done that in their first six months in this town, let alone one day."

Kozue is carefully organizing the stash of *meishi* she collected from staff and House members, each with blue or black engraved lettering, some with a gold emblem. She pauses, holding one of them. She says quietly, "I haven't had time to tell you guys. Congressman Perry pulled me aside at the end of our meeting. He asked if I'd like to work on the Hill as a page."

"Whoa." Brad twists to look back at Kozue.

"I thanked him, of course. Then he said I should get in touch with his Stockton office people. Maybe we should talk about this sometime."

"We absolutely should, Kozue," says Brad. "It would be an honor, and educational."

Amaya turns her face to stare out the side window. "It would be a year of living in Washington."

Kozue leans against her and says, "It would be at least five or six years from now. That's about the time I could enter the police academy. A lot can happen between now and then. What should I call the boat?"

Brad shrugs. "Whatever you want. Make it something personal to you. Something meaningful." He gets an idea. "Driver, could you turn up Seventeenth Street and let us out by the Reflecting Pool?"

The driver slows and moves to the right lane.

"Tree, wanna try to sail that boat?"

Kozue lights up. "Sure!"

The three clamber out of the cab and stroll toward the long, rectangular pool that stretches between the Lincoln and World War II memorials. It's hot in late afternoon, but at least there's a breeze. Brad carries the model in both arms. They stop at the east end of the pool. On the outer edges of the National Mall, softball games with Hill staffers have just started up. Brad hands the model to Kozue. She is in her Quadrangle upper-division uniform and has on a narrow-brimmed white straw hat with a green ribbon. She takes the ribbon off the hat and uses it as a makeshift towline to pull the boat in the water. She sets the model gently on the surface. It floats!

As she walks along the edge of the pool with the model, the wind picks up. Suddenly, the towline slips its knot, and the model is blown sideways. It slowly turns in the wind and heads west toward the center of the pool.

"Daddy-Brad!"

The wind gusts. The model bobs a few times and then begins to list. Its glued seams have dried and cracked over the years in the Capitol Building. It rides lower and lower.

"Do something!" shouts Amaya.

Brad calculates he really does need to do something before the boat takes on any more water. *What the hell.* He steps into the shallow edge of the pool and starts sloshing toward the boat, which is now listing badly. The bow dips below the surface. In a minute, the *El Caballo* slips underwater, headed to the bottom. Fortunately, the bottom is only thirty inches below the surface. Unfortunately, Brad can make only halting, awkward progress on his rescue mission. He straddles the sunken ship and reaches his hands under her keel. His entire front is soaked. The wind has picked up. The sky has darkened.

Filled with water, it now won't budge. He bends his knees, sending his waist below the choppy surface, and starts to raise her. Once out of the water and hugged to his chest, the model makes streams and spurts of water from her damaged seams. As it does, Brad's load lightens. He is able to slowly turn and march back toward his wife and daughter, who are snapping photos.

As he draws closer, a mounted Park Service policewoman eases her horse a little closer to Brad's family. They have now switched their phones to video. Soon, the episode will be on its way to the Elgar Steel plant in Stockton. From there, Eddie Sandoval will forward the footage to Jerry Hiwasaki in Tokyo. Amaya will send hers to the prime minister of Japan.

Brad extends his arms at the end of the pool and rests the boat at Kozue's feet. She is limp with laughter, unable to pick it up. Brad steps up to the edge where he stands, his pants legs draining.

"Good afternoon, sir," the officer says. "I take it you're from out of town."

"Yes, Officer, and we'll be returning tomorrow."

"The Capitol Reflecting Pool is under the jurisdiction of the National Park Service, sir. Mind if I ask you something?"

"Not at all, I need to stand here and sort of air out."

"Would you please confirm what I suspect, namely, that you do not hold a license for maritime salvage in National Park Service waters?"

Kozue says, "Is that a crime? Are you going to arrest him?"

"Hi, is that your dad?"

"Yes, his name is Brad Oaks, and he lives at 2403 Larkin Street, San Francisco. I'm Kozue, and this is my mom, Amaya."

"Are you the owner of …" She leans over her horse's neck and squints. "I can't make out the name of the vessel."

"Right now, it's the *El Caballo*, but I'm going to rename her."

"Well, Kozue, what I'm seeing here is a case of real bad judgment mixed with good intentions. They sort of cancel each other out. Anyway, bad judgment is not a crime in the District of Columbia. We wouldn't have enough jail cells if it was. What's the new name going to be?"

Kozue wraps her arms around Brad's sopping-wet leg and presses her cheek to his trousers. Her straw hat slips off. She picks it up and says,

"One Times One."

CHAPTER 47

With Kozue in the front and Brad in the stern, Amaya rides in the center of the green aluminum canoe mid-morning in a marshy estuary of San Francisco Bay, near the Marin County end of the Richmond-San Rafael Bridge. She stares up at the bridge's span, and her mind goes to the Nagasaki ship channel and the Megami Bridge. Brad and Kozue are not looking up, however. They are spotting the avocets, herons, sanderlings, willets, and oyster catchers in the murky ooze where mud meets the Bay. The morning fog has burned off. The sun warms the canoeists, and the mud bank begins to give off steam.

Amaya often thinks of herself as a privileged Egyptian queen at times like this, on an outing on her barge, scanning the shoreline for birds. Some of the birds would have been of the same species as a Cleopatra might have seen. Kozue keeps a running account of her sightings. Her favorite is the American avocet, with upward curving long bill, extraordinarily long, thin black legs, and soothing coloration of black, white, and cinnamon feathers.

Brad has just laid out the invitation made by Masako Daigo to head up the new Honshu subsidiary in America. Kozue stops paddling and twists herself to face Brad. "So then, Daddy-Brad, if you could have an office in San Francisco, you wouldn't have to drive to Stockton." She and Amaya can't quite get their heads around the idea of Brad leaving Elgar for Honshu America.

Amaya lets out a breathy laugh. "Tree, his office would always be at thirty thousand feet. Look what he does now when his business is all on land. The new company would have hundreds of boats going from one place to another everywhere in the world."

Brad says nothing. He is enjoying the sound of his Tree and his Amaya bantering over his future. Hah. *They* are his future, just inches in front of where he crouches on the damp bottom of this small canoe.

"Remember, Kozue, Yuko says she is pretty."

"That's a great point, Mom. Dad goes for pretty. You throw pretty in with a jet airplane and hundreds of big boats, and I don't see how he can turn this down."

Brad wisely says nothing, thus eluding disaster.

Kozue breaks the silence. "You brought us out here in the canoe to tell us this story about the tempting job offer of the beautiful shipping vixen. So, tell us what you want. What are you going to do? What are we going to do, Cap'n Ahab?"

Brad brings his paddle out of the water. The canoe drifts listlessly. The air is soft, salt-smelling, and filled with muted sounds of marsh grass rustles. "Well, don't forget about the new development with Shin. Sarah Jane is very excited about the prospect of a merger. It's something even her dad talked about. It's been our pie-in-the-sky objective, and now, it's taken a big step forward. I was on the phone with her every day I worked on the plan with Jerry. Actually, I believe she has counted those unhatched chicks in deciding to move to Washington, although she's never said it directly."

Kozue shakes her head. "The question was to you, Cap'n Ahab. Mom and I need to hear from you."

"I was reminded twice on this trip of two essential touchstones in Japanese culture. Mariko reminded me of *on*, obligations we acquire in relationships through life. Before I left Tokyo, Jerry spoke of *chusei shin*, the ultimate loyalty, and the essential task of everyone to identify his and her own *chusei shin*. Because of what they did for me twenty-two years ago and ever since, I acquired and still wear compelling *on* to the Elgar family. I include the steel plant and coal mine in that family as much as

Sarah Jane and June. I owe my sanity to those twins and their business during my darkest days. I have you two, and you are my *chusei shin*. The shipping vixen's offer does not reconcile with my *on* and my *chusei shin*."

Kozue bores in, "Dad, you are being vague again. Is that the way you are choosing to talk right now, or is it the way you think?"

"OK, Tree, I'll give you specifics. The Shin merger will happen in the next year or two. Then what do I do? I suppose I would always have my current job after the merger, but Shin Steel might have other plans."

Amaya looks into the marsh grass. "I have seen Japanese companies expand this way. They will always have American senior management, but the Tokyo head office and board will always have autonomy. That is what you must recognize, Brad. When Shin buys Elgar Steel, they buy autonomy. You have always had great influence on the Elgar family. That influence will change. It will be Shin that replaces the family. Your relationship with Shin is about as good as it gets, but you are not their adopted son."

Brad grunts in acknowledgment. "I'd be working for my best friend. That would be uncomfortable. So, instead of discarding the Honshu Lines offer altogether, it may be how I step away from the new Shin Steel."

Kozue says, "That's nuts, Dad. That just substitutes one big Japanese company for another. Where's the autonomy in that?"

Amaya twists as far as her life jacket allows in order to see Brad. "You will forever work? Work until you drop, as the expression is? You could retire now. You must retire in another ten or twelve years. Do you know how you would spend retirement? I mean in terms of intellectual capital."

"It's not something I think about a lot. I'm not such a workaholic that I will postpone retirement. The main thing I look forward to is giving full-time attention to us."

Amaya shifts so she is riding backwards, looking at Brad carefully. "I hope those are not empty words, Brad. To achieve that, you would have to achieve much at work by way of preparation. You always think ahead. You would need a succession plan in the business. Do you have such a plan for yourself, your working self?"

"Nothing specific. But you are right, now is the time to plan."

Kozue says, "You two are talking around in circles. Not exactly circles, it is more like this paddle, the flat end. There is one side, and then there is the other side, and then there is the thin edge. All you are doing is spinning the flat blade in circles. We are talking about life, and that's three-dimensional."

Brad says, "Tree, that is very good. A much better way to visualize it."

Amaya throws up both hands. "But bring that to this discussion."

Brad says, "This discussion is about balance. But how do we look at balance? If this summer has shown us anything—if our lives up to this point have shown us anything—balance is not constant equilibrium. It is not a fixed, unchanging condition, like a rock balanced on top of a cliff, and if it moves, there is catastrophe."

Amaya relaxes more. "The old houses of Japan survived earthquakes by being able to sway and move on foundations. Their posts were cupped at the end where they rested on rounded stones. They were not attached there. So, they rocked and swayed. If they were ridged beams and posts that couldn't move, they would have broken."

Brad says, "I think we have balance if you look at it that way. We are able to make adaptations if something interrupts the regular pattern. But we always come to rest on our foundations. Our moorings."

"So now, Brad, what about Alden's offer of USTR?" Amaya asks.

"I have ruled out Alden's suggestion. It's not even an offer. It is too tenuous. It depends on too many changes that may not come about. Alden's working on a change that will take thirty or more years, I'm afraid. For one thing, Thad Maxwell is still in his party's leadership. Alden was hoping that he'd avoid financial scandal but somehow lose footing when Alden and his friends get back into it. Well, Maxwell dodged the scandal, but look at the price to him. He had no problem with the idea of sinking an unarmed ship to save his job. When that failed, he sank his marriage. There's no way I want to get involved in party politics with that kind of guy around. So, no, Alden's pipe dream is not a good prospect for us. I don't want us sucked under."

Amaya turns and repositions herself, facing forward. "The answer does not lie in attempting to avoid extraordinary lives at work, but to avoid the unnatural, unusual surprises that come from it. I have learned that in America, there is greater freedom to change than in Japan. There can be a danger in too much change. I like the expression, 'If you don't have what you like, like what you have.' To me, balance is to find wonder in an ordinary life between the extraordinary surprises—to find the joy of ripe fruit in season. To express joy when one or the other of us succeeds at something, to cry when it is called for. I think if we make the ordinary come alive, we can live through the extraordinary events without breaking."

Brad picks up his paddle. "So, USTR is off the table, Shin is on the table, and Honshu is on the table. We need more canoe time."

Kozue says, "Can we come back tomorrow?"

With sweeping strokes, Brad turns the bow of the canoe back to the direction they came from. "Yes, absolutely."

Then he braces his thighs against the sides of the canoe where he's kneeling, and in long, slow J-strokes, he eases the canoe, his Tree, and his Night Rain back to where they started this morning's excursion.

———

Back inside their apartment, Amaya stoops to pick up today's mail, deposited through the letter slot onto the hallway carpet. Two envelopes catch her attention immediately. When Brad and Kozue have settled into their rooms, Amaya makes green tea and sits in the living room near the rounded bay windows. The first envelope she opens is from Emiko Sugawara.

Dear Mori-sensei,

I write this letter to complete our recent story. I am grateful you came to Arita to tell me yourself about the possible reunion with my mother. I am proud that I was able to perform a small duty to assist. You may think that in the end, my heart fell and broke. It did not. It was the outcome I had anticipated for some reason.

So, to put a conclusion on it, let me tell you what I have done with my mother's remains. The North Koreans had cremated her body. The box contained her ashes and her wedding ring. I have transferred them to a blue-and-white porcelain funerary vessel. It is not antique, but it is tasteful. I then took her back to Okawachiyama. I have buried the vessel in the Korean hillside with a very simple shrine. You may think me perverse, but somehow, it is a fitting resting place. I will be able to visit there whenever the spirit moves me.

Your faithful friend,
Emiko

Well, Amaya thinks, *it may be appropriate for Emiko. She is so filled with sorrow. I won't question her judgment.* She puts down that letter and picks up the other, a larger, square one on official stationery. She shudders, but she opens it. A stiff, white card is engraved on one side:

Greetings, Aya-chan

The Prime Minister of Japan, Yuko Kagono, and the Ambassador to Japan from Switzerland, Marcel Bourquin, request the pleasure of your company together with one guest to a joint Oktoberfest celebration at the Embassy of Switzerland on Sunday, October Seventeenth, Twenty Twenty-Seven at three o'clock in the afternoon. Alpine attire is optional.

The "one" before the word "guest" is struck out and a "two" is handwritten above it.

On the reverse of the card, there appears,

Since I know how well you can keep a secret, let me say that at this occasion, Marcel and I will be making a significant personal announcement. There may be "intriguing chat." Marcel and I would love to see you here if you can possibly break away again from your busy lives. My best regards to your Brad, and my enduring love to your Treetop.

Orchid Petal

Amaya quickly opens her laptop and loads the family calendar. She scrolls to October. Oh. Brad has filled Monday the 18th with "NYC for Honshu IPO." She closes the laptop.

"Brad? Can you come here, please? We need to talk."

The book is dedicated to the family of
Suzanne Fountain, in her memory.

ACKNOWLEDGMENTS

For certain insights into Japanese cultural touchstones, I acknowledge: De Mente, *Japan's Cultural Code Words: Key Terms That Explain the Attitudes and Behavior of the Japanese* (2011; Tuttle Publishing). For a glimpse into North Korea's creative ways around sanctions, see: *The Diplomat*: *Anatomy of a North Korean Coal Smuggling Operation* (April 16, 2020).

I gratefully acknowledge the insights and discoveries of my developmental editor, Marcia Trahan. Again, Domini Dragoone captured the spirit of the text in her cover design, as she has with the other books in *The Three Heirs* series.

John W. Feist frequently travels to Japan, pursuing his interests in ceramics and writing. He used to go there often as a lawyer for steel, coal, and shipping companies. *Ship of Perils* borrows from those experiences, as do *Night Rain, Tokyo, Blind Trust*, and *Doubt and Debt.*

He was raised in Kansas before his parents moved to a San Francisco apartment like the one in the book. He and his family have canoed in estuaries of Marin County. He has lobbied for steel and pipe manufacturers in Washington, D.C. Now he lives in Falls Church, Virginia, where he enjoys the music, theater, and museums of Washington at a safe distance from the other madness there.

I'd like to ask readers to please put up a review of *Ship of Perils* on Amazon. I'm sure other readers would appreciate your thoughts; I know I would. I also invite any comments you'd like to leave about the book on the feedback form on www.johnwfeist.com. Thanks!

—John

The Color of Rain: A Kansas Courtship in Letters (Winter Wheat Press, 2021) is Feist's debut literary novel. set in 1896-97 and created from the complete courtship correspondence between Frank Wilson, a widowed banker in Horton, Kansas, and Irene Webb, a young schoolteacher in Nortonville, Kansas.

Pocket Japan, a nonfiction, concise guidebook for business travelers to Japan. If you're headed for Japan on business and the prospect of navigating the traditions and cultural differences has you overwhelmed, then *Pocket Japan* can provide a concise and informative approach for conducting business and forming relationships with Japanese business partners.

He has written four geo-political suspense thrillers set in Japan:

Night Rain, Tokyo brings Brad Oaks and Amaya Mori together amid sniper fire and abduction aimed at preventing Elgar Steel from realizing an innovative infrastructure pipedream.

Blind Trust, the second in the series, brings them back to Japan at the request of the first female prime minister to navigate political intrigue and restore the country's electric power grid after a domestic terrorist attack.

Doubt and Debt, set against the backdrop of a 2026 Iranian-North Korean nightmare alliance, pits Brad and Amaya against ruthless monopolists to rescue Elgar Steel from a hostile takeover.

Ship of Perils launches Brad and Amaya into separate adventures in Japan and Kozue into a gun violence reform campaign as they cling to family loyalties

Night Rain, Tokyo, Blind Trust, Doubt and Debt, and *The Color of Rain* are available in audiobook editions.